Read My Beak

Overhead fluorescents flickered for a second—I needed to replace one of the tubes—then came on bright and clear.

The shop was trashed.

The vintage magazine rack lay on its side, blocking the path to the counter. A quilt, fallen off the wall, draped across the jewelry display case. Antique newspapers covered the counter, their pages spread open as though someone had been interrupted while reading.

Behind me I heard Karen's soft "Oh no!"

I set the box of bakeware on the floor and turned to take the quilts from Karen, placing them on top of the box before I picked up the magazine rack.

Bluebeard woke up from his nap, glaring at me as though I were the intruder. He muttered something cranky and spread his wings to their full width before settling back down. He fixed his eyes on me and ruffled his feathers, then he spoke again. This time his voice was clear and precise.

"It wasn't an accident."

Murder Buys a T-shirt

Christy Fifield

BERKLEY PRIME CRIME, NEW YORK

THE BERKLEY PUBLISHING GROUP
Published by the Penguin Group
Penguin Group (USA) Inc.
375 Hudson Street, New York, New York 10014, USA

Penguin Group (Canada), 90 Eglinton Avenue East, Suite 700, Toronto, Ontario M4P 2Y3, Canada (a division of Pearson Penguin Canada Inc.) • Penguin Books Ltd., 80 Strand, London WC2R 0RL, England • Penguin Group Ireland, 25 St. Stephen's Green, Dublin 2, Ireland (a division of Penguin Books Ltd.) • Penguin Group (Australia), 250 Camberwell Road, Camberwell, Victoria 3124, Australia (a division of Pearson Australia Group Pty. Ltd.) • Penguin Books India Pvt. Ltd., 11 Community Centre, Panchsheel Park, New Delhi—110 017, India • Penguin Group (NZ), 67 Apollo Drive, Rosedale, Auckland 0632, New Zealand (a division of Pearson New Zealand Ltd.) • Penguin Books (South Africa) (Pty.) Ltd., 24 Sturdee Avenue, Rosebank, Johannesburg 2196, South Africa

Penguin Books Ltd., Registered Offices: 80 Strand, London WC2R 0RL, England

This is a work of fiction. Names, characters, places, and incidents either are the product of the author's imagination or are used fictitiously, and any resemblance to actual persons, living or dead, business establishments, events, or locales is entirely coincidental. The publisher does not have any control over and does not assume any responsibility for author or third-party websites or their content.

PUBLISHER'S NOTE: The recipes contained in this book are to be followed exactly as written. The publisher is not responsible for your specific health or allergy needs that may require medical supervision. The publisher is not responsible for any adverse reactions to the recipes contained in this book.

MURDER BUYS A T-SHIRT

A Berkley Prime Crime Book / published by arrangement with the author

PUBLISHING HISTORY
Berkley Prime Crime mass-market edition / March 2012

Copyright © 2012 by Chris York.
Cover illustration by Ben Perini.
Cover design by Sarah Oberrender.
Interior text design by Kristin del Rosario.

ISBN: 978-0-425-24666-5

BERKLEY® PRIME CRIME
Berkley Prime Crime Books are published by The Berkley Publishing Group,
a division of Penguin Group (USA) Inc.,
375 Hudson Street, New York, New York 10014.
BERKLEY® PRIME CRIME and the PRIME CRIME logo are trademarks of
Penguin Group (USA) Inc.

PRINTED IN THE UNITED STATES OF AMERICA

10 9 8 7 6 5 4 3 2 1

ALWAYS LEARNING   **PEARSON**

In loving memory of my father,
Gerald Eugene Fifield.

I miss you.

Acknowledgments

My sincere gratitude to:

First reader and friend Colleen, for your cheerleading, support, and attention to detail.

Agent Susannah Taylor, a consummate professional and my personal champion. Thanks for being on my team.

Editor Michelle Vega. Your help and understanding make my job as a writer a real joy.

Pal Cindie, for the parrot.

Husband Steve, for, well, just everything.

And to all the friends and family who helped me through an incredibly tough year. You know who you are.

Chapter 1

"NO, PETER. IT IS *NOT* A GOOD IDEA."

I gripped the phone tightly and rolled my eyes. My cousin Peter Beaumont owned half of Southern Treasures—well, he owned 45 percent and I owned 55 percent—and he thought he knew everything about everything, just because he had a master's degree from the University of Alabama.

Never mind that his degree was in mechanical engineering, he'd never worked in retail, and he lived more than a hundred miles away. He was *educated*.

"But Glory, honey, coffee is big money. Do you know how many Starbucks there are, just here in Montgomery?"

"That's not the point—"

"There's seven, Glory. In just a couple miles, I swear. And plenty of others, too."

"And there's a coffee shop right next door to me, Peter." The Lighthouse was so close I could get a caffeine high just from the aroma of fresh-roasted beans. "We don't need an espresso bar."

I glanced around the crowded store: odd bits of vintage furniture, books and magazines from the turn of the *previous* century, and shelves crowded with a jumble of knickknacks and oddments. Collectible midcentury kitchenware vied for shelf space with a display of the latest in silly souvenirs. A spinner of postcards stood near the front door, and hand-made quilts covered most of the walls.

Even if I wanted to put in a coffee bar, there was no place for it.

"Coffee!" squawked Bluebeard, the middle-aged Amazon parrot I'd inherited from our great-uncle Louis Georges, along with my 55 percent. Bluebeard wasn't allowed to have coffee, but that didn't stop him from demanding it.

"No coffee, Bluebeard," I called to him.

He ruffled his feathers and loosed a string of angry chatter, laced with an occasional clear profanity.

I sighed. "And no coffee, Peter. It just doesn't make sense for Southern Treasures."

"But, Glory," Peter started up, a faint whine creeping into his voice.

The bell on the front door rang as someone pushed the door open.

"Gotta go," I interrupted him. "Give my love to Peggy and the kids."

I flipped the phone shut, cutting off Peter's protest, and shoved it in my pocket before looking up to see who had come in.

Bluebeard wolf whistled as I caught sight of Karen Freed, my best friend and "Voice of the Shores" for WBBY, the local radio station in Keyhole Bay, Florida. With her wavy shoulder-length chestnut hair and willowy build she was wolf-whistle material and Bluebeard seemed to know it.

"Shut up, Bluebeard," Karen laughed.

She set two tall paper cups on the counter, the aroma of espresso and chocolate teasing my nose.

"Hot, not iced?" I asked, eyeing the cardboard sleeve with The Lighthouse's logo.

"It's Tuesday after Labor Day, Martine," she said. "Officially the end of tourist season. I'm pretending it's fall."

I grinned and took a sip.

"It's only September, but I'll play along for a free mocha." I sighed. "I hope the season isn't over yet. I could use a few more busy weekends."

The shop had been empty all morning, and I'd been working on the books and straightening shelves when Peter called. It seemed like there was always something out of place in the store.

Initially, I had blamed it on customers, but lately I was beginning to wonder. I had even suspected Bluebeard for a while.

Now I had some new suspicions about the constant shuffling of merchandise. But I wasn't about to tell anyone I thought the shop was haunted.

Even Karen.

"I guess we are in the quiet time, though, aren't we?" I continued.

"Yes. But that isn't why I stopped by," Karen said, pausing to sip her own drink. "My calendar is a mess, and I need to double-check who's hosting dinner Thursday. Do I have to get ready for company?"

We had dinner every Thursday with Felipe Vargas and Ernie Jourdain, each one of us taking a turn at hosting and cooking. Karen claimed it was the only way she could make herself clean house.

I laughed. Karen was the most organized person I knew when it came to her job and her news stories. She had files within files and a color-coded labeling system to organize all her contacts and sources.

But when it came to her personal schedule, she couldn't keep track of anything. Without the deadline of company every fourth Thursday, her house sagged under multiple layers of clutter. I called them her middens and told her someday an archaeological dig would unearth all the things she'd lost over the years.

I often wondered why her organizational skill didn't translate, but I'd given up trying to find an explanation. It was just part of her charm.

"I'm hosting," I said, the schedule fresh in my mind. "Felipe next week, and you the week after."

I went back to sorting T-shirts. "Not sure what we're eating yet. It'll depend on what kind of fish I can get fresh."

Recently, we'd decided to concentrate on traditional Southern dishes. I knew there would be field peas with cornbread and fried fish, and banana pudding for dessert. A second, or third, vegetable would be good, but that would depend on Thursday morning's grocery shopping.

I slid three size-small shirts back into their proper place on the rack. Why couldn't people put things back where they belonged?

"Going to visit my ex?" Karen sounded worried. "You looked like you were about to belt his deckhand when the four of us went looking for fish last month."

"He was a jerk." I shrugged. Karen's ex, Riley Freed, ran a fishing boat. He usually had the best, and freshest, catch. But a couple of his deckhands were redneck idiots. "Not every-body thinks Ernie and Felipe are a cute couple."

"Well, I don't think I'd seen you that mad since Cherie Gains made a play for Keith Everett."

I planted my fists on my hips in mock indignation. "He was my boyfriend! And that's very important when you're fourteen."

"Yeah, right." Karen set her cup down and helped me finish sorting the T-shirts. "But it didn't last."

I gave a dramatic sigh. "My first lost love," I said.

"At least you found out early," Karen said, stepping back to admire our handiwork. "Saved yourself a divorce."

"Oh, please!" I walked to the front of the store, and cast a critical eye on the merchandise in the window. It needed *something*; I wasn't sure what. Maybe I'd step outside later and try to come up with a new display.

"You and Riley are still friends, Karen. It wasn't exactly the end of the world."

"True." Karen's usual sunny outlook had replaced her earlier concern. "Riley isn't a bad guy. I actually kinda like him—just as long as I don't have to live with him."

She took a last pull on her mocha and tossed the cup into the trash can behind the counter. "So, Thursday? You need any help?"

"If you're offering, I won't turn you down." I grinned at her. "About six work for you? I told Felipe and Ernie we'd eat at seven."

Karen nodded. "Got an appointment," she said, waving over her shoulder.

As she reached for the door, it swung in. A middle-aged couple, south of retirement age but past the kids-in-tow stage, stood in the doorway.

Karen moved aside, holding the door for the couple. "See you Thursday," she called over her shoulder as she walked out.

I smiled at the new arrivals and went back to my paperwork. I'd learned early that one sure way to drive customers right back out onto the sidewalk was to make them feel like they were being watched.

Even when they were.

Southern Treasures was the kind of place where customers had to wander to investigate the one-of-a-kind pieces that were my specialty. Not upscale antiques like Ernie and Felipe carried at the Carousel Antique Mall, with price tags to match—my treasures were quirkier. And cheaper, except for the handmade quilts.

I did carry the standard stuff—postcards, shells, and shot glasses—to fill out the shelves when my inventory ran low and provide a steady cash flow. Still, nothing matched the thrill when a customer's eyes lit up over one of my garage-sale finds.

I kept an eye on the couple's progress, glancing up at the concave mirrors in the corners of the store. The woman was especially taken with several of the quilts, but her husband was clearly not opening his wallet this morning.

As I watched-without-watching, the woman made her pitch, but hubby kept shaking his head. The only thing in the shop he appeared to like was Bluebeard, and he wasn't for sale.

They spent half an hour wandering around, occasionally arguing in lowered voices over an item but never actually carrying anything to the counter. In the end, she bought a single postcard "for the grandkids" and slipped it in her giant purse as they headed out the door.

I shrugged. Typical. All that drama for a lousy fifty-cent postcard. And she'd made a mess of the postcard spinner.

Oh well. It needed restocking, anyway.

I straightened the cards, lining them up in the pockets of the spinner. I didn't realize I was muttering to myself until Bluebeard chimed in.

"Dammit."

I glanced up at the bird. "Language, Bluebeard."

He ruffled his feathers and turned away, pretending I wasn't speaking to him.

Bluebeard had a salty vocabulary, and I wondered where he had learned it. From Uncle Louis?

I barely remembered him. I was only ten when he died, and my mother didn't talk about him much as I grew up. I always assumed I'd get the real story when I was older, but my parents were killed in a hit-and-run when I was in high school, and no one else seemed to know much about Uncle Louis.

Now I wondered about the man who had left me 55 percent of the store that supported me—just barely—and a foul-mouthed parrot.

If only Bluebeard could really talk.

Chapter 2

BY THE NEXT MORNING, THE MYSTERY OF UNCLE Louis had been tucked back away. One of these days, when I had some free time, I would try to find out more about him.

And pigs would fly. Running a small business in a tourist town didn't leave a lot of free time, and what I did have, I used to treasure hunt for the oddities that gave Southern Treasures its personality.

I used to have a hired manager, but eventually I knew the store better than anyone I could hire. Three years ago, I let my last paid manager go and quit my job as an elementary school office aide in Pensacola. Now I just had part-time help in the summer.

The phone rang before I could make it to the front door to turn over the "OPEN" sign.

"Southern Treasures; how can I help you?"

"Play hooky," Karen said without preamble.

"Uh, Freed? Hello? I have a store to run." What if my quilt

lady from yesterday managed to pry some money out of her husband? The sale of a five-hundred-dollar quilt would sweeten my week a lot.

"Linda will cover for you. Besides, it's the quiet time; you said so yourself. Your inventory is down, and you need a treasure hunt. And I just got called to go over to DeFuniak on a story this afternoon. We could treasure hunt on the way."

I hesitated. She was right about the inventory. The shelves were full but only because there was an extra load of T-shirts. The walls of my tiny stockroom were empty and the shelves bare.

The invitation was tempting. I just hated to impose on Linda.

Linda Miller and her husband, Guy, owned The Grog Shop next door. She was more than a neighbor; she was as close to family as I had in Keyhole Bay. She had been my babysitter and a friend of my mom's. She had also been my guardian during the months between my parents' deaths and my eighteenth birthday, and we were closer than many "real" sisters.

But Linda had her own business to run.

Before I could answer Karen, someone tapped on the glass in the front door. Bluebeard squawked a greeting as I made my way to the door.

Out on the sidewalk, Linda stood with a fat paperback book tucked under her arm and a full cup of coffee, waiting for me to open the door.

I shook my head. I'd been played.

Linda grinned at me and gestured at the lock.

"All right, Freed. How soon will you be here?"

"I'm just pulling onto the highway," Karen replied. Her voice held a barely concealed note of laughter. "Three minutes, unless there's traffic."

I punched the disconnect button on the phone and unlocked the door for Linda. She gave me a quick hug and made a beeline for the tall director's-style chair behind the counter.

"I want to finish this book," she said, setting her coffee on the counter. "If I'm babysitting Southern Treasures, Guy can't interrupt me every five minutes."

"And what if my customers interrupt you every five minutes? Did you think about that?" I asked.

She shrugged. "They'll pay for the privilege. It all works out." Pointing to the staircase in the back that led to my apartment over the store, she continued, "Better grab a bottle of water before you go. It's gonna be hot out there."

Good advice. I hurried up the stairs, grabbed a tote bag, and stuffed in the necessities for a day trip: sunglasses, purse, bottled water, cell phone, and checkbook. I ducked into the bathroom and quickly pulled my long, dark-blonde hair into an untidy knot to keep it off my neck.

At the last minute I remembered sunscreen. I didn't mind when my pale complexion freckled with a little sun, but the difference between freckles and sunburn was about a nanosecond. I wasn't taking any chances today.

I heard Karen's SUV pull up outside as I headed back down.

One last detour. I opened the door of the heavy iron safe under the stairs and counted out eight hundred in cash. For some people, cash talks louder than a check, especially when you're buying odds and ends out of their backyards. I'd closed a lot of deals by offering folding money.

"Thanks, Linda," I said, stopping to give her another hug. "I owe you for this one."

"Got my book and my coffee," she said. "I'm good for the day."

"Coffee?" Bluebeard said. He sounded hopeful. It was

odd sometimes how human he seemed. Or maybe I was just spending too much time with him.

"No coffee," I answered. I stopped to check his water dish and offered him a shredded-wheat biscuit from the canister under his cage. "You behave while I'm gone."

Karen handed me a coffee when I slid into the front seat. "Twice in two days? I could get used to this," I said as I fastened my seat belt.

"Don't," she answered, silencing the chatter of the police scanner next to her seat. "You've already used up your allotment for the month. Next time it's your treat."

We left the highway, heading north. Karen knew treasure hunting almost as well as I did by now.

Just south of Keyhole Bay, I-10 was a freeway across the southern states. Even the old highway that formed Keyhole Bay's Main Street was heavily traveled. Everything there would be picked clean. We needed rural routes and county roads.

That was where we were headed—into the piney woods of Florida's Panhandle, maybe up into southern Alabama. It was the long way around to get to DeFuniak Springs, but it took us through lots of places too small to be called towns and past a couple of my favorite quilt makers.

Five hours and several stops later, we hit I-10 just outside DeFuniak. Stowed in the back of the SUV were a pile of cast-iron bakeware from a company that went out of business in the 1950s, several new quilts, and an antique crazy quilt in silks and velvets that should bring at least a couple thousand dollars.

Fortunately for me, some of my suppliers hadn't yet heard of eBay.

We grabbed a late lunch, and Karen dropped me in front of the library while she went to do her interview. Not that I intended to go inside, I just wanted to walk Circle Drive around the unusual, perfect circle that was Lake DeFuniak. I had spent too many hours indoors during the summer, and the walk would do me good. I just had to remember to pace myself.

As I strolled, stopping every few yards to admire the picturesque houses that ringed the lake, I thought about Uncle Louis. He never married, which I found curious. In a region where family was everything, he never had one of his own.

Karen returned as I was completing my second leisurely lap around the mile-long path surrounding the lake. The long walk in the afternoon sun had left me pleasantly worn out.

We left DeFuniak on I-10, heading west into the sunset. Karen regaled me with the story of her interview; an hour with a retired chorus girl who had become a volunteer dance coach with a high school drill team.

"She's a real character," Karen laughed. "She showed me pictures of her in Las Vegas and Atlantic City. I had to keep reminding myself that I couldn't put them on radio. But I got a couple, anyway. We can post them on the station website when the story runs."

Taking the freeway, we would be home in just over an hour. Plenty of time to tidy up for tomorrow night, finish the book I was reading, and get a good night's sleep.

I'd be up late tomorrow. No matter how hard we tried, how often we promised ourselves we'd break up early, dinner with Felipe and Ernie always ended after midnight, and Friday morning always came too soon.

As we crossed the line back into Escambia County, Karen kicked the volume up on the scanner. She kept it on whenever she was in range, just in case.

It immediately crackled to life with heavy traffic. The voices of local police, many of them men and women we knew well, filled the car.

"Patrol 15, this is Dispatch. Repeat, please."

"Traffic accident. County Road 198, milepost 27. Single car." Tension crackled in the officer's voice. "Need rescue unit and paramedics."

Karen stepped hard on the brakes, cutting across two lanes of traffic and speeding down the exit ramp. She hung a right at the end of the ramp, heading north.

"Hope you don't mind a little detour," she said. It wasn't a question; she was going to the scene. My agreement wasn't a consideration.

Karen drove fast, with an assurance that came from familiarity and experience. The location was north of Keyhole Bay on a lightly traveled county road, and she didn't need to consult a map or GPS to find her way.

The radio crackled again. "Patrol 15, Dispatch. Rescue and medics on the way. ETA six minutes."

"Copy that, Dispatch. Where's my backup?" Urgency pushed his voice up an octave.

"Right here, Patrol," a third voice answered. "FSP unit 47, about one minute away."

"Thanks, FSP." The patrol officer paused for a few seconds, his silence as tense as his voice had been. "Think I hear your siren."

Karen roared down the country road as I listened to the scanner. The patrol officer was joined by two state patrol officers, and the rescue unit reported that they were only two minutes away.

"Vehicle is off the road about twenty yards," one of the state officers reported. "On its roof in a field. Driver still in the vehicle. We are attempting to extricate, but it looks like we'll need hydraulics."

"Roger that," the rescue unit replied.

For the next few minutes, there was constant chatter as

official vehicles and equipment arrived on-scene. Orders were radioed from one crew to another as the dispatcher tried to direct traffic between the crews.

Then the radio went quiet. No one spoke. No chatter or requests. No orders.

"Patrol 15, this is Dispatch. Do you read?"

Silence.

"FSP 47?"

No response.

"Rescue 19. Respond."

A pause.

"Somebody respond!" The dispatcher yelled, but he got no reply.

"FSP 24 here, Dispatch. We're almost on-scene." In the background, we could hear the patrol car's siren.

"Update me when you arrive, 24. Seems like everyone out there's gone tunnel vision. I need to know what's happening."

"Will do."

Tunnel vision. It was a phrase Karen had explained to me several months back. Something—something bad—had so consumed the crew's attention that they no longer responded to the dispatcher's calls. Focused on the problem in front of them, they couldn't hear, or respond to, the voices on the radio.

We drove in silence for a couple minutes, waiting for the second state car to arrive and hoping to hear their report to the dispatcher.

Karen's face was grim.

Her hands wrapped around the wheel so tightly that her knuckles gleamed as white as bone as she glared at the road ahead.

Karen spun the SUV around a tight left turn, heading west and south. In the distance, we could hear the faint wail of a siren. A minute later, we caught sight of red and blue strobes cutting through the growing dusk. Karen tapped the brakes, slowing down as we approached the scene.

She nosed the SUV to the shoulder and cut the engine. Just as she reached for her digital recorder, the radio sputtered to life again.

"Dispatch, this is FSP 24. Stand down medical. We need Doctor Frazier, and transport." The officer's tone was flat and matter-of-fact as he called for Doctor Marlon Frazier, the county medical examiner.

The coroner.

In the distance, the siren faded and choked into silence. Nobody was in a hurry, not anymore.

I looked over at Karen. She stared into the distance, where a knot of blue and khaki uniforms surrounded the overturned vehicle.

She gasped, and I followed her gaze.

The car was instantly recognizable. A fully restored baby-blue muscle car rested on its top, the window openings mashed to only a few inches high.

A crumpled echo of its former glory as the pampered baby of its teenage owner, the car belonged to Kevin Stanley.

Kevin, the hero of the local football team. The quarterback who was scouted by college teams two years ago, as a sophomore, and was expected to lead the locals to a state championship this fall.

Kevin, the golden boy of Keyhole Bay High School.

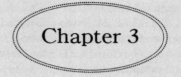

Chapter 3

KAREN DREW A SHARP BREATH AND SHUDDERED slightly before squaring her shoulders and climbing out of the SUV. She had been on-scene at accidents before, her posture said; this was just another one.

Except.

Except we all knew Kevin. We knew his parents and his grandparents. We had watched him grow up in Keyhole Bay. This time it wasn't some anonymous tourist, speeding by on the old highway.

I climbed out of the SUV and walked with her along the ditch toward the cluster of police and rescue vehicles a few yards ahead of us. As we got close, Police Chief Barclay "Boomer" Hardy walked back to meet us.

Boomer shook his head. "You don't want to see this, ladies."

I felt Karen stiffen beside me. She was a bit prickly about any attempt to "protect" her, and I knew this wasn't her first encounter with Boomer.

"Chief Hardy," I said, stepping in front of Karen, "I don't think we want to *see* what happened, but we heard the call—"

"And my listeners will want to hear about what happened," Karen interrupted, clicking the record button on the digital recorder she carried with her everywhere.

At least I had managed to draw her attention away from Boomer's remark and focus her back on the accident.

"We're investigating," Chief Hardy replied, aware of the recorder. He chose his words carefully. "For now, all we know is that there appears to have been a single-car rollover accident."

"Injuries?" Karen asked.

She didn't need to. From where we stood, even with Boomer Hardy trying to shield our view, we could see that someone had draped a dark-blue blanket over a body on the ground.

"I can't release any more information, Ms. Freed—"

The chief's careful voice was interrupted by chatter from the radio hanging on his Sam Browne belt. He stepped away without hesitation, keying the radio and responding to the call.

Karen and I waited, straining to hear at least the chief's side of the conversation. He kept his voice and the radio low, but an occasional word could be discerned.

"Thompson's Corner."

"Underage."

"Kegger."

The chief walked a few steps farther away, and Karen tugged on my sleeve.

"Let's go," she whispered, pulling me toward her SUV.

I could guess where she was headed, and I knew it would be useless to argue. We were going to Thompson's Corner, to check out the kegger.

I called Linda and told her to close up and go home. I wasn't likely to get back to town any time soon.

As we left the accident scene and headed for Thompson's Corner, we passed the tow truck from Fowler's Auto Sales, headed toward the accident site.

I had the ugly feeling I knew how Kevin Stanley's car had ended up on its roof in the cornfield.

BY THE TIME WE PULLED UP IN FRONT OF SOUTHERN Treasures, the streetlights had flickered to life. Inside the store, night-lights glowed dimly.

The events of the afternoon had unsettled us both, and I invited Karen in for a cup of tea. I don't think either one of us really wanted to be alone with our thoughts.

We'd seen the aftermath of the kegger. A couple dozen local kids carted off to the police station, their cars impounded.

Usually these things resulted in a flurry of calls to parents, who retrieved sheepish—and tipsy—teenagers from a gathering in the backwoods of the Panhandle. And usually the parents ferried the kids home, while other relatives retrieved the cars from wherever they were parked.

But usually no one died.

Especially not the hometown hero.

The chatter on the scanner was subdued as the local and state police rounded up the partiers and questioned them. Although no one actually said so, the assumption was clear: Kevin Stanley, his celebrated reflexes and physical conditioning impaired by alcohol, had left the kegger in a high-powered vehicle and ended up dead in the middle of a cornfield.

A horrible accident.

In a town as small as Keyhole Bay, everyone would know

the details by morning. And by the day after, he would be a tragic figure cut down in the prime of his youth. The sordid details would be whispered from one gossip to another, but publicly he would be remembered only for his promise and talent.

It's how small towns hold themselves together.

Karen and I dragged ourselves from the SUV and retrieved my treasures.

I stacked the bakeware on the sidewalk while I wrestled the front door open. I carried the heavy box into the dimly lit store, intending to deposit it on the counter.

I was too drained to deal with the new merchandise tonight. I could process it into inventory in the morning.

Karen didn't know the store as well as I did, so I reached out with my elbow and flipped the light switch inside the door. Overhead fluorescents flickered for a second—I needed to replace one of the tubes—then came on bright and clear.

The shop was trashed.

The vintage magazine rack lay on its side, blocking the path to the counter. A quilt, fallen off the wall, draped across the jewelry display case. Antique newspapers covered the counter, their pages spread open as though someone had been interrupted while reading.

Behind me I heard Karen's soft, "Oh no!"

I set the box of bakeware on the floor and turned to take the quilts from Karen, placing them on top of the box before I picked up the magazine rack.

Bluebeard woke up from his nap, glaring at me as though I were the intruder. He muttered something cranky and spread his wings to their full width before settling back down. He fixed his eyes on me and ruffled his feathers, then he spoke again. This time his voice was clear and precise.

"It wasn't an accident."

Chapter 4

KAREN TURNED TO ME, HER MOUTH OPEN, BUT NO words came out. For the first time ever, the "Voice of the Shores" was speechless.

Not that I was doing any better.

I tripped over the box I'd just set down, catching myself on the magazine rack and nearly toppling it back over.

Karen grabbed my arm, whether to stop my fall or to steady herself, I wasn't sure.

Silence stretched for seconds that felt like hours. Karen's voice was a barely controlled croak when she finally managed to speak. "Did you hear that?"

I nodded, still not trusting my mouth to work.

Bluebeard's pronouncement was unsettling, but I knew something Karen didn't. I recognized the voice that had come so clearly from his beak.

A vague memory from childhood, a man I never really knew.

Uncle Louis.

I clenched my teeth to stop them from chattering. Of course he sounded like Uncle Louis. Who taught him to talk, after all? That's all it was.

Nothing spooky, or ghostly. No reason to fall apart.

And, of course, the chaos in the shop wasn't an accident. It looked as if someone had been searching through old newspapers. Seemed pretty deliberate to me.

I pulled in a deep breath, then let it out slowly, forcing away my suspicions.

"I can clean this up in the morning," I said to Karen. "Bluebeard's sick idea of a joke, but I'm too damned tired to deal with it tonight."

Karen didn't buy that Bluebeard was responsible for the chaos in the store. She offered to help me clean up, even suggested she should stay the night so I wasn't alone in the shop.

"At least call the police and make a report," she said.

I shook my head. "They have bigger problems than my parrot trashing the store while I was gone. I'll talk to Boomer in the morning, I promise."

She still wasn't convinced, but she accepted my promise to call the police in the morning. One thing she could count on—I always kept my promises.

"If you're really sure?" she asked, blocking the doorway as I tried to get her out onto the sidewalk.

"Absolutely." I nodded firmly and gave her a push. "I'll call Boomer in the morning, and I'll see you for dinner tomorrow night and give you a full report."

Her expression clearly conveyed her continuing doubts, but she allowed herself to be propelled through the door. She turned back, watching to make sure I locked the door and threw the deadbolt before climbing into her SUV and pulling away from the curb.

Once I saw Karen pull away, I turned around to survey the mess. Magazines cascaded across the floor at the foot of the magazine rack, 1950s *Popular Mechanics* mixed in with mid-century *Life* and *Look*, and *Ladies' Home Journal* from the 1930s. I winced at the damage to the volumes, but the ones on display weren't the most pristine. Those were in Mylar sleeves in the locked case next to the counter, fortunately undisturbed.

The quilt that I'd retrieved from the top of the jewelry case was a modern reproduction of a Victorian classic, and it appeared undamaged.

The rest was just shelves in disarray and T-shirts unfolded and strewn across the floor. It looked like Bluebeard had grabbed whatever items were in his path with his claws and displaced them.

Except for those newspapers.

There were no rips or tears, no hint of beak or claw touching the fragile half-century-old newsprint. They lay open on the counter as though the reader had just walked away when we unlocked the front door.

Despite my claim that I was too tired to deal with the mess tonight, I started folding T-shirts and putting them back into neat stacks on the shelves. I straightened the miniature snow globes and lined up the glassware in tidy-looking rows.

I folded the quilt and left it on top of the jewelry case. Even at five-seven, I would need to drag out the ladder in order to hang it back on the line near the ceiling.

The new bakeware and quilts got stowed in the nearly empty storeroom in back. I would have to price and label them after I'd had a chance to verify the value of the cast-iron pieces.

Outside, the dark night was quiet and empty, as though I were the last person on earth. Inside, the newspapers lay on the counter, their arrangement too precise to be the accidental result of one of Bluebeard's tantrums. I passed the counter one last time, but I couldn't bring myself to look at them. That would have to wait until daylight.

I took a last look around and turned off the fluorescents, leaving only the pale glow of the night-lights as I ascended the stairs to my apartment.

I was sure things would look better in the morning.

I WATCHED THE SUN COME UP OVER THE BAY AS I sipped my first cup of coffee. My sleep had been fitful, filled with dreams of Bluebeard driving a tiny car through Southern Treasures, knocking over shelves and scattering merchandise.

Not too hard to figure out what *that* meant! But as a result, I was out of bed, though not really awake and ready to face the day, when the sun came up.

The view from the back windows of my little apartment was one of my private joys. Looking over the rooftops of the neighborhood behind the string of shops that lined the highway, I could see the bay in the distance.

I sometimes saw the look on the face of a tourist who realized I lived over the shop. Concern, a touch of pity, sometimes a smug glance that asserted his superiority because he had a "real" home.

But he didn't know about my view.

I refilled my coffee cup and headed downstairs. I still had the newspapers to clean up, and there was the call to Boomer I'd promised Karen I would make.

Once downstairs, I switched on the radio to WBBY, hoping to catch Karen's first broadcast of the day. I knew what story would lead: the death of Kevin Stanley, football hero.

I steeled myself, remembering the upside-down car and the blanket-covered body. It took me a few seconds to realize why this death felt so intensely personal: Kevin's accident was a painful reminder of how I had instantly become an orphan at seventeen.

I hadn't been at the scene of the accident in which my parents died, never looked at the crumpled remains of their imported sedan. But I would never completely be without the pain that came with their sudden loss—and the way it occasionally resurfaced.

I should have expected my response, and probably would have, had it not been for the chaos in the shop when I got home. Distracted by Bluebeard's destruction, I had focused on the immediate problem and ignored my growing distress.

I drew in a deep breath, telling myself I could handle whatever was coming. Over the years, I had learned to allow myself a moment of sadness before I moved on, as I did now. I puttered around as I let the emotional rush pass, straightening the last of the shelves and feeding Bluebeard while I waited for the newscast.

I tried to get Bluebeard to talk, wondering if he really sounded like Uncle Louis, but he stubbornly refused to do anything but let out the occasional squawk.

I still hadn't gone near the newspapers. I told myself I didn't want to be distracted by the radio while I was sorting out the fragile newsprint.

In a couple minutes, WBBY's news jingle played, followed by a recorded ad for Beach Books, the store directly across the street from Southern Treasures.

Jake Robinson had bought Beach Books when the previous owner had moved to Atlanta to be near her grandchildren. In the three months he'd owned it, he had expanded the magazine section and beefed up the stock of popular fiction. As a result, Beach Books was one of the most popular tourist attractions in town.

Jake was rather an attraction himself. A little over six feet tall, with dark wavy hair and deep blue eyes, he could have been a cover model for the romance novels he stocked.

Not that I noticed or anything.

I didn't know much about Jake. He was friendly enough when I went into the store, and he'd been in Southern Treasures a couple times. I *did* know he was single—an important detail—and Felipe and Ernie swore he was straight. Beyond that, Jake was pretty much a mystery.

Karen's voice cut through my speculation about Jake. As I expected, the lead story was Kevin's accident. Karen played bits from an interview with Boomer, who described the accident with uncharacteristic restraint. There were also comments from Danny Bradley, the high school football coach, and the principal, Hank Terhune.

Everyone was shocked and saddened by the tragic accident. Kevin was lauded as an outstanding athlete, which he was. His tone formal and restrained, the coach spoke of Kevin's incredible potential, demonstrated by the continued interest of the college scouts. The principal noted solemnly that Kevin was well liked by classmates and teachers alike.

Karen returned to close out the story, careful to say that the accident was still under investigation.

The station switched to an ad for the local car dealer, thinly disguised as an interview with the owner.

There had been no mention of the kegger.

Chapter 5

I HAD UNDERESTIMATED KAREN. SHE HAD TO PUT the commercial break between her segments, but when she returned, she had the story of the kegger. Several law enforcement agencies had been involved, and they had issued more than twenty citations for "Minor in Possession." Those arrested, their names withheld because they were minors, had all been released to their parents.

She went on with a piece on the latest city council antics and a list of upcoming municipal and county board meetings. Local government was a primary source of entertainment in Keyhole Bay, after "stupid tourist" stories.

For the most part, the visitors to Keyhole Bay were lovely people. They brought money into our little community and allowed us to live in one of the most beautiful places on the planet. But occasionally one of them did something so outrageous that it provided amusement for months on end, in conversations that always started, "Do you remember that time . . . ?"

The newscast concluded, and Karen segued into her morning call-in show. WBBY was a small station, and she wore a lot of hats. Usually I enjoyed listening to her, but today I switched the radio off. I had too much to do.

Setting aside my empty coffee cup, I reached for the first newspaper on the counter. It was the local weekly, the *Keyhole News and Times*, from May 1987, open to the "Passings" page. There, at the top of the page, was the obituary for Louis Marcel Georges. Uncle Louis. The man whose voice I had heard from Bluebeard just last night.

Okay. That was creepy.

I carefully folded the yellowed newsprint and set it aside. Beneath it was another copy of the *News and Times*, this one from before my parents were born. Open to the "Business" section, it featured a story about Uncle Louis buying Southern Treasures.

I quickly closed the page, not reading beyond the lead paragraph.

I glanced at the date on the final newspaper—October 1938—but didn't even look at the stories on the open page. I didn't want to know if there was something about Uncle Louis.

How had Bluebeard managed to pick out those particular papers and leave them on the counter? And how had he managed to do that without damaging a single page?

A chill ran up my back. I knew the answer, but I didn't want to think about it.

It wasn't Bluebeard.

It wasn't a practical joke.

The shop was haunted.

By Uncle Louis.

I shook my head to clear away the nonsense. There was no such thing as ghosts. The shop couldn't be haunted. I was spooked by last night's accident, and the feeling would pass.

I just had to give it a little time.

Time I didn't really have. It was Thursday, my weekly dinner with Karen, Ernie, and Felipe. And it was my turn to cook.

I glanced at the clock. Dinner was in less than twelve hours, I hadn't shopped or cleaned, and I needed to log my treasures from yesterday.

I tucked the folded newspapers in their proper places in the rack—out of sight, out of mind—hauled the bakeware from the storeroom, and booted the computer to log the inventory.

I didn't have time for ghosts.

I also didn't call Boomer.

Sure, I'd promised Karen I would, but there really wasn't anything for him to do. Nothing was missing, there was no damage to any of the merchandise, and I saw no sign that anyone had been in the shop who didn't belong there.

With an efficiency born of long practice, I managed to get the shop put to rights and my bookwork up-to-date in short order. No one had come in to interrupt, and it didn't look like anyone was going to.

I made a quick list of errands, left the "CLOSED" sign in the window, stuffed my wallet in my jeans, and grabbed a shopping bag.

I'd need the car to go down to the docks for fish, but that would have to wait until the fleet returned in the afternoon. For this morning, I could walk. It might help clear my head.

I glanced at the clock. Karen would be on the air. I dialed her cell phone and waited while the call went to voice mail.

"Hi. It's me. Running out to shop for dinner. I'll see you about six." I paused, then hurried ahead before my time ran out. "I didn't call Boomer after all. Nothing to report, really, and he's got to be busy with last night's accident."

I gave Bluebeard a stern look before I left. "I don't want another mess like last night."

Bluebeard opened one eye and glared back but said nothing. Apparently, he wasn't speaking to me.

Really? I was being dissed by a bird? I couldn't decide if that was pathetic or just crazy.

The morning air was still cool, but I had warmed up by the time I walked the few blocks to Frank's Foods.

I headed straight to the produce section, looking for ideas. Traditional Southern cooking included a lot of vegetables, and I needed some inspiration.

Frank was unpacking sweet corn from a farm crate and stacking it on the display table. I waved as I approached, and he waved back with an ear of corn.

"Morning, Glory." It was an old joke, one I'd heard a million times, but coming from Frank, it always made me smile.

"Morning, Frank. How you doing?"

He shook his head, his mouth turned down. "Not so good. You heard about the Stanley boy?"

I nodded, and he continued. "Damn shame." He shook his head again. "Just a damn shame."

I didn't need to ask if he knew Kevin. In Keyhole Bay, with about six thousand year-round residents, everybody knew everybody. The only question was how well.

"I didn't know him real well," I said. "But it sure looked like he was going places."

"You know my sister's girl, Tricia? They used to go out."

"Used to?" I said, picking through the corn.

"Yeah." Frank picked out a couple ears and handed them to me. "Broke up a few months back," he said as he continued to examine the corn. "How much of this do you want?"

"There's four for dinner," I answered. "What do you think?"

"You making creamed corn?"

I thought for a minute. "That might be good, but I've never tried it. How's it done?"

Frank started to tell me, and I held up a hand to stop him. I grabbed a paper bag from the bin under the table, and he offered me a pen from his pocket.

I scribbled his directions on the bag, then filled it with the eight ears he said I'd need.

"Thanks, Frank. We're supposed to be cooking traditional Southern recipes every week, but I never learned much cooking from my mom, so I'm always grateful for help." I glanced around the produce section. "Especially with the vegetables."

He grinned sheepishly. "I get a little carried away sometimes, I guess. Cheryl says I do, anyway."

I grinned back. Cheryl, his wife and co-owner of the market, adored Frank, and he returned the favor. They hadn't had any kids, but they were deeply involved with their nieces and nephews who lived in town.

Which reminded me of our earlier conversation. "How's Tricia handling the news about Kevin? Even if they broke up, it's got to be hard for her."

Frank's expression instantly sobered. "Yeah. Especially since she thought they might be getting back together. She broke it off, said he was getting too wild. But lately it seemed like he'd got his head back on straight and was cleaning up his act, and Tricia said she wanted to get back with him. You heard he got the lot-boy job for Matt Fowler?"

I shook my head, but I wasn't surprised.

The lot boy was usually one of the football stars, and the job mostly consisted of standing around the lot looking like a jock and occasionally driving one of the new cars on a delivery. It was basically a way for the Booster Club to funnel money to whichever player they'd anointed, in the guise of an inflated paycheck.

And a way for men like Matt Fowler to associate themselves with the local team. Sure, the Booster Club members did a lot of good. They raised money for new uniforms, and their ads paid for printing the game programs. They underwrote the cost of the annual awards banquet, and they quietly provided money to cover the activity fees of a talented player whose family couldn't afford them.

In theory, they followed the same rules as college alumni groups, altruistically providing financial support when school budgets ran short. But, in practice, some of them turned every game and pep rally into a none-too-subtle ad for their businesses.

"Yeah," Frank continued, "sure looked like things were going his way."

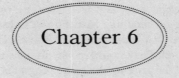

Chapter 6

FRANK'S WORDS ECHOED ALL THE WAY HOME. IT CERtainly did look like things were going Kevin's way, right up
to the point where he rolled his baby-blue Charger.

Frank had said it was a shame, and that was true. But soon
some intemperate soul would have the gall—or the whiskey—
to say what many of us were thinking: What was he doing at
a kegger?

The answer was, unfortunately, simple. Kevin was participating in the time-honored ritual of teenagers everywhere, and he hadn't thought about the consequences.

He believed he was invulnerable. I'd seen the same kind
of reckless behavior in the kids I went to school with and in
the spring-break crowd that flooded into the Florida Panhandle. The belief that they would live forever, no matter
what fool thing they did.

Truth be told, I hadn't been any better than my friends,
sneaking out to parties I wasn't supposed to attend, drinking

a furtive beer under the bleachers at a football game. But I escaped unharmed, unlike Kevin.

I tried to shake off the dark thought as I unlocked my front door, hoping there wouldn't be a repeat of last night's chaos.

The shop was calm and quiet. Bluebeard dozed on his perch—an arrangement of smooth wood branches hanging above a display rack on the far side of the shop—as though nothing had happened, and everything appeared to be in its proper place.

Upstairs, though, I still needed to clean the apartment and cook for tonight's dinner.

I turned the sign from "CLOSED" to "OPEN" and set the door alarm to ring upstairs if anyone came in. I doubted I would be interrupted.

Cleaning my little apartment didn't take long. Without a roommate or a pet to pick up after, I managed to keep the place tidy most of the time. By lunchtime, the kitchen and bathroom were scrubbed, the floors cleaned, and the table set for dinner.

Now all I needed was the food.

I still didn't know what kind of fish we were having, since that would depend on today's catch, but the rest of the menu was settled. I'd decided on hush puppies instead of cornbread, and there would be creamed corn, along with the fresh field peas and the banana pudding.

The alarm sounded, signaling an open door downstairs. Abandoning my kitchen duties, I hurried downstairs, hoping for a paying customer. For once I was in luck. It was my quilt lady from Tuesday, without her husband and with a large wad of cash.

"We went over to Biloxi," she explained as she counted out twenties and hundreds on the counter. There was a twinkle in her eye as she continued. "I told Bill it was my money, I won it, and I could decide how to spend . . ." Her voice trailed off and her eyes went wide as she looked past me to the back counter.

"What is *that*?" she whispered.

I turned my head, not sure what to expect.

On the counter behind me was the silk and velvet crazy quilt from yesterday's treasure hunt—a quilt I was sure I'd left on a storeroom shelf for when I created the perfect display space.

Quilt Lady reached in her purse and drew out another wad of cash. "I hit two jackpots," she said, her voice still barely above a whisper. "How much is that quilt?"

I hesitated for a split second, then quoted her a number that took my breath away. She would haggle; they always did, and I was prepared to drop my price a few hundred dollars to make the quick sale.

To my astonishment, she laughed. "What the heck! I'm spending the casino's money, not mine."

I tried to hide my excitement as I carefully wrapped the treasure in layers of tissue and packed it into a sturdy box for the journey to its new home. Normally, I charge for special packaging, but I was just going to box up her quilt and thank my lucky stars that it had been where she could see it, right at the moment she came in with cash money in her hand.

She chattered the whole time I was wrapping, telling me all about hitting the jackpots while her husband played poker. "He lost, of course," she said. "But he had his allowance and I had my own, and he knows better than to argue with me about what I do with my winnings."

By the time she left the store, we were fast friends. She promised me she would send all her friends from "back home" in Ohio to visit Southern Treasures.

"Do you have a website?" she asked as she picked up her package. "I could tell them about it."

I pointed at the business card taped to the box. "It's on there." I didn't tell her the website wasn't much more than a name, address, and phone number. I kept meaning to update it with some real merchandise, and I'd promised myself I'd do it right after tourist season. Which was now.

Once she was out the door, I allowed myself a whoop of joy. Quilt Lady—she'd told me her name was Margie—had just made my month.

I shoved a few twenties in my pocket and put the rest of the cash in the safe. Not only had I made a tidy profit, but I had saved a trip to the bank to replenish the cash depleted by my last treasure hunt.

But I was sure I'd left the quilt in the storeroom, and I really didn't want to think about how it had moved.

Bluebeard chose that moment to repeat his phrase of the night before. "It wasn't an accident."

I jumped.

The blasted bird hadn't made a sound since last night. This was getting creepy. No, it *was* creepy. No *getting* about it.

I was living with a ghost.

Chapter 7

I PUSHED THE THOUGHT ASIDE. I WOULD THINK ABOUT it later.

Much later.

Right now I had to get down to the pier and see what Riley Freed had caught today.

I left my car in the fisherman's lot a block from the waterfront and walked down to the pier. For once my timing was excellent, and Riley was off-loading the day's catch from the *Ocean Breeze*.

"Hey, Glory!" Riley called when he spotted me headed his way. "What's up?"

"Dinner," I said, stopping a few feet up the dock, out of range of the fish his deckhands were rapidly loading into totes. "What's good today?"

Riley bit his lip. "I was line fishing, Glory. Got some nice grouper, but it's pricy." He shrugged. Riley knew I was usually very frugal, even when I entertained. "You know how it is; line fishing's expensive."

I fingered the twenties in my pocket and smiled. "Just for today, money's no object. I need enough to feed four—and maybe your recommendation of how to cook it."

His eyebrows rose. "Must have been a real good day if you aren't concerned about prices."

"Let's just say I love tourists who hit it big over in Biloxi and stop here on their way home."

"Well, my price may have just gone up," he teased.

I grinned at him. We'd been friends for years, both before and after he married my best friend. Even through their divorce, I had managed to stay friends with both of them, just as they had stayed friendly with each other.

"Don't make me haggle," I whined in mock supplication. "You know how much I hate to haggle."

Riley shook his head. "Yeah, right," he said drily. He knew my reputation for bargaining with tourists, and he knew I usually came out ahead.

He scanned the totes on the dock, quickly filling with wiggling fish the color of underripe tomatoes. After a few seconds, he plunged his gloved hand into the mass and pulled one out.

"Should run about three pounds, which ought to do you. I'll clean it for you." Riley knew I hated cleaning fish.

He slapped the fish on a work table on the deck, and with a few deft strokes, he cleaned it and cut off the head. "You cut it in steaks, season with salt and pepper, and coat with a mixture of lemon juice, mayo, and mustard."

I nodded as he wrapped the fish in a sheet of brown butcher paper while he continued. "Broil it until the coating's crusty. If it isn't done enough, finish it in a hot oven."

"And can I call you if I forget any of that?" I kidded.

"You can try." He glanced at the deckhands, who were beginning to move the totes off the dock toward the sales shed.

"But I'm probably going to be buying the guys a round at The Tank in about thirty minutes, so you're gonna be out of luck."

I was still chuckling when I climbed back in the car for the short drive home. Quilt Lady had definitely improved my mood, and bantering with Riley always lifted my spirits.

But when I got home, I approached my back door with trepidation. What was I going to find inside? What might Bluebeard—and Uncle Louis—have been up to while I was gone?

Luckily, nothing.

I hoped moving the crazy quilt was enough disturbance for one afternoon, and there wouldn't be any more surprises for the rest of the day.

Back upstairs, I went to work on dinner.

I had the pudding in the refrigerator and the field peas simmering on the back of the stove by the time Karen arrived. The alarm sounded on the front door, and she called up as she came in, "Don't need to come down; it's just me."

"Lock it behind you," I called back. "It's closing time."

I met her at the top of the stairs and was greeted with a hug before she took me by the shoulders and shook me gently. "What do you mean, there wasn't anything to report? That's for Boomer to decide, not you. Besides," she continued, following me into the kitchen, "you promised."

"Yes, I did." I lifted the lid on the field peas and stirred, releasing a rich aroma of earthy peas and ham hocks into the air. "And I really meant to call him. But when I looked at it again in the morning, I realized there really wasn't any reason. Just some stuff Bluebeard moved around, and a magazine rack he knocked over."

"If you say so." Karen didn't sound convinced.

"I do." I took a pitcher of sweet tea from the fridge and

poured two glasses without asking. Karen was always ready for a glass of sweet tea.

"I know I promised," I said. I took a long pull at my own glass. Cooking was thirsty work. "I take that seriously; you know that. It just seemed so silly the next morning."

Karen wrapped her arm around my shoulders and gave me another hug, this time without the admonitory shaking. "Okay. I'll take your word for it." She took a sip of tea. "Now what can I do to help?"

I ran down the menu with her. "The corn needs about half an hour, and I need to make hush puppies. The fish is ready for the broiler, but it should only take about ten minutes to cook, so I'll wait until the boys are here to start it."

Glancing at the clock, I worked backward to figure out what to do next. "Sit and relax for a few minutes," I said. "I'll get the corn started and then do the hush puppies. I'll holler if I need an extra hand."

Karen pulled out one of my mismatched vintage dining chairs and sat down. "You don't have to ask me twice."

The apartment had been furnished on treasure hunts over the years. Somehow, it all worked together, but nothing matched exactly. Sort of like my life.

"Did you hear anything more about the accident?" I asked, as I started the hush puppies.

Karen shook her head. "Just what was on the news."

"I only heard the morning broadcast," I admitted. "Was there anything after that?"

"Just a statement from his folks. They're ripped up pretty bad. Kevin was basically a good kid, and he was in line for a free ride at whatever school he decided on."

I added the egg and buttermilk, stirring the thick batter to mix it well. "I heard he'd got a little wild."

"Doesn't everyone? Heaven knows we had *our* moments!" She chuckled at some memory, then immediately sobered again. "Where did you hear that? Not that I'm saying he wasn't," she added hastily. "Just wondering where you heard."

"Frank Beauford. I talked to him when I was in the store this morning. His niece—you remember little Tricia, Shandra's girl?—used to date Kevin. Frank told me they split up a few months back because, Tricia said, Kevin was getting too wild."

"I heard some rumors," Karen said. "But you hear that about all the kids, one way or another. Especially when they hit senior year. Didn't know it was bad enough to dump the quarterback."

I nodded. When I attended Keyhole Bay High School, dating the quarterback was the top of the social pecking order. Breaking up with him would have been the equivalent of social suicide. "Frank said Tricia thought they might be getting back together. Said Kevin seemed to be cleaning up his act, and Tricia wanted him back. Don't know what Kevin thought about that idea, though."

"Yeah, she dumps the biggest of the BMOC and then wants him back? That doesn't sound very likely to happen."

"Not unless high school has changed a *lot* since we were there," I agreed.

"The other thing Frank said—" I was interrupted by the buzzer on the deep fryer, signaling the oil had reached frying temperature.

"Now I can use your help." I gestured at the heavy cast-iron skillet on the stove. "The corn needs to be stirred while I'm frying hush puppies. Okay?"

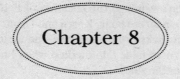

Chapter 8

TWENTY-FIVE MINUTES LATER, THE BELL RANG AT the back door. Karen abandoned her post to look out the window. "Felipe and Ernie," she confirmed. "Right on time," she added unnecessarily as she headed down to let them in. No surprise. Those two never arrived late for *anything*.

Felipe gave me a hug, while Ernie stowed the six-pack he was carrying in the refrigerator.

"Good to see you," Felipe said, his dark eyes level with mine. Ten years in New York and another ten in Keyhole Bay hadn't completely erased his Puerto Rican accent.

"My turn." Ernie's long arms wrapped around me and I rose onto tiptoe to return his embrace. He lowered his face to kiss my cheek as he said, "You tryin' to steal my boyfriend?"

"Never," I answered. "I know better than to mess with you!"

He threw his head back and laughed, white teeth flashing against his cocoa-colored skin. "Smart girl!"

"Besides," I continued as I slid the fish under the broiler, "I wouldn't stand a chance."

As if to underscore my point, Felipe slid his arm around Ernie's waist. "True. But something smells divine in here. I just might be tempted. What are we eating tonight?"

With Karen's help and the heckling of Felipe and Ernie, dinner was soon on the table. Karen and I switched our sweet tea for the longnecks Ernie offered us, and we took our places at the dining room table I'd inherited when I moved into the apartment over the store.

For the first several minutes we discussed the menu, and I answered questions about the preparation of the meal. Thursday dinners had been a tradition for nearly five years, but recently we'd decided to try adopting a theme, and traditional Southern had seemed like a logical choice.

Finding recipes had become a kind of treasure hunt, and I was pleased to share what I'd found, along with their origins.

"Frank Beauford gave me the creamed-corn recipe when I was in the store this morning," I told Felipe and Ernie.

"Which reminds me," Karen said. "You were going to tell me something Frank had said about Kevin Stanley."

"Oh, right." I put a couple more hush puppies on my plate and passed the platter to Ernie. "Frank told me Matt Fowler just gave Kevin the job of lot boy."

Felipe's elegant eyebrows drew together in a scowl at the mention of Matt Fowler's name. "Of course he gave the boy the job," he said. "Thought he could make something off the deal. Man never does something without a percentage off the top for Mr. Fowler."

Karen raised her eyebrows. "Gee, Felipe, tell us what you really think!"

Ernie quickly spoke up. "He's a self-serving jerk, that's all." He patted Felipe's hand. "We already knew about the lot-boy job—Fowler made a big deal of announcing it at the last Merchants' Association meeting." He gave me a reproachful look. "Which you would have known, had you been there."

I shook my head. "We've had this conversation a million times, Ernie. I'm too young and too female for that group."

"And it'll never change as long as people like you take that attitude," Karen said.

"Et tu?"

"Just saying, Glory. It will be an old boys' club as long as the girls refuse to change it."

"Well, this girl has plenty to do without tilting at the windmill that's the Merchants' Association."

The other three let the subject drop. They knew my reasons for not joining the association, and that I wasn't going to change my mind, but it didn't always stop them from mentioning it.

"Anyway," Felipe circled back to his original point, "Fowler made a big announcement, complete with a special guest appearance by the Stanley boy. Like it was a surprise to anyone in town."

I nodded. We'd all expected Kevin to be the new lot boy. "But so what? He does that every year. And we all know he's fronting for the Booster Club, funneling money to their star. I never really understood why these guys do that. What do they have to gain by basically bribing a high school athlete?"

Karen shrugged. "On the college level, there have been scandals about gambling and fixing games, but that hardly applies to high school ball. Makes 'em feel important, I guess."

I looked back at Felipe. "Anyway, the money isn't even really coming out of Fowler's pocket. Why are you so hot about it this time?"

"It was the way he did it. There was something almost, I

don't know, almost predatory about it. Like he was expecting something more this year." Felipe pushed a crumb of hush puppy around his plate with his fork. "He even hinted that the kid was going to continue working for him after he graduated—like Fowler was going to be part of the University Booster Club."

"It's no secret that's what he wants," Karen said. "He hasn't been exactly discreet about his ambitions. Even when I have my recorder running. He intended to ride that kid's coattails into the university athletic system. For Fowler, Kevin was just one more promotional opportunity—a chance to take his dealership places he couldn't get to on his own."

"I guess that shouldn't surprise me," I said. "He was the same way in high school." I shook my head at the puzzled expressions around the table. "He was a few years ahead of me, but some of my friends had older sisters and brothers."

Karen's dark-blue eyes widened in sudden recognition. "Didn't he have some trouble with Linda over the prom fund?"

I shook my head. "Her youngest sister, actually. I never got the whole story—I was only a freshman when it happened—but it got whispered all over school."

Felipe's dark eyebrows drew together. He pointed at Ernie and back at himself. "And he thinks we're a scandal?" he asked, his voice rising. "What did he do?"

I shook my head. "I don't really know."

Karen grinned her I-know-a-secret grin. "You remember Larry Carter, the guy who used to have my job?"

All three of us nodded for her to go on.

"We threw him a party for his retirement. It got a little, um, lubricated, and he told some stories he had never been able to put on the air. Annie was treasurer for the prom, but Fowler managed to get his name on the bank account. There was a rumor that he'd 'borrowed' some money. Had some kind of deal going on and figured he could get it back in the bank before anyone missed it, but Annie noticed. The money got repaid, and it all got hushed up, but Carter said Fowler doubled the money and pocketed the profit."

Matt Fowler was a prime example of why I didn't want to belong to the good ol' boys club. He was the kind of guy who called every woman under eighty "honey," sucked up to anyone more powerful than he was, and stepped on anyone who wasn't. Using Kevin Stanley as a stepping-stone to the next level of power was entirely in keeping with his methods.

"The kid didn't seem too happy about it, to tell the truth," Ernie said. "Looked like he didn't want to be at the meeting, and like he really didn't want to work for Fowler."

"But that job isn't work," I said. I stood up and started clearing the dinner dishes. "All he had to do was stand around, look like a star quarterback, and once in a while drive a new car around town."

I took the banana pudding from the refrigerator and put it on the table with a fresh pitcher of sweet tea. Beer was fine with fish and hush puppies but not with banana pudding.

I also started the kettle and put fresh grounds in the French press. Felipe always wanted coffee with his dessert, even if everyone else was drinking sweet tea.

The conversation moved away from Matthew Fowler and his attempts to exploit Kevin Stanley. Not that it much mattered, with Kevin dead. Fowler would quickly switch his allegiance to another player.

But in a town the size of Keyhole Bay, everyone went to the games and knew the players, and we all knew there wasn't anyone else on the team nearly as talented as Kevin.

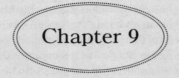

Chapter 9

THANKFULLY, FRIDAY MORNING WAS QUIET IN SOUTH-
ern Treasures. Karen, Ernie, and Felipe had stayed until after
midnight, and after Quilt Lady's visit, I didn't even mind the
lack of business.

I debated what to do about Uncle Louis. I was convinced
he was responsible for both the mess on Wednesday and the
quilt sale yesterday, but what could I do about it?

I had always dismissed the odd things Bluebeard said,
maybe because I hadn't wanted to admit my suspicions. But
now it was more than just the random comments of a talking
bird. And why was he interfering now, after all the years I'd
been here?

He could have chosen so many times: the death of my parents; my high school graduation, a couple months after my
eighteenth birthday; the milestone birthdays that followed at
twenty-one or thirty; or when my finances forced me to quit

community college after a year and find a job in Pensacola. Or even when I took full control of Southern Treasures.

What had changed? Had Kevin's death somehow triggered a reaction from Uncle Louis?

"Bluebeard."

The parrot looked up as I crossed the shop to his perch. He had been here when Uncle Louis was alive, but he wasn't exactly going to carry on a conversation with me.

Still, he had commented on both the mess in the shop and the quilt being out of place.

"Coffee?" he said expectantly.

I shook my head. "No coffee, Bluebeard. You know better."

I reached in the plastic bag I'd carried down from the kitchen above. Taking out a single hush puppy, I put some of the seasoned cornmeal in the center of his dish.

He let out a squawk and dived for the dish. Corn was one of his favorite treats. He needed a low-fat diet, but an occasional hush puppy was a treasure in his eyes.

He devoured the hush puppy crumbs and followed them with a drink of water before eyeing me intently.

"More," he said.

I put the rest of the treat in his dish and quickly tossed the bag in the covered trash can. I'd empty the can before I left him alone; otherwise, he would dig through it. Both the greasy crumbs and the bag could be dangerous for a parrot.

When he finished the treat, Bluebeard hopped over and landed on my shoulder. He rubbed his head against my cheek, his signal that he wanted pets.

I scratched his chin. "I wish I knew what you were thinking, big guy. You've been around here longer than most anybody, and you know all the secrets, but you're not telling."

"Secret," he repeated. "Tell the secret."

"But you won't tell me," I sighed. "And that is the problem."

Bluebeard leaned forward to look me in the eye. He might be just a parrot, but parrots were smart animals, and this one was scary smart. Especially when there seemed to be an almost-human intelligence in his gaze.

I held out my arm and Bluebeard walked down it from my shoulder to my wrist. His claws were strong, and I could feel the tips of his sharp nails through the sleeve of my sweat-shirt. I'd need to trim those nails soon.

I carried Bluebeard back to his perch and held out my hand for him to step across.

"Coffee?" he asked once he was settled.

I shook my head. "No coffee, Bluebeard. It isn't good for you. And you already had a hush puppy."

I pulled the liner out of the trash can and knotted the top. Pulling a fresh bag off the roll at the bottom of the can, I quickly relined the can and dropped the lid back in place.

"I'm going next door to talk to Linda for a few minutes, Bluebeard. I do not want another mess, understand?" I paused a moment and continued. "If this keeps up, you'll be seeing more of that closed cage than you're used to."

I had a large cage that sat in the corner of the shop, but I usually left it open for him to come and go as he pleased. I had almost put it out for sale in the shop, but now I was glad I hadn't. If Bluebeard kept disrupting the shop, I would have to keep him locked up in the cage when I wasn't watching him.

Bluebeard didn't care for the closed cage, enjoying the freedom of the shop, and he recognized the word. He un-leashed a string of profanity in protest.

"Language!" I said sternly. Even though the shop was empty, I wanted to curb his vocabulary. I never knew when a customer would be offended by an outburst, and I couldn't afford to offend the people who kept me in business.

His voice dropped to a mutter, and though I could still discern a word or two, I let it slide for now.

I flipped the "OPEN" sign over, threw the deadbolt, and went out the back door to drop the bag of trash in the bin. I let myself in the back door of The Grog Shop, calling out to Linda and Guy as I came in.

I had lived with them for several months after my parents died, and their shop was almost as familiar as my own. I threaded my way between stacked cases of beer and wine and passed tall metal shelves with liquor bottles carefully lined up and labeled.

"Up here," Guy called from the front of the storage room.

He had several cases of beer piled on a hand truck, ready to restock the walk-in cooler up front. I squeezed past and opened the door for him.

"Thanks, Glory," he said, maneuvering the loaded hand truck through the door.

I moved ahead of him again, and pulled open the heavy glass door of the cooler. Cold air flowed out, chilling my feet as it slid across the floor.

Guy pushed the hand truck inside, and I let the door close behind him as I turned to look for Linda.

As usual, she was at the register, ringing up a purchase for a customer. I waited for her to finish the sale and hand over the receipt before I approached.

As soon as she caught sight of me, Linda came around the counter and gave me a quick hug. At five-two, she was shorter than me by several inches, but that didn't stop me from feeling protected by her embrace.

Linda had been my mother's neighbor growing up. She'd

attended Mom and Dad's wedding with her parents and been my first babysitter, and I'd been a junior bridesmaid when she married Guy. And at thirty years old, with no children of her own, she had taken me in as a teenage basket case when my folks were killed.

It wasn't until I turned thirty myself—and understood how young she had been—that I realized just how phenomenally lucky I had been to have her. My life could have taken so many wrong turns without Linda and Guy, and I still depended on her to steer me straight.

Like today.

"You got a minute?" I asked, returning the hug.

"For you? Always!"

Guy emerged from the cooler with the empty hand truck. He pushed it through the door into the storage space and came right back.

My worry must have been all over my face, because he gave me a long look and said, "Why don't the two of you go get a coffee? I'll take care of the shop."

I ran over and gave him a hug of pure gratitude. There are times a girl just needs her mom—or the closest thing she has to a mom—and this was one of them. Lucky for me, Guy was one of those men who understood that bond. Lucky for me *and* Linda—that she had found him.

"You're the best," I said as I gave him another squeeze.

As Linda and I walked past the front of Southern Treasures, I examined the window displays. They definitely needed updating, but that was a project for another day. Today I wanted to learn about Uncle Louis.

Walking in the front door of The Lighthouse was olfactory overload. The heady aroma of roasting beans and brewing coffee was laced with the sweet warmth of treats, fresh from the oven. It made my mouth water before I even looked in the case to see what the special was today.

I ordered lattes and lemon scones before Linda could object. If I was going to ask for her help, the least I could do was pay for the coffee.

Before we could sit down, we had to spend a few minutes chatting with Chloe at the counter while she made our coffees. A student at Keyhole Community College, Chloe wanted to talk about the accident.

"I was just a couple years ahead of Kevin," she said. "I was a senior when he made varsity his sophomore year. He was an amazing ballplayer. Way better than Jimmy Parmenter, and he got a full ride at State."

"Parmenter?" Linda asked. "Is that one of the Parmenter boys from out on Highline Road?"

Chloe nodded. "Jimmy's a couple years older than me. Went down to State, but he came back a couple months before we graduated. Said he blew out his knee and lost his scholarship."

She handed over a tray with the lattes and scones. "Now this happens to Kevin. Man, I don't know if being a football star is a good thing in Keyhole Bay."

I led Linda to a table in the back of the store, as far as possible from the hum of gossip. Now that we were here, I didn't know quite where to start.

Linda took my hesitation as sadness over the accident. "Did you know Kevin?"

I shook my head. "I knew who he was, but I didn't know him personally." I paused again, trying to find a way into my questions. "I was out there Wednesday, at the accident. Karen and I were on the way back when we heard the call, and she headed over there. We saw the car." I stopped, remembering the sight of the baby-blue Charger sitting upside down in the middle of the field.

Linda reached out and put her hand over mine. "You went out there? Are you okay?"

"I, I think so. We didn't get that close, but it was obvious it was a bad one."

Anger twisted Linda's features. "It shouldn't have happened. Those kids shouldn't have been out there. Not with a keg, certainly."

"Where did they get the beer?" I knew it sure wasn't The Grog Shop; Guy and Linda were careful who they sold to, especially kegs.

She shook her head. "I don't know, but I don't think anyone in town sold to any of those kids. Either they went down to Pensacola or someone bought for them."

I didn't want to think about it. It made sense, and I wanted to believe no one in town would sell beer to kids. But no matter who sold the beer, the outcome was the same. Kevin Stanley was dead.

"That was why you were late getting back, wasn't it?"

"Yeah. We were out at the accident scene, and then we went to Thompson's Corner, where the party was. Lots of kids picked up and taken into the station instead of just calling their parents."

"Is all of this bringing up memories of *your* parents? Is that what has you so upset?"

"Yes. No. I don't know." I fiddled with my scone, breaking it into pieces and exposing the tiny fragments of lemon peel. I hadn't actually eaten any of it.

My throat was suddenly dry, and I took a swallow of coffee.

"I need to know about Uncle Louis."

Chapter 10

"UNCLE LOUIS?"

"Yeah. I don't know anything about him. I mean, why did he leave me his shop?"

"Who else would he have left it to? He never got married or had kids of his own. Your mom and her brother were his only close relatives."

"But why did he leave me a bigger share than Peter?"

Linda sipped her coffee, as though she were stalling. "I didn't know Louis that well," she said finally. "He died before Guy and I bought The Grog Shop, and he was always kind of a private person." She stopped, her eyebrows scrunching together in concentration. "I'm not sure if anybody knew him that well."

"But he lived here his entire life."

She nodded. "Sure, but Louis was already middle-aged when I was a kid, and he kept to himself a lot. If he hadn't had Southern Treasures, I think he would have been a hermit, living out in the woods by himself."

She studied me for a minute. "Why the sudden interest? You've been in the gift shop for almost fifteen years, at least part-time. Why now?"

That was a question I didn't want to answer, but I needed to share my concern with someone. And if there was one person I could count on, one person I could trust, it was Linda.

I hoped.

But I couldn't just blurt it out. I had to go at it kind of sideways. "Was there anything out of place when you locked up the shop the other night?"

Linda shook her head, her expression puzzled. "You know I would have put it away if there was. But what does that have to do with your sudden interest in your uncle?"

"Well," I swallowed hard and forged ahead. "There was a mess when we got back."

"What?!" Linda almost yelled, and a couple people turned to look at us. "What do you mean 'a mess'?" she said, more quietly this time. "Everything was just fine when I left."

"I didn't mean *you* did anything, honest. And that's what makes this so, well, strange. The magazine rack was knocked over and there was stuff on the floor. I just figured Bluebeard had thrown a tantrum and made a mess because I was late coming home."

Linda chuckled. "That's not strange. He's just the most spoiled parrot on the planet." Her expression got serious again. "So what has you so upset? One of Bluebeard's tantrums shouldn't be the cause of this much concern. There's got to be something else."

For a moment she actually sounded like my mother. That not-so-subtle demand, mixed with just-tell-me-what's-wrong concern, brought back the feeling of being sixteen and facing my mom when there was something I didn't want her to know.

And yet I wanted to tell Linda my suspicions, if only to have her laugh them off and reassure me.

"There was," I admitted. "There was a stack of newspapers on the counter, all open like somebody had been reading them." When I said it out loud like that, it sounded pretty silly.

"Karen wanted me to call Boomer. It looked like someone had trashed the shop. But I knew Boomer was busy with Kevin's accident, and I figured it could wait till morning." I shrugged. "By morning, it just didn't look that serious. No sense in calling Boomer for a parrot tantrum. But when I started putting those newspapers away, it seemed like every one was open to a story about Uncle Louis, and it got me thinking. I really don't know much about him."

Linda patted my hand, and I looked up. She wasn't laughing anything off, but I hadn't said anything about a ghost.

Yet.

"You were just a kid when he died, Glory. You never got a chance to know him. And, like I said, he kept to himself a lot. This is what I can tell you. Louis Georges was born right here in Keyhole Bay. His dad was from up North, but he ended up here after World War I and married a local girl. Your granny idolized her older brother, but she was a lot younger than Louis—she was just a little girl when he enlisted in the army."

I nodded. I'd seen pictures of Uncle Louis in his army uniform, and he looked like he wasn't much more than a kid himself.

I thought for a minute. "So he enlisted? I saw pictures from the war, and just figured he was drafted."

Linda shook her head. "I think your mom told me once that he was already in the army before they started drafting anybody."

"But he obviously came back to Keyhole Bay," I said, remembering the "Business" section headline from the news-paper. "He bought the shop before my mom was born."

Linda finished her coffee and stuffed a crumpled paper napkin in the empty paper cup. "That's all I know," she said. "The *News and Times* keeps an archive, though. You should be able to go down to the office and look up the stories about your uncle. It might be a place to start."

Linda paused as though there were something more she wanted to say. But she seemed to think better of it and gave me another questioning look instead. "Still, why were you upset about newspapers on the counter? They weren't dam-aged, were they?" She waited, taking my silence for agree-ment. "Then what has you in such a state?" She was starting to sound irritated by my stalling.

I squeezed the napkin I was holding into a tight ball. "Linda," I said, my eyes on the table and my voice almost a whisper, "do you believe in ghosts?"

Linda was quiet for so long I was afraid to look up. She was probably trying not to laugh out loud at the ludicrous question I had asked.

Finally, I couldn't stand it any longer, and I slowly raised my eyes to look at her.

She wasn't laughing. In fact, she didn't even look like she wanted to laugh. Her expression was dead serious.

Ooh. Bad word choice there!

She studied me for a moment, as though trying to guess why I was asking.

After a couple of minutes that felt like centuries, she smiled at me. "Honey child," she used my childhood nickname, "of course I believe in ghosts. We live way south of the Mason-Dixon Line, and we have a fine tradition of ghosts. Besides, we aren't that far from the bayous, and there's way worse things than ghosts in those swamps."

Chapter 11

RELIEF FELT LIKE A WARM GULF WAVE WASHING OVER me. "You mean that? You don't think I'm going crazy?"

Linda smiled and nodded, and I felt my stress level drop about a thousand percent. "And you think it's Louis, and that's why you wanted me to tell you about him. Right?"

It was my turn to nod. "Those newspapers all had stories about him," I said. "That has to mean something."

"Do you remember any of the dates? That's probably where you should begin."

I thought for a minute as I gathered up the empty cups and carried them to the trash. One of the papers had been Uncle Louis's obituary, and there was one about him buying Southern Treasures. I didn't remember the third one, but it had been even older.

It was a place to start.

When I came back to the table, Linda stood up. "I better get back, before Guy thinks I ran off with the beer man."

It was a running joke between Guy and Linda. The delivery man from the local beer distributor was approaching retirement. His pot belly and bald head didn't stop him from flirting with every woman on his route, and he always asked Linda if she was ready to run away with him.

We left the store and stepped back onto the sidewalk. Midday traffic had picked up, locals waving to us as they drove past. We waved back, continuing our conversation as I unlocked the front door of Southern Treasures.

"You really don't think I'm nuts?" I asked again.

In reply Linda gave me a hug. "Not for a second." She stepped back and turned toward The Grog Shop.

I started to call after her, but the phone rang in the shop, and I ran to answer it.

"I'm back on the air in three minutes," Karen said without saying hello. "Just wanted to thank you for dinner—it was great—and to see if you had plans for tonight."

"Nothing important," I answered. To tell the truth, the plans I had involved leftovers and the television. I didn't have what you would call an active social life.

"There's a place in Pensacola I want to check out," Karen said.

I interrupted her before she could go any further. "I don't feel much like going out. Why don't you come over here? Dinner and a DVD, maybe? And I, uh, I have something I want to talk to you about, anyway."

"Great!" Karen accepted the invitation so quickly that I wondered if that was her intention all along. "I'll pick up burgers from Curly's." She named our favorite fast-food drive-through.

"Sixish?"   •

"Works for me. Gotta run," she said, and disconnected.

Within seconds I heard her voice on the radio, announcing "News at Noon."

I told myself it was no big deal. Burgers and a movie. It was a typical Friday night with Karen.

Except that most Friday nights I didn't tell her I was living with a ghost.

Between customers, I started leafing through the back copies of the *News and Times*. I had put the papers back in their proper places and tried to forget about them, but I knew when Uncle Louis died, and I was able to find his obituary:

> *Louis Marcel Georges, 67, passed away on Thursday. The owner of the Southern Treasures Gift Shop, Mr. Georges was a native of Keyhole Bay. He attended Keyhole Bay High School, and served in the U.S. Army during World War II.*
>
> *He is survived by his sister, Antoinette Georges Beaumont; niece Alexis Beaumont Martine; and nephew Andrew Georges Beaumont; as well as a great-niece and -nephew.*
>
> *Services are pending.*

He had lived in Keyhole Bay his entire life, except for the years he was in the army, and that was all they had to say about him? Sixty-seven years boiled down to two paragraphs?

It seemed like there should be more, somehow.

I looked at the other two obituaries on the page. An elderly woman whose husband had retired to Keyhole Bay from Michigan. The story ran for an entire column full of family and hobbies and jobs. She had clearly lived a full life.

Had Uncle Louis? Linda said he kept to himself; maybe no one knew what to write about him.

The day seemed to fly by. Between customers and phone calls, it was late in the afternoon before I got a chance to do more reading. When I glanced at the clock I was surprised to see that Karen was due in about half an hour. I only had time to look for one more article.

I tried to remember what other dates had been on the newspapers. They had been a few years apart, and both from before my parents were born, which narrowed the search to the 1940s or earlier.

My stock of papers was far from complete, but I had several issues from most years. When I first took over Southern Treasures, I'd found bundles of *News and Times* tied with yellowed string and stacked in the attic.

I had almost tossed the papers, but Linda stopped me. "There are people who collect old newspapers," she told me. "Put them in the store and see what happens."

I had selected a few issues from each year, and slowly started adding them to my stock. Even if they didn't sell, they attracted attention, and often shoppers would stop to thumb through the plastic-covered papers in the display.

I flipped through the rack looking for the 1940s and had selected a half-dozen issues when the phone rang.

Dumping the stack on the counter, I grabbed the handset and answered. "Southern Treasures; this is Glory."

My mistake. The whiny tenor on the other end told me it was Peter before he could even get past hello.

Not tonight. Please, not tonight.

But Peter was in full-on "helpful mode," and I wasn't fast enough. He plowed right in.

"Glory, I've been watching the news, and I heard about that poor high school kid that got killed out in the woods down there. Must have been awful. A real tragedy."

"Yes, it was—"

He didn't let me go on. "I was thinking," he said, a signal that trouble was coming.

I tried to head him off. "It was tragic, Peter. A terrible accident." I kept my voice soft, soothing. "The star quarterback, just as school is starting—"

"I know," Peter cut in. "That's why I called you. I think we need to act fast. Very fast. If we get on this *right now*, we should be able to make it work. We need a memorial T-shirt, Glory. In memory of the star of the football team. And this is the great part: we contribute part of the proceeds from every sale to support the team! I think it could be great for raising the profile of Southern Treasures. You might even get some TV coverage—it's hit the regional news all the way up here. Isn't it genius?"

Peter finally paused, as though allowing me time to appreciate his splendid idea. And for a moment I couldn't speak.

I quickly found my voice. "That is very probably the worst idea you have ever had, Peter. It's horrible!" I was shaking now, the anger and pain I'd suppressed bubbling to the surface. "A seventeen-year-old boy is *dead*, Peter," I shouted. "He took his prized baby-blue muscle car out on a country road and flipped it, and he died. I cannot believe you want to capitalize on that tragedy. Do you think someone should have made freakin' T-shirts when my parents were killed? And maybe given me a few cents for each one to help 'support' me? Is that what you think?" I wanted to wring his scrawny neck with my bare hands for his callousness.

"No, no, not at all. I didn't mean anything like that, Glory. I just thought we could do something for the school; that's all. And maybe get some good publicity for us as kind of a bonus. It wasn't about the money."

"That's the kind of thing the Booster Club does, Peter. They build themselves up by very publicly supporting the sports stars." I brought my voice under control with an effort. "I have never been a part of that, never wanted to be a part of it, and I certainly don't want to be part of it now. Especially not this way."

I drew a deep breath and spoke softly. It was usually more effective than yelling, once I had Peter's attention. "The answer is no. Absolutely not. Never. I am going to hang up now and try my damnedest to forget we ever had this conversation."

I broke the connection with trembling fingers, the adrenaline rush of anger draining away, leaving me weak and shaky.

I'd lost my temper, something I rarely do. I had been on my own since I turned eighteen, and in the last fifteen years, I had learned a few things about maintaining control of my emotions.

The flare of temper had caught me by surprise, unleashing a flood of anger and loss that was usually tightly controlled. Somehow, Peter had managed to push a button I wasn't even aware of, to expose the pain of my parents' death.

Which explains how Karen caught me in a weak moment.

Bluebeard left his perch and made his way across the shop to sit on my shoulder. There wasn't enough room for him to actually fly; instead, he hopped from the perch to a display rack and across the gondolas of T-shirts and souvenir glasses.

"Good job," he said in Uncle Louis's voice.

I was startled for a moment but nothing like a few days earlier. Maybe I was getting used to the idea of sharing my store with a ghost.

Or maybe I was just too overloaded to react. Either way, I actually felt grateful for the reassurance. I reached up and petted his head, getting a nuzzle in return.

I laughed, my voice still a little shaky. "I lost my temper. Not such a great idea. Besides, you don't know Peter, so how do you know?"

"You'll find out," he replied.

I think my mouth was still hanging open when Karen

opened the front door, carrying a cardboard tray with burgers and shakes from Curly's.

"I figured after the week we had, we deserved a treat," she said, nodding at the shake cups. She glanced up and caught the surprised expression frozen on my face.

"Wow," she said. "You look like you've just seen a ghost."

Chapter 12

"YOU HAVE NO IDEA," I MANAGED TO SQUEAK OUT. I tried to calm my shaking and control the tremor in my voice.

Bluebeard moved off my shoulder onto the counter, peering at the cups in Karen's tray. "Coffee?" he asked.

"It's not coffee, and it's not for you." It occurred to me that his obsession with coffee might have another explanation. In fact, Uncle Louis might be the explanation for a lot of things. Not that the idea made me happy.

Karen set the tray on the counter and put her arm around my shoulders. "Glory? What's wrong? I mean, you *really* look upset."

"I haven't seen a ghost, Freed. Just, well, *heard* one." I winced at the startled look on Karen's face. "Let me lock up," I added hurriedly, "and we can take our burgers upstairs. I promise I'll tell you everything."

Telling Karen everything took a lot longer than I imagined. At first she simply stared, but she quickly recovered her natural curiosity. Soon she was interrupting to ask questions, and then she began reminding me of incidents I had forgotten. As she did, I realized there were a lot of little things I'd chosen to ignore: lights that went on and off when I wasn't in the room, locks that opened themselves, merchandise moved around the store.

I'd dismissed the lights as old wiring, and the locks as my own forgetfulness. I'd blamed Bluebeard for the merchandise. But now, after Kevin's death, I was looking at all of it in a different light.

"When we came back after . . ." she hesitated, as though looking for the right word. "After the *accident*," she continued, "Bluebeard said, 'It wasn't an accident.'"

I nodded, afraid of what was coming next.

"Do you think he meant the shop? Or did he mean Kevin?"

It was the same question I'd been asking myself for days, and I didn't like my answer.

"I don't know," I confessed. "At first I just thought he meant the shop—that Bluebeard was pitching a fit and he wanted me to know he was angry. But then there were all those newspapers, and I wondered if it might have something to do with Uncle Louis."

I couldn't sit still any longer. I stood up and carried the burger wrappers and empty cups to the trash. I got a dishrag and wiped down the table, even though there wasn't anything to clean.

"I think," I said, dropping the dishrag in the sink and turning to face Karen, "I think he meant Kevin."

I sat back down again, sighing. "But how could he *know*? How could he . . ." I forced myself to say his name. "How could Uncle Louis know what happened? He wasn't there!"

Karen laughed, but not like there was anything funny. "How do *we* know? If he's a ghost—and I'm not saying he is—but if he is a ghost, we don't know what the rules are for him. Maybe he can come and go, and he was out on County Road 198, or at Thompson's Corner. Or maybe he's been talking to Kevin. Maybe Kevin told him what really happened, and all we have to do is ask and he'll tell us."

"But why now? Why not when my parents died, or when I took over the store? There has to be some reason, some connection, that made him start talking now."

Karen got up from her seat at the table. "We need to figure out what we're going to do about this ghost," she said. "So let's go downstairs and see what we can find in those old papers. We're not going to fix this sitting around watching a movie."

I led the way back downstairs into the shop. Bluebeard had retreated to his cage to sleep, and he gave us a sharp look when we came in. I tossed a worn dark-green blanket over his cage, and he went back to sleep.

For the time being, I would rather not have his help—or his comments—while we looked for clues to Uncle Louis.

Searching the back issues went a lot faster with Karen's help. She took the stack I had already sorted out, and I started back through the display.

Karen slid the yellowed newsprint from its protective sleeve. "At least now I understand why you didn't call Boomer," she said.

"Yeah." I shifted a stack of papers to the counter. "I hoped it was just Bluebeard. And if it wasn't, I didn't want to tell the police a ghost had trashed my store. Just easier to clean it up and forget it."

"But you looked at the papers?"

"Not at first. I wanted to just forget about it. Then today I decided I had to figure it out. I'd just started through the stuff down here when Peter called." I stopped, remembering the insane idea he'd proposed and feeling the same rush of anger. "Did I tell you his latest scheme?"

"You told me about the coffee idea. Was that it?"

"No." I launched into the story of Peter's memorial T-shirt idea, and soon we were both giggling. Karen could see the absurdity in every one of Peter's brilliant plans, and she pointed it out each time he called with his latest idea.

"Is all his taste in his mouth?" Karen asked between gales of laughter. "I mean, this gives a whole new meaning to the word *tacky*!"

"The part that amazes me is how crass he is. I've always thought his mother—you've met my aunt Missy, right?—I always thought her name rhymed with *prissy* for a reason. She's the type who never says a bad word."

Karen set one paper aside and carefully opened another, scanning the stories as she gently paged through the brittle newsprint. "Isn't she the one who always said, 'Do you kiss your mother with that mouth?' if we slipped up in front of her?"

I nodded. "Her favorite was always 'Bless her heart,' though."

It was a great Southern tradition. We never spoke ill of someone directly. But if we said something that could be construed as critical, the proper formula was to add the phrase "Bless her heart," or "his heart," as though the individual in question just couldn't help whatever harebrained thing she or he had done.

"Of course!" Karen said. She dropped her carefully trained voice and exaggerated her drawl. "Now, Glory, you know Peter is just tryin' to help you. You bein' just a lil' ol' girl and all. Bless his heart."

At first, when Karen whooped loudly, I thought it was part

of the hysterical laughter we'd shared. But as she carefully picked apart the pages of the paper she had in front of her, I realized she'd found something.

"Here it is," she said. Her normal voice—a hint of the South overlaid on a trained broadcaster's diction—couldn't hide her excitement.

I set down the paper I was working on and moved around the counter to read over her shoulder.

The date at the top of the page read October 17, 1945. A banner proclaimed it the "Business" section. In the center of the page, a photo of Southern Treasures looked both familiar and strange. Next door, where The Lighthouse stands now, was a produce stand full of pumpkins. The other side was an empty field where The Grog Shop would be built.

Cars parked diagonally against the curb, but a few spaces were empty directly in front of Southern Treasures. On the sidewalk, a man stood next to a window displaying a giant sign proclaiming "Under New Ownership."

The caption identified the man as Louis Georges, new owner of the Southern Treasures Gift Shop. Below, a two-column story gave more detail:

Local serviceman Louis Georges has purchased the Southern Treasures Gift Shop on Main Street.

Mr. Georges, a graduate of Keyhole Bay High School, recently returned to our fair city after a seven-year absence, serving in the U.S. Army Air Corps. He saw action in both the European and Pacific theaters as a flight engineer.

Upon his return, he purchased Southern Treasures from Mr. Ernest Willingham. Mr. Willingham and his wife are retiring to Montgomery, where their daughter and son-in-law reside.

Southern Treasures provides a diverse assortment of mer-

chandise, including many souvenir items suitable for gift giv-
ing. The store caters to the visitors whom peacetime will bring
to enjoy the delights of a coastal vacation, and to local resi-
dents looking for the perfect gift for friends and family.

Centrally located on Main Street, with street-side parking
for shoppers, Southern Treasures is sure to achieve contin-
ued success.

When asked about his decision to return to Keyhole Bay
as a shopkeeper after his many adventures abroad, Mr.
Georges said he simply wanted to come home and enjoy the
peace and quiet of his hometown.

"I lived in Keyhole Bay from the day I was born until I
left to serve my country," he said in response to questions
from this newspaper. "It is my home, and I can't think of a
place I would rather be."

Assisting him in the shop is his younger sister, Miss An-
toinette Georges. A popular student at Keyhole Bay High,
Miss Georges says she is looking forward to working with
her brother as he moves forward with his new venture.

The shop will be open Tuesday through Saturday from
10 A.M. to 6 P.M., although Mr. Georges says he hopes to
extend the hours during the summer.

"I wonder why he wasn't open on Sundays? You would
think that was a good day for tourist business."

Karen smiled at me, and I was sure she knew the answer,
just from the smug, I-know-something-you-don't look on her
face.

"It was 1945, Glory. Ever hear of blue laws?"

"Of course," I replied. "No Sunday sales. But I thought it
just meant booze. And I thought they repealed all that a long
time ago."

"They repealed the last of them when we were in grade

school. But there were lots of local ordinances back in the first half of the century. For a while, the only place that could legally open on Sunday was the drugstore, because there might be a medical emergency. And even then, there were often laws about what they could and couldn't sell on Sunday."

I thought back to my grade-school days. My parents weren't particularly religious, and though I occasionally went to church with my grandmother, it wasn't a regular thing. I had spent a lot of Sundays playing in the schoolyard or riding my bike down to the bay to watch the fishing boats.

"That's why Doc Bowen's was the only place to buy a soda on Sunday." I had never made the connection before, but it all made sense. "I always assumed the stores were closed because they all went to church. But if there was a law . . ." I shook my head. "But why would you know that and I wouldn't?"

Karen looked sheepish. "Actually, I was doing research for a series I'm planning about the local businesses that have been here for a long time. The station's fiftieth anniversary is coming up, and I'm trying to talk the manager into letting me profile any company that's older than we are. It's just something that came up when I was reading about some of the older businesses."

Before I could respond, she hurried ahead. "Oh! I forgot in all this talk about your uncle—Felipe called just before I left the station. The memorial for Kevin is set for Monday afternoon. He said they intend to close Carousel for the afternoon, and he wondered if we wanted to go together."

"Sure."

We went back to searching. After a few minutes of silence Karen stopped, a puzzled look on her face. "Why seven years?"

I shook my head. "Huh? Where did that come from?"

She picked up the 1945 paper we had set aside and opened it on the counter again. "Why was he in the service for seven years? That seems like an odd length for an enlistment."

It was my turn to feel smug. "It was wartime, Freed. Everybody stayed in until the war ended."

"But we were only at war about four years. Why was he in for seven?"

"I don't know. He went into the service, the war started, and he stayed in until the end. Seems to make sense."

Karen shook her head and returned the paper to the back counter, along with the 1987 obituary. "Still seems odd to me."

Chapter 13

THE WEEKEND PASSED IN THE USUAL WHIRLWIND OF boredom and business. The shop would be empty and busy by turns, a syncopated rhythm I had grown used to over the years behind the counter.

In the quiet moments, I thought about what Karen had said. I didn't really know why Uncle Louis had enlisted. Why did anyone enlist? My dad had talked about enlisting in the U.S. Air Force right out of high school so he wouldn't be drafted. But there wasn't a draft when Uncle Louis graduated—I'd been able to do a quick online search and found out the draft started in 1940.

It was one of the many questions I had about Uncle Louis, but no one seemed to know the answers.

I even toyed with the idea of calling my uncle Andrew, Peter's dad and my mother's brother, but that would mean talking to Aunt Missy for half an hour, listening to her tales of distant relatives I didn't know. Missy had a standard litany of news that always involved someone I'd never met or didn't remember, and she could not be sidetracked.

I put off calling Uncle Andrew. Maybe when I made my semiannual visit I could ask him what he knew. In the meantime, I would see what I could learn in Keyhole Bay.

It was late on Sunday afternoon, and the tourists had either headed home or settled into their hotel rooms and rental houses for the night. The shop had been quiet for more than an hour, and I was considering closing early when the phone rang.

Someday, I swear, I will learn to check my caller ID before I answer the phone. Of course it was Peter. It was as if just thinking about his family had triggered the idea of calling me. But no. It was much worse.

"You did what?!" I nearly exploded when he told me his latest escapade.

"I offered the Booster Club the services of Southern Treasures as a distribution point for the memorial T-shirts."

"I thought I told you—"

"I did just what you said." Peter cut me off. "You said the Booster Club would probably do something, so I called them. The high school gave me the contact information for Matt Fowler—great guy, Matt—over at Fowler's Auto Sales. He was real happy to have a place that would stock the shirts and sell them for the club. Said he usually does that sort of stuff himself, but he's a little shorthanded, what with one of his most valuable employees being killed in that tragic accident—"

"Peter!" I had to yell to get him to stop running on. "I told you I didn't want to be involved."

"You said you didn't want any part of making a T-shirt,

and I completely understood that. But this isn't the same thing. This is providing support for the local team while they are mourning a loss. Not the same thing at all."

I needed to count to ten. Hell, I needed to count to ten thousand. But I couldn't let Peter start talking again.

"So you volunteered me to do all the work of handling the shirts? Because Matt Fowler is shorthanded? Peter, you *do* realize that I run this shop by myself? As in, there is no one else to do anything around here? You can't get more short-handed than that."

"But, Glory," his whine returned. "Just think of all the great free publicity you'll get. That's all Matt gets out of it, and he does this stuff all the time for various events. It's for the kids, Glory, and for all those people who've been asking Matt how they could help."

This time I stopped myself. There was no way Peter would ever understand that Matt Fowler didn't do anything that didn't benefit Matt Fowler in some way. The only reason he didn't want to handle the shirts was because he couldn't see any advantage in it. Kevin—the football star who was his ticket to the University Booster Club—wasn't around any-more. I know it sounded awful, but the plain truth of it was that he was glad to have someone else do the work this time.

As for the free publicity, it would be worth just about what I paid for it. Keyhole Bay had about six thousand full-time residents, and Southern Treasures had been in the same place on Main Street since their grandparents had been children. They all knew the shop and saw it every day when they drove through town to the post office or the grocery store.

I let the silence stretch. There was no answer that would change what was done. Kevin's face, square-jawed and with buzz-cut hair, would be plastered across piles of T-shirts in Southern Treasures for the next few weeks. I would have to face the tasteless reminder of this tragedy—and of my parents'—every day, thanks to my clueless cousin.

"Peter, I will do this. Just once. But if you ever pull another stunt like this, if you commit Southern Treasures to *anything*, I will come to Montgomery and purely knock the stuffing out of you. And then I will call whoever you made the deal with and cancel it. You do not have the authority to make a deal like this and to commit *me* to do the work. I know you think you're helping, and I admire your enthusiasm. But you are not here in Keyhole Bay, and you are not in the shop." I drew a deep breath, silently congratulating myself on holding my temper. "In the future, please make sure we are in agreement before you make these kinds of decisions."

"Sure, Glory. But you're the one who said to talk to the Booster Club, so I figured you were good with their tribute to Kevin."

That wasn't what I had said, but it was what he'd heard.

"Matt will probably call you," he went on. "But if you don't hear from him in a day or so, you might want to give him a buzz. I know he's pretty busy right now."

I think that was the point where I started wondering how I could manage to buy Peter out.

Chapter 14

MONDAY MORNING STARTED OUT COOL. SOFT GRAY fog blanketed the bay and spread inland across houses and shops. It felt as though the entire town were shrouded in melancholy.

Perfect weather for a funeral.

The fog persisted, and as I climbed into Felipe and Ernie's van with Karen, the chill in the air reminded us that fall was on the way. There would be several weeks of good weather ahead before winter, but not today.

The memorial service was held in the high school football stadium, which had been chosen for its size, not its significance. As we cruised the ranks of cars looking for a parking place, Ernie observed that the entire town seemed to have turned out for the service.

I wasn't surprised. Kevin had been a local star who had died in a tragic accident, and we were all here to participate in the community ritual of grief and bonding.

But no one except me—and now Karen—knew that there was any hint of something more troubling than a young driver, a couple of beers, and an overpowered car.

No one else had heard a ghost tell them it wasn't an accident.

We parked about three-quarters of the way back in the lot and climbed out. Ernie and Felipe wore white shirts and dark suits, Karen had a stylish black trouser suit, and I'd managed to find a navy-blue dress in the back of my closet.

At the entrance to the stadium, where the ticket-takers usually stood on game nights, football team members acted as ushers. Wearing ill-fitting dark suits—many of them obviously borrowed from older brothers or fathers—and stricken expressions, they struggled to control their emotions as they handed small programs to each of the mourners.

Travis Chambers thrust a program into my hand and offered a muttered, "Thank you for coming," before turning to the party behind us. Travis headed the defense for the Keyhole Bay Buccaneers, and on any other team, he would have been the standout star. With Kevin gone, everyone was expecting him to move into the position of captain.

Bluebeard's pronouncement came back to me again as I passed through the gate and followed Karen into the stadium. Was there someone in the crowd who knew more than he should? And if there was, how could we find him?

To one side of the entrance, a news crew from one of the local network affiliates had set up cameras to record the ceremony. A too-tan newscaster with an expensive haircut and a dark suit was interviewing anyone who would stop to talk, but he was getting few takers. I winced, thinking about Peter watching the coverage in Montgomery and congratulating himself on his publicity coup.

The stadium continued to fill with students and parents,

business owners and their employees. I spotted Kevin's family sitting on the field in a row of chairs covered with dark drapes. His parents appeared to have aged a decade in the last five days, and his younger sister sat with her head bowed, as though she carried the weight of the world on her shoulders.

Matt Fowler stood near the small podium that had been set up midfield, huddled with Coach Bradley and Principal Terhune. Fowler's carefully tailored suit was in marked contrast to the ill-fitting, off-the-rack versions on the principal and coach. From their body language, it was clear Fowler was trying to issue orders, and the other two were having none of it.

Fowler was a powerful man in Keyhole Bay, and he was used to getting his way. His usually jocular mask slipped for a moment as I watched, his face clouding with anger. Just as quickly, the mask was back in place. He raised his hands, palms facing the other two men, as though in surrender. I doubted Fowler ever surrendered. He'd just figured out another way around to whatever it was he wanted.

The stands were a mass of dark suits and dresses on local residents who only brought them out for graduations, weddings, and funerals. A few of the older women wore hats and gloves, a nod to proper Southern manners.

Above us in the stand to our right, the students clustered together, sitting in a group apart from their families. Several of the girls clung to each other, a knot of misery and support. They were the age I had been when my parents died, and I felt a wave of sympathy, knowing they would carry this memory forever.

A few couples sat together, the girls teary-eyed and clinging to the arms of their boyfriends and the boys struggling to maintain a manly exterior though their puffy eyes and red noses gave them away.

In the center of the unofficial student section were the kings and queens of the school: the sports stars and the cheerleaders. Several seats remained empty, undoubtedly reserved for the football heroes who were still greeting new arrivals.

I spotted Tricia Lincoln, Frank's niece, in the center of the group and remembered what he had said about her wanting to get Kevin back. Although Frank had said they hadn't reconciled, the girls around Tricia hovered protectively, as though she deserved special consolation.

The stream of arrivals slowed to a trickle, and the football players began leaving their usher posts and making their way into the stands. One by one they took their seats, clapping teammates on the back and hugging the weeping cheerleaders.

One man, older than the rest, looked out of place in the cluster of jocks, and it took me a moment to recognize him. Jimmy Parmenter.

Jimmy had been the golden boy when he was in school, a standout athlete who thrived on the recognition and reward that went with being a star. He was scouted by several colleges and supported by the Booster Club.

I wasn't sure quite what happened, but Jimmy had come home during winter break his sophomore year and never gone back to the university. I remembered Chloe telling me he'd had a knee injury, but I didn't know for sure if that was what ultimately kept him in Keyhole Bay.

What I did know was that he'd married his high school sweetheart, Julie Nelson, and gone to work for her father as a maintenance man at the small hotel the Nelsons owned.

Jimmy sat with the athletes even though he had graduated before any of them were on the team. Still, they all knew Jimmy; he'd been a star when they were in junior high, and they greeted him as one of their own.

He moved easily into the group, almost as though he had never left his exalted position at the top of the high school social pyramid.

Karen nudged me, and I turned away from watching the students.

"Did you see that?" she said in a whisper. She nodded toward the field, and I followed her gaze.

Down on the field, Fowler, Bradley, and Terhune had approached the podium, but the power struggle was still taking place. Fowler was standing a step back from the microphone, with Principal Terhune in front of him, as though blocking his path.

I glanced around the stands, but the rest of the crowd appeared to be preoccupied with their conversations and oblivious to the drama playing out in front of them.

Karen and I watched as Bradley took Fowler by the arm and pulled him back toward the chairs behind the podium.

Karen nudged Ernie, who in turn nudged Felipe, and the four of us focused on the field as Bradley continued to press Fowler away from the microphone.

Clearly there was some dispute over who would speak first.

Fowler had a solid work-out-in-the-gym-every-day build, but Bradley kept up with two squads of high school football players. When it came right down to it, Fowler didn't stand a chance. Bradley had an iron grip on his arm, and it would be nearly impossible to pull away without attracting a lot of unwanted attention.

Fowler backed off, though with poor grace. He plopped into one of the folding chairs, and Bradley took the seat next to him, his lips pressed into a tight line.

Right now I wouldn't want to cross the coach, though I

didn't know what to expect from Fowler. The man wasn't one to back down.

Conversation in the stands began to fall off, and Principal Terhune nodded to the band director. The director tapped his baton against his music stand, looking expectantly at the band members arrayed in the stands in front of him. After a moment, he brought his baton down, and the band began a slow, soft arrangement of "Swing Low, Sweet Chariot."

The assembled crowd took the cue, and conversation died off. By the second verse, a few voices joined the band, singing in little more than a whisper.

More voices joined in on the chorus, and by the time the song finished, the entire stadium was singing softly in tribute to their fallen friend.

Principal Terhune opened the memorial, saying all the things we expected and knew were true. He spoke of Kevin's generous spirit; his quick wit and sense of humor; his respect for his family, his teachers, and his teammates; and, finally, of his athletic talent.

When he finished, he introduced Coach Bradley, who rose and reached for the microphone. As their coach took over the podium, the entire team stood and bowed their heads.

Jimmy Parmenter stood with them.

Watching these young men fighting back tears, I found myself choking up. No matter what the reason, they had lost one of their own, and their grief and bewilderment were genuine. And heartbreaking.

It was a feeling I knew all too well.

The coach led his team in a heartfelt prayer. Maybe we were technically on school grounds, but at that moment, I don't think anyone in that stadium would have objected. When he finished, there were murmurs of "Amen" from most of the crowd—those who could still speak—and I saw a lot of tissues applied to eyes and noses of adults and teenagers alike.

Coach Bradley continued for several minutes, praising Kevin's accomplishments, both as a player and as a team leader, and he asked the crowd to offer their support to the team—both on and off the field—as they faced the coming season.

When Bradley reached the end of his remarks, the band director once again signaled his musicians, and they began playing.

By the end of the number, Fowler was on his feet at the podium, waiting with barely concealed impatience for his turn in the spotlight. I caught him cutting his eyes to the cameras focused on the podium, and he stood a little straighter and arranged his expression to reflect a proper somberness.

Fowler leaned into the microphone and spoke in a low voice.

"Keyhole Bay has lost a great young man," he said. "A leader of our younger generation, Kevin Stanley was a role model and a fine example of what a young man should be."

From below me I heard a muffled sob, a sound that seemed to escape in spite of a futile effort to contain it. Lots of the mourners had been moved by the music and the speakers, but this was more than that.

I glanced over the crowd, curious as to who would be so overcome. I spotted a young blonde woman bent over, her hands covering her face and her shoulders shaking silently.

Next to her sat Gordon Nelson, owner of Seaside Guest House, the small hotel where Jimmy Parmenter worked. As he reached to put a comforting arm around the stricken young woman, I realized who she was. Julie Parmenter, Jimmy's young wife and Gordon's daughter.

It seemed odd to me that Julie was sitting with her father,

while her husband—they'd only been married a little over a year—was in the midst of the high school athletes. Then again, maybe they each needed to join the group that offered them the most comfort.

I put Jimmy and Julie out of my mind and focused back on Fowler. He was going on about what a terrible loss we had all suffered and taking the opportunity to point out his own connection to Kevin and how much he would miss him.

Fowler droned on for what seemed like forever until finally he paused. The band director took that as his cue to begin the school hymn. Terhune stepped to the podium while the band played, and Fowler retreated in confusion.

Terhune then introduced Warren Stanley, Kevin's father.

An oil-rig worker who looked decidedly out of place in a suit and tie, Warren's sun-darkened face stood in stark contrast to the blazing white of his dress shirt. He gripped the sides of the podium with hands roughened by years of hard work on the rig, hanging on as though it were the only thing keeping him upright.

When he spoke, it was in a voice made husky by too many cigarettes, and thick with grief.

"My wife and my daughter and I want to thank y'all for bein' here today. Losing Kevin . . ." He swallowed hard and continued. "Losing a son is about the worst thing can happen to a man. All that hope and wishin' for the future, just gone."

He shook his head. "It'll be a long time before I get used to his being gone, and I don't know that our lives will be quite right ever again. But there are so many of our friends and neighbors here." He looked up at the crowd, shaking his head as though he couldn't quite believe how many people had come to pay their last respects to his son. "It humbles me to see how many lives Kevin touched, and how much he meant to all of you. Thank y'all for coming. Thank you."

He stopped, unable to go on, and Principal Terhune quickly returned to the microphone.

"Mr. Stanley," the principal said, "we all offer our sympathy and support during this dark time. Please remember that we all are here for you and your family."

Warren Stanley nodded without speaking and slowly moved away from the podium. He gathered his wife and daughter into his arms as he sat down, the three of them a tableau of loss.

Chapter 15

PRINCIPAL TERHUNE MADE A FEW CLOSING REMARKS, the choir started singing "Will the Circle Be Unbroken," and the crowd began making their way to the exits.

The four of us lingered in our places, letting the surge of departing mourners wash past us. There was no sense in trying to hurry out of the stadium; we'd just be stuck in the traffic jam leaving the parking lot.

From my vantage point, I was able to see Matt Fowler working the crowd. First he made a beeline for Kevin's family. He put an arm around Warren Stanley as though the two of them were fast friends, though I doubted Mr. Stanley really knew him.

The two men inhabited very different social circles. Warren Stanley, a blue-collar workingman, spent weeks at a time separated from his family, living on an oil rig in the shallow waters of the Gulf. Even when he was home, he hardly

moved in the socially elite, powers-that-be crowd where Matt
Fowler saw himself.

I wondered as I watched him inserting himself into the
family circle whether Fowler was actually as connected and
powerful as he wanted everyone to believe. He certainly had
the attitude; but did the other members of the Chamber of
Commerce, the Merchants' Association, and the Booster
Club see him that way? Or did they see through the bluster
and the posturing to the grasping self-interest that was at the
center of Matt Fowler?

Finished with the family, Fowler surrendered his grip on
Warren Stanley. The stricken man and his wife turned back
to Coach Bradley as Fowler moved away—and directly into
the path of the television cameras.

From where we sat, we couldn't hear his remarks to the TV
reporter, but we could see his chest swell with importance.

The reporter listened attentively. He occasionally asked a
question, but Fowler clearly took charge of the interview, just
as he had tried to take charge of the service.

The difference was the reporter didn't know Matthew
Fowler, and Principal Terhune did.

When the reporter edged away to speak with Terhune,
Fowler set his sights on another target.

Travis Chambers.

Kevin's family was still standing just a few yards away,
accepting condolences from a crowd of other parents who
surrounded them. Fowler was looking for a new star to hitch
his wagon to.

The stands had nearly emptied, and Ernie rose to his feet.
"Ready?" he said, looking at me with concern. Apparently
my watchfulness hadn't gone unnoticed.

"Sure." I pulled my jacket a bit tighter against the damp

and followed Ernie down the steps toward the exit. Behind me, Felipe leaned forward and spoke quietly.

"He's evil, that one," he said, his lips near my ear. "I tried to get Ernie to put a hex on him, but he swears he doesn't know how."

I chuckled, instantly feeling guilty for my amusement. Despite many years in New Orleans, Ernie swore he knew nothing about voodoo or black magic, and Felipe refused to believe him.

"Well," I replied, "I can't think of a more deserving target."

We made our way to the exit gate, trailing along behind a group of teenagers with Jimmy Parmenter in their midst. Jimmy stopped for a second and swiveled his head, like he was looking for someone. I wondered if it was Julie, since I didn't see her with the group. Maybe she'd already left with her dad.

Jimmy shrugged and kept moving along with the athletes and cheerleaders, as though he had never left high school.

I glanced back to check on the small group of people left on the field. The Stanleys and Principal Terhune stood together in an informal greeting line, shaking hands and exchanging hugs with the last of the mourners.

Coach Bradley huddled with Travis Chambers. Travis looked somber, but he couldn't completely conceal his pleasure at what the coach was saying.

My guess? Travis was already the new captain of the football team.

"Travis looks happy," Karen commented.

I jumped, startled at the sound of her voice. None of us had said more than a few words since we'd entered the stadium, each of us lost in our own thoughts most of the afternoon.

I caught sight of Fowler once again, scanning the crowd

as if looking for his next target. He spotted me and headed in our direction, but I avoided eye contact and hurried toward the van.

The only thing he could possibly want to talk about was T-shirts, and I hoped it could wait another day or two. Or more. He would eventually insist on cashing in on Peter's offer, but for today I would avoid him if I could.

We reached the van and climbed in, Karen and Felipe in the back, Ernie driving, and me next to him in the front seat. Ernie didn't start the engine right away, since the lot was still jammed with the steady stream of cars trying to funnel through the two exit lanes.

"If you left your car at Carousel, why don't you give me a lift home, Karen? Save the guys an extra stop."

"Sure," Karen answered.

Felipe leaned forward between the front seats and looked from Ernie to me and back again. "What did you make of all that?" he asked. "Fowler was up to something, and I thought Bradley was going to take him apart, right there in front of the entire town."

Karen leaned forward, too. In the relative privacy of the van, we were finally able to talk freely. "I wonder if there was some argument about Travis," she said. "Fowler sure looked like he was trying to get close to Travis after the service, and Coach Bradley practically body-blocked him."

I'd missed that. "When was that?"

"Just before you about jumped out of your skin," she answered. "I saw Bradley get between Travis and Fowler, and Travis looked like a drowning man who'd just got hold of a life preserver."

"Is that what you were talking about? I thought the coach was telling Travis something that made him happy. You think it was just the coach rescuing him from Fowler?"

"Oh, there might have been more to it," Karen said. "But it looks like there's no love lost between Fowler and Bradley."

"Bradley's a good guy," Ernie said.

"Yeah," cut in Felipe. "Anyone who stands up to Fowler is a good guy in my book."

"On the other hand," I said, "he may just be defending his turf. You know, as the coach, he's supposed to be in charge of the team. He might see Fowler as a rival for the loyalty of the players. I mean, how much are the guys doing what the coach wants, and how much are they sucking up to Fowler? He acts like he has a lot of pull with the college recruiters, and I've heard him brag about his connections."

Karen's snort of derision clearly expressed her opinion of Fowler's so-called connections.

Ernie shook his head. "Doesn't matter, really. I heard from Sean, a friend of mine in the math department, that Fowler and Kevin weren't exactly seeing eye-to-eye on some stuff. How much do you really think those kids are gonna listen to Fowler?"

I remembered the crowd of players leaving the stadium. "Some of them definitely will," I said firmly. "Did you guys see Jimmy Parmenter? He was here, sitting in the middle of the team, just like he'd never graduated."

"He was one of Fowler's favorites, remember?" Karen said. "Lot boy, got himself a nice truck his senior year," she stopped and looked at Ernie, and back at Felipe. "That was after you moved here. I think Jimmy graduated three or four years ago."

Ernie started the van. The traffic had eased up and he was able to pull out of the lot.

"Still," Karen continued from her spot in the backseat, "none of that explains why—" She stopped suddenly.

"Why *what*?" Felipe asked instantly.

I turned around to Karen with a don't-you-dare look, but it was too late. Felipe knew something was up, and he wasn't someone I could brush off easily.

"Nothing." Karen's voice wavered, and Felipe pounced on her hesitation.

"It's something," he insisted.

Ernie pulled into traffic, then shot me a quick glance.

"What?" I said.

"Something going on you're not telling us?" Ernie's tone was mild, but it was clear he wasn't going to be put off.

I glared at Karen, but she just shrugged.

I sighed in resignation. I'd known all along I would have to tell Ernie and Felipe about Uncle Louis, but I had hoped I could put it off a little longer.

"All right," I said finally. "I've got a story to tell."

Chapter 16

WE GATHERED AROUND THE SLEEK, MIDCENTURY modern teak dining table in Felipe and Ernie's elegant dining room. Although their shop ran to more ornate vintage and antique art and furnishings, their little house on the block behind the store was very much elegant 1950s modern.

I don't know whether telling Ernie and Felipe was easier than telling Karen, but it was certainly slower. Probably because Karen kept interrupting to add her own comments.

By the time we finished, the sun had set, the morning's fog had turned to drizzle, and we had all abandoned any plans to get back to work.

Even though it wasn't Thursday, Ernie had taken pity on us halfway through and thrown together a reasonable facsimile of jambalaya from leftovers in the refrigerator.

Although he was still learning traditional Southern style along with the rest of us, Ernie was already a pretty amazing cook. I attributed it to his years growing up in New Orleans, a city known for its great food. He claimed it was all about growing up poor and knowing how to get the most out of what he had.

Whatever the reason, the rice, chicken, sausage, and shrimp was just the right dinner for a rainy evening. The peppery smell cut through the chill, just as the spiced rice and hot link sausage spread a bit of fire through our stomachs.

"This doesn't get you out of taking your turn," Karen said as she ran a piece of bread around the inside of her bowl, soaking up the last drops of broth. "This isn't traditional Southern, anyway."

Ernie jumped to the defense of his home state. "Louisiana cooking is *definitely* Southern!"

"*Traditional* Southern," Karen argued.

"This is traditional in my part of the South," Ernie shot back with a grin, his New Orleans drawl deliberately exaggerated. It was a lighthearted argument the two of them had had several times over the last few months, and it didn't appear to be ending any time soon.

I wasn't sure whether Karen really believed what she said or if she just liked pushing Ernie's buttons. Either way, the two of them seemed to relish the argument.

"Let me get this straight," Felipe jumped in, drawing the conversation back to my story. "You think you have the ghost of your great-uncle living in your shop. And you think he's moving stuff around and talking to you through the parrot, right?"

I nodded, trying not to feel defensive. It still sounded pretty far-fetched, even though I believed it was true.

"And he told you Kevin's accident wasn't an accident?"

I hesitated. "What he said was, 'It wasn't an accident,' and we had just come from the scene. At first I thought he meant all the tearing up he'd done in the shop, but now I think he meant Kevin. I have no idea how he would know that, though."

Felipe turned a questioning glance at Ernie, who held up a palm. "Do *not* ask me, cher. I keep telling you I don't know about haints, or voodoo, or gris-gris neither. If the girl says she's got a ghost, I will purely take her word for it."

Felipe turned back to me. "So what you want to do?"

Karen interrupted, outlining the research we'd already done and the few facts we had gathered about Uncle Louis.

"No, no, no," Felipe said, shaking his head for her to stop. "I mean, what do you want to do about Kevin? If that wasn't an accident, and everybody thinks it was, don't you think we should tell somebody?"

Ernie laughed harshly. "Oh, I can see it now." He waved his hand across the air in front of him. "A headline in the *News and Times*, 'Orphan, Gays, Claim Ghost Says Stanley's Death Was No Accident.' Yeah, that would work."

"How about we talk to Boomer?" Karen suggested. "Like Linda told Glory, there's a proud tradition of ghosts in the South. He might be willing to at least listen."

"To you, maybe," Felipe shot back. "They tolerate us, they let us have our Memorial Day gathering in Pensacola, but I can't see the police chief taking a ghost story seriously if Ernie and I are involved."

"Then I'll talk to him," Karen said, and it was settled.

So far, my friends had taken the news about Uncle Louis without telling me I was crazy, but I didn't have high hopes for the rest of the town. And if Karen managed to get Boomer to listen, whether he took it seriously or not, everyone would eventually hear about it.

Like I said, after crazy tourist stories, gossip was the major source of entertainment in Keyhole Bay. I just wasn't sure I wanted to be the subject of that gossip.

"Listen," I said, trying to throw water on the idea of talking to Boomer. "He rolled the car. It isn't like he was shot, or stabbed, or something. He died in that car."

"Maybe he was poisoned," Felipe said. "I bet it was Fowler. He was absolutely sure Kevin was his ticket to the big leagues, and if the kid wasn't doing what Fowler wanted, who knows what he might do?"

"My vote's on Bradley," Karen said. We all turned to stare.

"The coach?" I asked, my voice squeaking. Not that I didn't know who she meant, but I just couldn't believe she'd said that.

"Think about it," she answered. "Bradley has a tremendous amount riding on this season. There are budget cuts threatening, although they *never* touch athletics. More important, Bradley had his eye on moving up, too. Kevin was at that kegger, I'm sure. If he got caught, he could be suspended, and the scouts wouldn't come. If Kevin screwed up, he was hurting more than his own chances; he was messing things up for Bradley, too."

"But Bradley?" Felipe was incredulous. "I think Fowler's a lot more likely."

"You're both forgetting," I said, "that those two weren't out in the woods Wednesday, at least as far as we know. There is one person I'd bet *was* out there. Travis Chambers."

Karen shook her head. "He's just a kid. He wouldn't do that to a teammate, would he?"

"What if he thought he had a shot at Kevin's scholarship money?" I asked. "Don't you think that would be an incentive?"

"But to kill him? I don't think so." Ernie, reasonable as always.

"What if he didn't mean to kill him, just hurt him enough that he would be out the rest of the season? Isn't that what happened to Jimmy Parmenter? The kids had to know that. Maybe he didn't even intend to hurt him. Just get him caught drinking and driving and get him suspended. Then Travis could take over and look like a hero."

"But if he didn't mean to hurt him," Karen argued, "then him getting killed *was* an accident, and we're right back to where we started."

"It could have nothing to do with football," Ernie suggested, continuing his reasonable tone. We all turned to stare at him.

"Come on." Karen was the first to speak. "He was the star of the team. Football was the most important thing in his life. How could it be about anything else?"

In the end, Ernie couldn't convince any of us. If Kevin's death wasn't an accident—and none of us were quite ready to say it wasn't, but we were all leaning that way—then it had to be about football.

"I think it has to be football," I said. "But this is all based on the word of a parrot. Or a ghost." I shrugged, feeling lost. "Given that, anything is possible."

Chapter 17

KAREN DROPPED ME OFF IN FRONT OF THE SHOP A few minutes before nine.

I had expected to be home much earlier, but I hadn't planned on telling Felipe and Ernie about Uncle Louis, either. And I hadn't planned on finding a note from my across-the-street neighbor, Jake Robinson, of Beach Books.

"Have a package for you," the note read. "Stop by when you get home, and you can pick it up. Jake."

I looked across the street at Jake's store. The door was closed and most of the lights were out, but someone was still moving around behind the front windows, and a couple of lights were on over the racks.

I'd better go see what he had.

Not that I objected to seeing what Jake had. In fact, most of the time I was quite happy to check him out: broad shoulders, a great smile, and—how do I put this?—nice-fitting jeans.

But a delivery for me? I wasn't expecting anything, and I

wasn't much in the mood for surprises. Still, I didn't like imposing on the neighbors. Especially a neighbor I would like to get to know a little better.

I looked up and down Main Street before I crossed. At this time of night there wasn't a car in sight, but despite feeling a little foolish, I still checked for traffic.

I was a couple of steps from Jake's front door when he swung it open for me.

"I was just straightening up the shelves," he waved toward the racks of paperbacks, "when I saw you drive up."

I glanced around. There were boxes of books lined up at the foot of the shelves with packing lists on top.

"A never-ending battle," I commented. It was a very familiar chore, one I struggle to keep up with myself.

"Yeah. Seems like there's never time to do it while the store's open. I gave up trying within the first month. Now I just wait until I close."

He went behind the counter and came out with a giant box. He carried it easily, setting it on the counter next to the cash register with a thump. It must have been heavier than he made it look.

There was a label on the top of the box with my name and address, but no shipping stamp or postage.

"A kid came by this afternoon in a pickup, looking for you. When he saw you were closed, he tried a couple places, but I guess most everyone was at that memorial service."

I nodded. "Most of us know the Stanleys, and we've known Kevin since he was a little kid. The whole town was there."

Jake bobbed his head in acknowledgment. "I figured. I knew who he was, but I'm too new to town to really know him or his family, so I didn't go."

"Oh, sorry!" I said. "I didn't mean—"

"I didn't think you did," Jake said at once. "No offense taken, believe me. I'm just the new kid in town, that's all."

"Well, it wasn't very friendly of me to point it out." I appreciated the low lighting; Jake wouldn't be able to see the blush I felt creeping up my face.

I didn't blush often, but Jake was a special case. There weren't many men in Keyhole Bay who fit his description: single, attractive, and smart (well, he loved books, didn't he?).

So, yeah, I blushed.

"I knew what I was getting into when I moved to a small town," Jake said. "I've only been here three months, whereas most of the people have been here at least three generations. I *am* the new kid."

Without a good answer to that, I kept my mouth shut, so I didn't put my foot back in again, and moved to inspect the box on the counter.

The printed address was on a plain white shipping label, the kind you buy in the office-supply store by the hundreds. There was no return address or any indication where it had come from.

"What in the heck?" I twisted the box around, looking for some explanation of its origin, but I couldn't find any answers.

I decided the best thing to do was take it home and open it. Besides, I'd imposed on Jake long enough.

But when I started to lift the box, it turned out to be even heavier than I expected. Jake had lifted it easily, but, then again, he was used to hauling around boxes of books.

"Here," he said, coming to my rescue. "Let me carry that for you."

I surrendered the box without argument. I suppose I could have tried to carry it across the street, but I think I might have injured myself in the process. Anyway, those shoulders I'd admired were obviously for more than looks.

I thanked him and held the door open as he hefted the box onto one shoulder. I tried to ignore how close he got as he walked past me onto the sidewalk.

I closed the door behind us and trotted to catch up with him. I moved ahead of Jake on the crosswalk so I could reach the door to Southern Treasures and open it for him.

At the sound of the door opening, Bluebeard ruffled his feathers and squawked at us for disturbing his nap. He gave Jake a beady-eyed stare, then moved his gaze to me.

"Tryin' to %^*$ sleep here," he said.

Jake nearly dropped the box. "Did he just say . . . ?"

I nodded. I used to be amazed at the breadth of Bluebeard's vocabulary, both standard and off-color. Now I was pretty sure it wasn't always the bird putting together full sentences.

"Sorry," I said, grabbing the box, which threatened to slip from his arms, and guiding him to the counter. "Just set it here." I hefted the corner onto the counter, while Jake slid the box to rest next to my sales terminal.

"I apologize for Bluebeard. He doesn't seem to have his company manners in place today."

Jake laughed. "It wasn't his swearing. I heard a lot worse in the service. But I've never heard a parrot quite that articulate. How long have you had him?"

As I fed Bluebeard and checked his water, I found myself telling Jake Robinson an abbreviated version of how I came to live with a foul-mouthed parrot in a crowded souvenir shop. He was easy to talk to, and he asked questions with a show of real interest.

After a few minutes I stopped, amazed at how much I had revealed to this relative stranger.

"I shouldn't be running on like this, keeping you from your work," I apologized. "I appreciate you carrying that box over."

I realized I hadn't even opened the box because I'd been so distracted by Bluebeard. And, if I was honest, by my conversation with Jake.

I stepped behind the counter and got a small box cutter, but I really didn't need it. The box was held shut with just a couple strips of carelessly applied packing tape. I was able to pick up one end of the tape and pull it across the box.

My heart sank when I pulled back the flaps. A packing slip on Fowler's Auto Sales letterhead was the first thing I saw, and I didn't need to see anything else to know what I had.

A box of Kevin Stanley memorial T-shirts, courtesy of Matt Fowler and my meddling cousin Peter.

Jake read the dismay on my face. "Not something good, huh?" he asked, stepping closer to peer into the box. I guess he felt some responsibility for it, since he was the one who took the delivery.

"They're T-shirts," I said unnecessarily.

Jake glanced at the shelves, racks, and spinners in the store and back to me. One eyebrow rose in question. "And?"

"And they're part of a fund-raiser for the high school athletic program." I sighed. "It's a long story, but I got volunteered to be a distribution point."

I debated trying to explain about my cousin Peter, but decided it would sound way too much like whining. Probably because it would be. I was tired, emotionally drained by the events of the day, and already unhappy about my responsibility for the shirts.

Fowler sending them even before the end of the memorial service pushed me close to the breaking point.

"That's very generous of you, Ms. Martine," Jake said.

The tentative note in his voice told me he realized I wasn't entirely happy about it.

"Call me Glory," I said. "All my friends do. And anyone who carts T-shirts around for me has earned that much, at least."

"Glory, then." Jake walked to the door. "I can see you're tired. I'm going to get out of your way and get back to work myself. Someday when you want to tell me the long story of your getting volunteered, I'd love to hear it. Maybe over coffee?"

Before I could say anything, he was out the door and trotting across the street. I watched, open-mouthed, as he let himself into Beach Books and went back to restocking his shelves.

Had he just asked me out? Or was I reading a lot more into the offer of a cup of coffee?

"Pretty boy," Bluebeard called. I didn't ask whether he meant himself or Jake.

I wasn't sure I wanted to know his answer.

Chapter 18

I TURNED BACK TO THE BOX OF T-SHIRTS AND PULLED out the packing list. According to Buccaneer Booster Club, via Fowler Auto Sales, I had six dozen memorial T-shirts in assorted sizes.

As much as I hated unpacking at that hour, I wanted even less to face the pile of shirts first thing in the morning. I figured I'd better at least verify the packing list and figure out where I was going to display them.

I reached in the box and plopped a stack of shirts on the counter. On the front of the shirt was a photo of Kevin in his football uniform, kneeling at midfield. I recognized it as the pose yearbook editors had used for as long as I could remember.

Below the picture was his name, his date of birth, and the date of his death, along with a line of flowing script reading, "We will miss you."

The irony wasn't lost on me. Everyone would miss Kevin, certainly. But many of the people involved in the memorial

T-shirts had their own selfish agendas and would miss Kevin for more than his great smile or his ready wit.

Some of them would miss the opportunity to turn a buck or build an empire on the back of a teenage football star.

The question was, who *wouldn't* miss him?

From across the room, Bluebeard started swearing loudly. He rushed across the shop, landing next to the shirts and screeching angrily.

I managed to shove the shirts back in the box before he grabbed them, but he clearly intended to tear them to shreds.

Adrenaline raced through my veins as I backed away from the furious bird. I had never seen him react that way to anything I brought into the shop.

"Bluebeard! Stop!"

He backed up a step but continued to glare at the box.

"What is wrong with you?" I scolded as I closed the flaps. If the blasted bird destroyed the shirts, I was sure Fowler would expect me to pay for them. "Those shirts are to make money for the football team. What do you think you're doing?"

Bluebeard blinked at me and slowly backed away. I could see calm returning as he settled down on the counter.

Gingerly, I took my hand away from the box and reached for his head. He let me stroke him, and I felt the tension recede. From both of us.

When Bluebeard had quieted down, I carried him back to his cage and gave him a biscuit. "What's wrong?" I cooed. I couldn't help it. The poor thing had been badly spooked by the shirts and I had to try to understand why.

"Bad man."

"Kevin?" I asked. "Kevin isn't a bad man. Kevin's just a kid who made a bad mistake and paid dearly for it."

"Not boy. Man."

Okay. It wasn't Kevin. There were two people involved

with the T-shirts, Fowler and Peter. Peter was in Montgomery, a hundred miles away, and besides, he didn't know anything.

That left Fowler.

"Did the bad man hurt Kevin?" I asked.

Bluebeard bobbed his head, and I took that as a yes.

"The bad man hurt Kevin, and somehow you know about it?"

More head bobbing.

I hesitated, glancing around the shop as though I needed to reassure myself I was alone. "Uncle Louis?"

Bluebeard sat completely still.

"Uncle Louis, do you need my help? Is there something I can do to help you?"

I waited, skepticism battling with conviction. One part of my brain told me I was acting like a fool, talking to a parrot and expecting a dead man to answer. But another part of me, a part that relied on faith in my own heart, told me I was on the right path.

"Do you need my help to, uh, move on?"

"Noooo! No move on," Bluebeard shrieked at top volume. He spread his wings and beat them against the air.

The sudden outburst startled me. He had calmed down, but the question clearly agitated him.

"No move on," he repeated. His voice had dropped from the initial scream to soft and pleading, almost pathetic. It reminded me of the robot in a movie I saw as a kid, a self-aware robot whose cry of "No disassemble" had brought tears to my nine-year-old eyes.

If Uncle Louis was in the shop—and now I was more confident of that than ever—he didn't want to leave. The ghost didn't want to move on to wherever ghosts go when they leave the world of the living. It seemed as though he wanted to stay in Southern Treasures with me.

"You don't have to go anywhere," I said, in what I hoped was a reassuring tone. I didn't really know what would reassure a ghost, but I did my best.

"Even if we figure out what happened to Kevin, you can stay here as long as you want to."

To my surprise, I meant it. For weeks—months, actually, if I was honest with myself—I had been fighting the idea of having a ghost living in my shop. But in the last few days, as I had slowly shared my secret with my closest friends, I'd come to accept his presence. Uncle Louis was as close to a blood relative as I had in Keyhole Bay, and I found I liked the idea of having him around.

I think.

After all, I didn't know what the rules were for ghosts. Did he get to talk to me whenever he wanted? Would he answer questions? Did he sleep? That part was kind of worrisome; was I going to have him wandering around the shop at all hours, doing whatever it was ghosts did while people were sleeping?

And would he want to talk to other people? Like Karen, or Felipe and Ernie, or Linda? Karen had already heard him, so I knew others could hear what he said.

Having a ghost around was a very complicated situation.

"It wasn't an accident."

Great! On top of all the questions swirling around in my head, Bluebeard had added one more. What really happened to Kevin Stanley?

"You said that before," I told him. "Do you mean Kevin's car crash wasn't an accident? Is that when the bad man hurt him?"

"Bad man!"

There were some serious limitations in questioning a ghost who spoke through a parrot. I was going to need a lot of patience to figure out the answers he gave me.

Bluebeard ruffled his feathers again, then retreated into his cage and settled onto his perch. He tucked his head into his chest. It was a signal he was tired. Like a small child, an emotional outburst often left him worn out and needing a nap.

I closed the door on his cage but didn't latch it, and draped the old blanket over it to provide him the restful darkness he needed.

Whatever else he had to say could wait until morning.

Unfortunately, the T-shirts had to be dealt with now.

I went back to unpacking, now that Bluebeard was sleeping, and sorting the shirts into stacks by size as I checked them against the packing list.

The six dozen shirts ranged from a handful of kid sizes to "XXX Large," with most of them in "Large" and "X-Large." I had to admit, Fowler knew what he was doing with his ordering. When most people bought "special" T-shirts, they wanted them a size or two larger than what they usually wore.

At the bottom of the list was a handwritten note. Shiloh Weaver, Fowler's office manager, had listed the sales prices for the shirts and my commission as sales agent. She said she'd check with me in a couple of days to see if I needed more shirts, and to call her if I had any questions.

Just one: *How do I get out of this mess?*

I remembered Jake Robinson telling me what a generous thing I was doing. If I went back on my agreement—well, *Peter's* agreement—to sell the shirts, I would have to face the disappointment of a town Fowler had probably already told about the shirts. A town now expecting me to provide them with a way to mourn their lost son and support their beloved football team—all in one simple gesture.

I sighed and cleared a space front and center. If I was going to be civic-minded, I might as well do it right.

Chapter 19

THE T-SHIRTS BROUGHT ME A STEADY STREAM OF LO-
cals all day Tuesday and Wednesday, though no actual business. No surprise there.

By Wednesday afternoon, I was sold out of everything but
a few size smalls, and I had already agreed to take another
four dozen. Shiloh promised me they would be delivered
later that afternoon.

Although it didn't bring me any business, I did get to talk
to a lot of people. Everyone expressed their shock and upset
over Kevin's death. I heard again and again what a nice kid
he was and how it was a terrible loss for everyone.

A group of four young women came in together early
Wednesday morning. One pushed a stroller, and one of the
others was visibly pregnant. It took a minute for me to place
them: cheerleaders from the squad of a few years back, when
Jimmy Parmenter was the football star and Julie was captain
of the cheerleading squad.

As they picked through the shirts looking for one that might stretch over a pregnant belly, I tried to be discreet as I listened in on their conversation.

"Julie should be here, too," the young mother said, maneuvering her stroller between the shelves. "She was team captain. You'd think she would want to come with us."

A tall brunette, still trim and athletic looking, waved her left hand, on which a large diamond sparkled as it caught the lights. "She said she just couldn't face it, bless her heart," she paused. "I can imagine, after what happened to Jimmy."

There it was, that whiff of disapproval masquerading as concern.

The other two nodded. The pregnant one sniffed slightly and held up the last size double-X. "Think this will fit?" She stretched the fabric across her belly. "I don't know what is wrong with Julie," she continued, twisting awkwardly to assess the fit of the shirt. "She cried her eyes out at the service, but she won't come with us to get shirts? What's up with that?"

The brunette cast a critical eye on her friend. "Like I said, I really think it's Jimmy. He lost his scholarship when he got hurt, and now another football star gets killed in a stupid accident." She shrugged. "That's got to mess you up."

I listened while they selected their shirts, and one by one, brought them to the counter to ring up. I didn't learn much of anything I didn't already know. Julie Parmenter was upset about Kevin's death, but I'd seen that for myself at the memorial.

As they left, I heard the young mother whisper something to her friends about driving drunk. The gossip was quickly spreading.

Shiloh Weaver delivered the new order of shirts herself

that afternoon. She was a short woman in her midtwenties, her brown pixie cut already showing signs of premature silver.

"Things are slow around the lot today," she said by way of explanation, "and it was a nice day to get out of the office."

I agreed with her. But Peter and Fowler had conspired to keep me trapped in the shop for the next few days.

"I really appreciate you taking these," Shiloh continued as we checked off the sizes together. "Usually I get stuck doing all this by myself. It's nice to get some help."

"I know what you mean," I said lightly. I didn't bother saying her boss had done exactly that to me, and he didn't even pay my salary. I didn't want to sound like a whiner.

To be fair, Fowler had just taken advantage of Peter's generosity with my time, but that didn't make me feel any more kindly toward him.

Shiloh seemed reluctant to go back to the office, so I offered her a cup of coffee as an excuse to play hooky a little longer.

I locked up the shop with a word of warning to Bluebeard, and we walked next door. Chloe was at the counter, and she took our order with her usual side of gossip.

She recognized Shiloh, and pounced instantly. "I hear you have a new lot boy."

Shiloh shrugged. "Yeah. Mr. Fowler offered the job to Travis Chambers, after, you know." She couldn't bring herself to actually say the words.

I wondered if I could get something more from her. "I saw them talking after the memorial," I said. "I wondered what that was all about."

Shiloh looked stricken. "Oh no! Mr. Fowler would never do anything like that. He's really sensitive about what happened to Kevin, and he really cares about those boys on the team."

I bet. "Those boys" make him look like a big man in town. He really cared about keeping them around. I wasn't so sure he actually cared about the kids themselves.

The Lighthouse was empty except for the three of us, and Chloe was quick to accept my invitation to join us at a table near the counter. "You can jump right up if anyone comes in," I said. "And I bet you'd be glad to get off your feet for a few minutes."

She hesitated for a second, then grabbed a cup and filled it from a carafe. "I am supposed to get a break," she said, slipping out from behind the counter.

"Me, too," I said as I sat down.

Shiloh gave us a conspiratorial grin. "I don't usually get a break when I'm in the office. Guess I might have to make up for that this afternoon."

While we drank our coffee, I tried to question Shiloh about Fowler and about the car lot. I agreed with Felipe that Fowler was a self-serving jerk, although I wasn't ready to label him a murderer—but I was curious how people closer to him saw him.

"Is Mr. Fowler really that much of a slave driver?" I asked. "You really don't get breaks?"

Shiloh tried to laugh it off. "I don't take them, that's all. We're usually pretty busy, and Mr. Fowler depends on me to keep things running smoothly."

"Isn't that his job?" Chloe said. "I mean, he's the boss. Shouldn't he make sure things go right?"

Shiloh shook her head. "No, he's way too busy. That's why he has me. I deal with the little things, and that lets him take care of the important stuff."

"What's more important than running his business?" The question was out before I could stop myself.

"It's not like that," Shiloh protested.

"I, I'm sorry," I stammered. I wasn't doing a very good job of being subtle. "I didn't mean it to come out like that. It's just that," I scrambled for a logical explanation, "I have a small business, and I do all the work myself, except for a part-time clerk during the busiest part of the year. One of these days, I hope to be successful enough that I can have more help. It makes me curious what the other things are that I would have to think about."

Shiloh brightened, and it looked like I'd recovered.

"He has a lot of community obligations," she explained. "He's the president of the Buccaneer Booster Club and he's on a couple committees at the Chamber of Commerce, and I've heard," she lowered her voice to a whisper even though we were still alone in the store, "he's going to run for the School Board."

I filed that piece of information away, wondering whether Kevin Stanley's death would have any effect on Fowler's political ambitions, if Shiloh's rumor was true.

By the time she went back to the car lot, the three of us were best pals. Shiloh even volunteered to pick up the money from the shirt sales the next week, so I wouldn't have to take the time to come down and hand over the proceeds.

I got the distinct impression it was an excuse to get away from Fowler Auto Sales for part of the day.

I didn't have the same luxury. The display of memorial T-shirts still needed to be restocked, and I was pretty sure there were no T-shirt fairies who were going to do it for me.

I was just putting the last shirt in place when Jake Robinson came in the door.

He walked over to the display and picked up a shirt, unfolding it and holding it up against his broad chest. "I figured I ought to have one of these if I want to be part of the town. Think this will fit?"

I tried not to show my admiration for what he'd look like in the close-fitting shirt. "It ought to," I said.

Jake carried the shirt to the counter, looking sheepish. "I probably won't wear it," he confessed. "I usually buy these things and then let them sit in the bottom of the drawer until I give them away."

I had to laugh. "I don't think anybody wears them, except maybe some of the school kids. It's really about supporting the team and remembering Kevin."

Jake handed over a check from the bookstore and tossed the shirt over his shoulder. "Thought any more about that coffee?"

I wasn't about to admit just how much I'd thought about it. "Coffee's good," I said as nonchalantly as I could muster.

He glanced around the shop. "You have time now?" he asked, careful to keep his tone light, as though the thought had just occurred to him.

I shook my head with real regret. "I'm sorry, I just got back from having a cup, and I have a lot to do this afternoon."

It wasn't the whole truth and nothing but the truth. Business was slow except for the T-shirts, my books were up-to-date, and I had cleaned the shop last night. The only thing I really had on my agenda was some more research on Uncle Louis.

Jake tried to hide it, but I thought I saw a flash of disappointment in his eyes, and I felt my resolve weaken.

No, I needed to figure out the mystery of Uncle Louis first. Jake was a mystery for another day.

"No sweat," Jake shrugged, and the shirt draped over his shoulder slipped. He grabbed it before it hit the floor.

"Good reflexes," I said.

He let the remark go without comment.

"Well, you're busy. I better get back to the store. Maybe some other time."

I nodded, biting back the impulse to say "Soon."

The door closed behind Jake, and I watched through the window as he crossed the street with an efficient long-legged stride that looked effortless.

"Liar!" Bluebeard shrieked.

Chapter 20

I IGNORED HIS SQUAWKING.

My search through the back issues of the *News and Times* with Karen had been incomplete. I knew there was at least one more issue with an article about Uncle Louis.

Checking the dates on the earlier stories, I started a time-line of my great-uncle's life. If he bought Southern Treasures in 1945 after seven years in the service, he'd enlisted some-time in 1938.

That was where I should start my search.

Setting aside the 1940s papers I had initially selected, I dug through the stack for the 1930s. There weren't many. I would have to get into the bundles I had stored in the attic at some point.

But there *had* been a third paper on the counter the night of Kevin's accident. I still thought of it as an accident, even though I had accepted Bluebeard telling me it wasn't.

Although I still had trouble calling it *murder*.

I locked the front door, flipped over the "CLOSED" sign, and laid the papers out on the front counter. Carefully turning the fragile pages, I scanned the headlines of each article for clues to Uncle Louis.

When I finally found the notice, it was a small box on the bottom of a page of wedding stories, birth announcements, and a column about several local students going off to college. Typical small-town news.

At the top of the page was the date: September 5, 1938.

Recent Keyhole Bay High School graduate Louis Marcel Georges reports for duty next week with the United States Army. Mr. Georges, Class of 1938, will report to Fort Knox, Kentucky, for basic training. The son of Mr. and Mrs. Emile Georges, Louis is well known as a standout on the Buccaneer football team, where he made his mark as running back.

That was all. A single paragraph and a grainy black-and-white photo a couple inches tall, a long shot of a slender teenager in a football uniform with a ball tucked under his arm. It was intended to be an action shot, and I had seen dozens exactly like it each football season.

I studied the photo, trying to reconcile the fuzzy image with the middle-aged man I remembered from my childhood.

Louis had been in his midfifties when I was born, and I had never known him as a young man. It was hard to connect his older self from my childhood with the scrawny teenager I saw in the photograph.

It was a familiar feeling for me. I had that same feeling looking at pictures of my parents as children. Recently, I'd begun to examine their later photographs, frozen forever in their early forties, just a few years older than the face I saw in the mirror every morning. I had my mother's blue eyes and fair skin, and I looked more like her with each passing year, just as they looked younger with each year.

I gathered up the three papers I'd found—the enlistment article, the one about Southern Treasures, and Uncle Louis's obituary—and carried them to my so-called office in the back. I didn't use the cubbyhole in the storage room much since I usually did most of my computer work on the terminal out front, but my printer and scanner were in the back, out of the way.

I fiddled with the scanner for a minute, finally figuring out how to temporarily remove the cover so I could lay the paper across the scanner bed without folding it. The paper was old and dry, and I was happy not to have to put any more stress on the fragile newsprint.

I made multiple copies so I could share them with Karen, Felipe, and Ernie at dinner Thursday night. Since Karen and I had told the guys the story, I might as well bring them up to speed on what I had learned.

I put the copies in a folder and replaced the originals in their plastic sleeves on the sales rack. There might be more articles somewhere, but for the moment I had found the three that Bluebeard—no, that Uncle Louis—had left for me to find.

Restless, I wandered upstairs and rummaged around the apartment, then came back down. I picked up a book and then abandoned it. I even considered walking across the street and telling Jake Robinson I'd changed my mind about that cup of coffee.

Bluebeard was sensitive to my moods, and I knew my fidgeting would eventually stress him out. Or was it Uncle Louis that reacted?

Either way, I'd have an agitated parrot if I kept this up. I needed to do something, anything other than wander around the shop and apartment aimlessly.

I'd had these symptoms before. I'd been inactive for too long, my stroll around Lake DeFuniak about my only exercise lately. I marched myself upstairs and changed into my workout gear. A workout was what I needed.

Fifteen minutes later I walked through the front door of the Community Center, next door to the high school.

The facility was a compromise between the City Council and the School Board; overlapping membership between the two groups sometimes made cooperation easier, and sometimes made it nearly impossible. The Community Center was in the "easier" category.

When the school district couldn't afford to upgrade the athletic buildings, they teamed up with the city to provide a multi-use facility. Now the sports teams had a state-of-the-art workout space that they shared with the rest of the town.

It had taken some time to get the schedules to mesh, and there were still occasional clashes, but for the most part it worked pretty well.

Climbing the stairs to the cardio room, I heard the whine of elliptical machines and stationary bikes, punctuated by the intermittent clang of pumping iron from the space below.

An antiseptic tang tickled my nose, and for a moment I thought I was going to sneeze.

At the top of the stairs, the expansive cardio room was emptier than I expected. Two thirtysomething women stood next to an elliptical machine where a third was just finishing her session. A white-haired man pedaled doggedly on a stationary bike, headphones clamped over his ears as he stared at the television screen suspended in the corner, where a helmet-haired newsreader silently mouthed her story.

I claimed an empty treadmill, and by the time I had my water and towel arranged, the women had left. I was about to start my walk, a book propped on the rack in front of me, when Coach Bradley walked in.

Danny Bradley was a couple years older than I, a friend of my cousin Peter's until Peter's folks had moved to Montgomery. I'd been a tagalong third wheel when Peter's mother insisted, though the boys hated the idea.

At the moment, he looked several decades older than me. He moved with the tentative step of an elderly man afraid of losing his balance, and his usually ramrod-straight posture—a reminder of his stint in the Marine Corps—sagged.

Danny spotted me as he came in. There was a flash of puzzled recognition, as though he knew he *should* know who I was, but he couldn't be sure.

I seized the opportunity, waving at him across the room. "Hi, Danny," I said, as though we'd been on a first-name basis all along, instead of twenty-five years ago. "How you holding up?"

It was a question he'd probably heard a million times in the last week. He shook his head slowly as he crossed the room to my perch on the treadmill. Our six-inch height difference camouflaged by the treadmill deck, I looked Danny in the eye.

He seemed defeated.

"It's a tough one for us," he said softly. "Kevin was a good kid."

It was the same thing everyone was saying. And I wasn't interested in whether Kevin was a good kid. I wanted to know why he died. Why, according to Uncle Louis, his death wasn't an accident.

"But how are *you* doing, Danny? It's not just the team; you're pretty tight with all your players. It must be hard."

Surprise registered on Danny's face. I doubt anyone had

asked about him personally in the last week, and yet he'd clearly suffered a loss. "He was special," he conceded. "The most talented kid I've coached, I think. He could have had a helluva future."

I stepped off the treadmill, moving closer to Danny, and lifting my face to look him in the eye. "He was that good? I'd seen him play, but I'm no expert."

Danny hesitated. I saw something shift in his eyes, and for the first time, I saw the man behind the tough shell of the coach. Hurt, loss, and anger battled for control.

"He was." Anger won out. "The whole team looked up to him, followed his lead. He could have made them all look good. Instead, he had them out slamming beers in the woods."

His mouth set in a grim line. "If he'd been caught I'd have had to suspend him for at least a month, but he'd be alive. Such a damned fool thing to do! Hurt the whole team."

He stopped, his face reddening as he bit back the rest of his tirade. Kevin's death had inflicted a lot of damage on the team and their chances, but Danny saw what might have been, and it made him mad.

How mad?

I wasn't sure, and he held back any more comments. Judging from his expression, he hadn't intended to share those feelings.

"I hadn't thought about that," I said, keeping my voice low in a show of confidentiality. The only other person in the room was the old guy on the bike, with his headphones firmly in place, but Danny was regretting what he'd said, and I wanted to reassure him.

"It's sad that sometimes kids can't see the bigger picture. I guess that's one of those lessons you learn as you get older," I said.

"Well," the anger was still in Danny's voice, bitterness

seeping into every word. "Kevin won't be learning any more lessons."

He muttered something under his breath. Anyone else would have just heard a vague growl, but I'd spent years listening to Bluebeard mutter, and I was pretty sure I understood what Danny said.

"And he won't be ruining anyone else's season."

Chapter 21

"THANKS, BY THE WAY, FOR TAKING CARE OF THE ME-morial T-shirts." Danny not-so-subtly signaled that the dis-cussion of Kevin was closed. "I appreciate it. Fowler would do it, but he's got a lot on his plate. The Booster Club will need all the help it can get this year, and your offer is really appreciated. It means a lot to the team, too, to know the town is behind them."

There was no sense in trying to tell him it wasn't my idea. And if Peter was going to volunteer me to do the work, then I'd take the gratitude. It was likely to be all I got out of the deal besides the tiny commission that would barely cover my expenses, so I might as well enjoy it.

"Thanks, Danny. I actually had to get another load of shirts this afternoon; we'd sold out of almost everything I had."

For a moment Danny's eyes glittered, and he blinked rap-idly a couple times. "That's good to hear. The team hasn't even been in to get their shirts yet." He snapped his fingers.

"I need to check with Fowler on that. He usually holds back a bunch for the players when he does something like this for special events and things like that, but I'm not sure if he did this time."

Did that mean he *gave* the shirts to the team? Since I was supposed to pay the Booster Club for the shirts, the added costs of the free shirts would pinch, but I could do it for the sake of the team, and the town. Still, it was another reminder of how Peter had dragged me into this situation and how little information I really had.

Danny moved away, toward a stair-climber in the far corner. He looked back over his shoulder, a sad smile on his face.

"Thanks for asking, Glory, and for everything else. I'm getting by, one day at a time." He flipped his hand in a desultory wave, as though dismissing his previous outburst, and mounted the machine.

Within a minute he was sprinting up an imaginary flight of stairs, working himself into a sweat. He ran with a desperate energy, as if some unseen demon was chasing him.

Maybe he was looking for the kind of physical exhaustion that would make him sleep soundly enough to forget the hurt and the anger.

I propped my book open and started the treadmill, blocking out the rest of the room.

When I looked up thirty minutes later, the stationary bike was empty, and Danny was climbing off the stair-climber with a red face and rubbery legs. He stumbled and caught himself against the handrail of the machine, wincing. He saw my glance and made a show of rubbing his calf as though he had a muscle cramp.

I gave him a few minutes as I finished my session on the treadmill. I didn't really want to run into him in the lobby or the parking lot; I needed time to think about what he'd said, and what it might mean.

The treadmill timer reached zero, and I breathed a sigh of relief. I hadn't been getting enough exercise over the summer—I told myself I didn't have time when I was busy in the shop, even though I knew that wasn't true—and I could feel the burn in my legs. Tomorrow I might be sore, and it would be my own fault for not sticking to a regular schedule.

I grabbed my book and my water bottle, wiped down the machine, and walked gingerly down the stairs. My legs were as rubbery as Danny's had been. The difference was he had been running stairs for thirty minutes and I had done a barely brisk two-mile walk on the flat treadmill.

I was nearly home when I realized I needed to buy groceries. My kitchen was getting bare, and even though Felipe was in charge of tomorrow night's dinner, I would have to eat tonight. Worse, I was out of treats for Bluebeard and had run out of apples, which he loved.

In spite of my sweaty T-shirt and baggy sweatpants, I turned into the lot at Frank's Foods and dragged myself out of the car. I grabbed my wallet and headed for the door. Might as well get this done.

I took a cart from the front of the store and headed for the produce section. Bluebeard loved fruit, and it was one way to get him to do what I wanted.

Frank waved to me from where he was working, stocking sweet potatoes. "How did your corn turn out?" he asked.

"It was great," I said. I walked back to the mound of lumpy, red-skinned tubers and picked out a couple to share with Bluebeard. Generally, he could eat anything I could—with the exception of chocolate, caffeine, and a couple other things—and I often gave him whatever fresh vegetables I was having.

"Did you go to the memorial service?" Frank asked.

I nodded. "I think most everybody in town was there. I didn't see you and Cheryl, but then, I didn't see a lot of people in that crowd."

"Yep." Frank moved on to piling bags of russet potatoes on a dry table, and I walked along with him. "We were up behind the Booster Club, down to the end of the field. Closed down the store for the afternoon; so many of the crew asked for time off to go that it just seemed easier to close."

"It looked like a lot of places were closed," I said. "I was, and I know Carousel was. I guess Fowler must have closed, too, since I saw him there. Although," I paused a moment, thinking, "he did have someone deliver those T-shirts to my shop that afternoon. Maybe he was the only one who got time off to go to the service."

Frank made a disgusted face. "That would be just like him. Make everyone else work while he plays the big man."

Was there *anyone* in this town who liked Matt Fowler? It sure didn't sound like Frank was in that category.

"Gee, Frank," I kidded, "why don't you tell me how you really feel?"

He reddened and ducked his head, suddenly intent on arranging the bags of potatoes. "Don't take that too serious," he said. "You know me, I'm just a country boy. I get my back up pretty easy over the salesman type of guy. It ain't Fowler's fault he's one of 'em."

In spite of his disclaimer, I wasn't sure I believed Frank. His distaste had been clear. And it wasn't just him. Plenty of other people had the same opinion.

Besides, I didn't buy Frank's "just a country boy" routine. He was a smart businessman who ran a successful grocery store, in competition with a chain store nearby and Pensacola just a few miles away.

No, he wasn't a bumbling country boy, despite what he said. As for Fowler, being an overbearing jerk wasn't criminal, just annoying, and he was arrogant enough not to care who he irritated.

I chatted with Frank a couple more minutes, as I picked out apples and carrots and some fresh okra.

"That came in yesterday morning," Frank gestured to the okra. "You're gonna want to cook it tonight, 'fore it turns."

"Sounds like a plan to me," I said, plopping the bag of small green pods in the cart. "Bluebeard will help me finish it if I don't eat it all."

Frank grinned. "That parrot eats better than some people I know."

"Some people won't eat their vegetables," I answered. "And Bluebeard doesn't get fast food. So, yeah, he probably does eat better than some people."

As I wheeled my cart down the next aisle, I caught sight of a young woman moving into the checkout stand to relieve Cheryl.

Julie Parmenter. I'd forgotten she worked for Frank.

I hurried through the rest of my shopping and wheeled my cart to the check stand within a few minutes. Julie was at the register, her puffy eyes and blotched complexion testament to her continued mourning.

She didn't speak as she took the groceries from my cart and passed them over the scanner, but she smiled weakly.

When I handed her my card, she swiped it through her machine and read my name. Recognition flashed in her reddened eyes as she looked up at me. "You're Miss Glory from Southern Treasures, aren't you? Sorry; I didn't recognize you at first. Did you do something different with your hair?"

Without thinking I reached up and patted my head. My hair, usually hanging long down my back, was twisted into a knot atop my head for my workout, as I was reminded by the presence of a pair of chopsticks holding it in place.

"Just put it up to go to the gym," I explained.

"That makes sense," Julie said, smiling a little more warmly. Her face clouded up again as she remembered what she had started to say. "You have Kevin's T-shirts, don't you? I need to get over there . . ." Her voice trailed off as tears welled in her eyes.

I nodded, a gesture of both agreement and sympathy. "When you get time, there's no rush. If you tell me what size you want, I can set one aside for you to pick up whenever."

Julie brightened a little at the prospect of putting off the chore, though I still didn't understand why she was so upset by Kevin's death. "I'd need a medium," she said. "It'll be kinda big, but that's okay. And could you give me a double-X, too? For my, um, husband?" Her mouth twisted on the last word, as though she had trouble saying it.

"Sure," I agreed. "I'll set them aside."

"How much?" Julie asked, reaching for the pocket of her jeans.

"Twenty bucks apiece," I said. "Just pay me when you pick them up," I added quickly. "It'll be easier for me to keep track that way."

Julie glanced past me to the next person in line. A look of dismay flitted across her features, gone in an instant as she pasted a wan smile in place.

"Hey, hon," a deep voice behind me said. I looked back to find Jimmy Parmenter looking at his wife, an easy grin on his face. "You okay?" he said, concern furrowing his brow.

"I'm fine," Julie said. The hastily suppressed dismay and

the quaver in her voice gave the lie to her words. "Just a little tired is all."

"Hey, Miss Glory," Jimmy said, acknowledging my presence. "Just stopped by on my way home from work to check on my little woman here. She's been a bit under the weather this week."

Under the weather? She'd been crying her eyes out. But he could call it whatever he liked.

Julie didn't respond to his expression of concern, turning back to me with my card. "Do you need some help out with that, Miss Glory?" she asked, carefully not looking at her husband.

"No, no," I replied hastily. "I've got it."

I grabbed the plastic handles of the three grocery bags and hefted them. They were heavy, but I could manage. "I'll try to remember my own shopping bags next time," I said to Julie.

I nodded to Jimmy and took a couple of slow steps, turning my back on the couple. I took my time moving away, straining to hear their voices behind me.

"What do you really want, Jimmy?" Julie's voice was low, a combination of misery and anger.

"I just wanted to be sure you were okay," Jimmy insisted. "I know you didn't feel none too good when I left for work, and I'm kinda surprised you didn't stay home."

"Like we could afford that," she snapped. "Besides, if you were so concerned, where were you at the memorial? Sitting with all your little friends."

"They're *our* friends, Jules. We're part of the team. You're the one who didn't want to be with them." Hurt tinged his words, and he was perilously close to whining.

"We *were* part of the team—" Julie's voice cut off.

"You need a break, Julie?" Frank spoke gently, but there was an undercurrent of reproach. He wasn't paying her to argue with her husband; he was paying her to wait on customers and stock shelves.

"I was just leaving, Mr. Beauford," Jimmy cut in. "Just checking up on Jules since she wasn't feeling so hot this morning."

"That's thoughtful of you, son. Julie, do you want to go ahead home? If you're not feeling good?"

"N-n-no," Julie stammered. "Jimmy's heading home. I'll just get back to work."

With no one else in line to wait on, Julie hurried away. In a few seconds, Jimmy spoke again. "She's real tore up over that poor kid, Mr. Beauford. You keep an eye on her for me?"

"Sure thing, Jimmy."

I was nearly to the door when Jimmy caught up to me. He reached out and held the door for me, then followed me out to the parking lot.

"Let me help you with those bags." He took the grocery sacks before I could protest, lifting them effortlessly into the hatchback of my battered compact.

Up close, he towered over me, probably six-four or -five to my five-foot-seven, and his chest looked as wide as my hatchback. Even though he wasn't playing football anymore, he was clearly working hard to maintain the athletic build that had made him a star.

"Thanks, Jimmy." I opened my door and climbed in the car.

The boy shrugged off my thanks and turned away. As I wrestled with the seatbelt, I saw him lope across the lot to a nearly new pickup with heavy-duty suspension lifting it high off the ground.

Julie said she couldn't afford to miss a day's work, but Jimmy was driving a new gas-guzzler with all the extras.

I watched him pull away and wondered which image was the truth. Was Julie's concern misplaced? Or was the real fight over something else? Something that had nothing to do with money?

I finally battled the seatbelt into submission and started the engine. As I shifted into gear, I remembered the visit of Julie's friends that morning with the strollers and maternity clothes, and another explanation occurred to me—one that would account for Jimmy's solicitous actions and for Julie's fragile emotions.

I wondered if Julie was pregnant.

Chapter 22

EARLY THURSDAY MORNING I GATHERED UP MY BANK-
ing, a couple pieces of dry cleaning, and an overdue library
book for a quick multi-errand run before I opened the store.

Which was a great plan, until the car wouldn't start.

I tried all the tricks I knew, which mostly meant opening
the hood and staring at the maze of wires and tubes that make
up a modern internal-combustion engine. I checked for dan-
gling wires and glared at various mysterious pieces of metal.

Finally I gave up and called for help.

I don't know if it was thanks to Peter's generosity with my
time, or my newfound pal Shiloh, but Fowler's promised to
have a service guy out to look at the uncooperative beast.

It only took him an hour to get there, which was pretty
quick by service standards in Keyhole Bay. One of the problems with a small town—you don't have a lot of choices when
it comes to things like electricians, or plumbers, or mechanics.

While I waited, I straightened up the storeroom and looked

for something to perk up the front window. I should do something with an autumn theme, something to attract the snow-birds who would flock to the Gulf Coast as soon as the cold weather hit up north.

I totally understood that. I had taken a class trip my junior year in high school, a January swim meet in Missouri. Leaving the overheated pool building with my hair still wet from the meet, I'd sworn I would never live anywhere that had snow.

I had a great deal of sympathy for people who lived in snow country as long as I didn't have to be one of them.

I heard the service truck pull into the tiny lot behind the store. When I stepped outside, I was surprised to see Jimmy Parmenter at the wheel. I thought he worked for his father-in-law as the maintenance man for their small hotel.

"Hey, Jimmy."

Jimmy jumped down from the cab of the truck. "Hey, Miss Glory."

That made me feel about a million years old. But it was how all polite Southern youngsters referred to people older than themselves, and I couldn't change that.

"What seems to be the problem?"

I shrugged and waved at the open hood of my high-mileage relic. "Won't start."

He ducked his head under the hood and looked around the inside of the engine compartment as though he actually understood what all the wiring and tubes and plastic and metal pieces were for.

I hovered nearby, trying to stay out of the way, but too anxious to go back to work. Car repairs were one of those great unknowns that could ruin an otherwise-profitable month.

I remembered that I had the T-shirts for Julie and Jimmy set aside behind the counter. I could send them home with Jimmy and save Julie a trip.

I hesitated, thinking back to the conversation in Frank's the day before. Julie told me to hold a shirt for her husband, but immediately clammed up when Jimmy appeared.

Maybe I should just wait for her to pick them up.

As I watched, Jimmy tugged on a couple of wires and tapped on the carburetor. At least I think it was the carburetor.

"I thought you were working for Stan Nelson," I said, trying to keep my voice from shaking with trepidation. Car trouble always made me extremely nervous.

Jimmy didn't look up from his exploration of my recalcitrant engine. "You know how it is," he said, "working for family. Not always a good idea."

He pulled a screwdriver out of his back pocket and tapped on something else.

"I suppose so," I answered. I'd never actually worked for anyone in my family, unless you counted Peter's part-ownership of Southern Treasures. Which I didn't. From my own experience, I could easily imagine the emotional land-mines that could result from mixing family and business, though, especially for newlyweds. It wasn't a pretty picture.

"I worked for Matt Fowler before college," Jimmy said, pulling his head out from under the hood and straightening his back. "When I wanted to change jobs, he offered me a spot in the service department."

I remembered that Jimmy had been the lot boy when he was the football star, though I didn't think that really constituted working.

He walked to the back of the truck and dug around in a chromed toolbox, coming up with what looked like an over-size scrub brush with dangerous-looking wire bristles.

"Been with Matt for almost six months now. Just got promoted last week to driving the truck." His broad chest puffed up a bit with pride. "Matt says that's the fastest he's ever put anyone on the truck."

Jimmy pulled on a pair of heavy leather gloves and ducked back under the hood. He disconnected some wires, scrubbed at the connection points with the brush, and reconnected them.

"Give it a try," he said, gesturing to the front seat.

I climbed behind the wheel and turned the key. To my delight, the engine coughed twice, just like it always does, and putt-putted into life.

"Wow! You're a miracle worker!" I called to Jimmy as he lowered the hood and latched it tightly.

He grinned and shook his head. "Nah," he said. "Just corroded battery terminals. It'll be fine now. All I had to do was clean 'em up a little."

He patted the hood. "You oughta bring it in for a checkup, though. Looks like you could use some attention." He glanced at me, looking for a reaction to his obvious double entendre.

I kept my expression as neutral as possible. I wasn't much of one for flirting, especially with someone young enough to call me "Miss Glory."

He held my gaze for a second longer, then lowered his eyes to the car again. "You know, let one of the mechanics crawl under the hood. Check the brakes. The usual."

His attempts to be suggestive and charming were both obvious and clumsy, and for a moment I felt sorry for Julie. Was he like this with all the women he met?

When I didn't react, he looked confused and quickly backpedaled. "I'm not gonna charge you for the service call," he said, "if you promise you'll bring the car in for service soon." He gave me a goofy grin designed, I was sure, to dispel the tension he'd created with his inept flirting.

I let it all go. He was just a clumsy, overgrown kid, used to getting by on his good looks and sports-hero persona. Give him some time and a decent role model, and he might grow up and turn out okay.

Then again, he was working for Fowler, and there had been rumors for years about Fowler and nearly every woman who worked for him. According to some people, the only way Fowler held on to his wife was expensive jewelry and a new Cadillac every couple of years.

Jimmy tossed the wire brush and the leather gloves back in the toolbox and climbed into the cab of his truck. "You be sure you get that car in for service real soon, Miss Glory."

"Just as soon as I can," I promised. I just didn't say how soon that might actually be. That would depend on having a few more visitors like Margie, the quilt lady.

Thinking about Margie reminded me of another nagging problem; I'd given her my web address, but there was nothing on my so-called website except an address and phone number. I was going to have to get that taken care of one of these days.

Jimmy waved as he pulled out of the patch of gravel that passed for a parking lot. He pulled into the narrow side street at the back of my store, the truck taking up most of the width of the street. I hoped no one would come along before he reached the highway. There wasn't room for another vehicle on the road.

Leaving my engine running for fear it wouldn't start again, I ran back and locked the storeroom door before I followed Jimmy's route to the highway. I didn't see any cars run off the road, so I guessed he had made it safely back to the wider main street.

I dashed into the dry cleaners, my car idling outside the front door. At the library, I dropped my book into the slot of the drive-through drop box; I could keep the engine running a little longer—and avoid the disapproving glare of the librarian when she inspected the due date.

By the time I pulled into the bank, I felt more confident of the car. I parked, took a deep breath, and turned off the engine, with a silent prayer that Jimmy had been right when he told me it was all taken care of.

At the teller window, I handed my deposit bag over to Barbara. I nodded at the poster taped to the wall just below the counter, a notice that the bank was accepting donations for the Kevin Stanley Memorial Fund. The proceeds would help Kevin's family with the funeral expenses and establish a scholarship fund in Kevin's name.

"How's the memorial fund doing?" I asked Barbara.

She didn't answer immediately, as she finished counting and stacking the cash in my deposit, and running the thin stack of checks through her scanner.

"I'm shocked," she said. She stopped to tap the totals into her terminal. On the counter next to her, a printer spit out a receipt.

"Good or bad?"

"Good." She lowered her voice as though unsure whether she should tell me the details. "Several thousand already, in one week. Lots of little donations, five or ten bucks. A bunch of the teachers challenged each other to raise a hundred bucks each, and I think a lot of them just took the money out of their own pockets."

"That's a lot, on a teacher's salary," I said.

Barbara nodded. "But that wasn't all. The Sea Witch— you know, the fish place where all the tourists go?—anyway, they came in earlier today with two grand."

"Wow!"

"Oh," she glanced around, making sure no one was listening. "It wasn't from them, really. They put a jar on the counter, told every customer about Kevin, and," another glance, "I hear they put a lot of pressure on the employees to contribute at least one shift's worth of tips."

Now it made sense. The Sea Witch was always getting its picture in the *News and Times* for something, but the owners were notorious penny-pinchers. They got their kudos for generosity by guilt-tripping customers and employees into digging into their pockets.

I shook my head as I accepted the receipt from Barbara. "That's worse than the teachers," I said. "Those guys live on their tips."

I hesitated. The car was going to need repairs soon, and I wasn't exactly rolling in dough. But this was something that the entire community should do, and I had been affected by Kevin's death in more ways than I ever expected.

I dug in my pocket and pulled out a twenty. It wasn't much, but it was something. I passed the bill over to Jessica. "Put this in the fund."

She took it and smiled at me as I turned to go.

"Wait," she called after me.

I turned back. She tapped a couple of keys on her terminal, then handed me another receipt. "We have to keep careful records," she said. "And you may need that for your taxes."

I climbed back in the car, fingers crossed. The engine coughed twice and sputtered to life.

Jimmy was, indeed, a miracle worker.

As I drove home, Jimmy was on my mind. There weren't that many tow trucks in Keyhole Bay. If Fowler's truck got the tow, maybe Jimmy would know what had really happened to Kevin's car.

Maybe I *should* get the car in for service soon.

Chapter 23

BACK AT THE SHOP, I WAS STILL THINKING ABOUT THE display window when Jake Robinson came through the front door.

Bluebeard roused himself from his nap and let out a piercing wolf whistle, too loud to ignore.

"Manners, Bluebeard," I scolded. Trying to avoid meeting Jake's gaze, I found myself staring instead at a broad expanse of muscled chest and chiseled arms, covered by a close-fitting polo shirt.

Safer to look him in the eye.

"Thanks, Bluebeard," Jake said with a chuckle. "But I don't think I'm your type."

"You don't like parrots?" I teased. Now who was flirting?

Bluebeard squawked and began muttering, an occasional profanity the only words that were clear.

"Language . . ." I dragged out the word in a warning.

The muttering muted, and I couldn't pick up on any more

recognizable words. Not that it mattered; his meaning had been quite clear.

"I like parrots just fine," Jake replied. "But I don't think they drink coffee."

"No, they don't. They can't deal with the caffeine. There are other things, too. Kidney beans. Avocados—" I stopped suddenly, realizing what Jake was actually saying.

"Oh, yeah, I, uh. No, no, Bluebeard doesn't drink coffee, but I do."

Jake bit his lower lip, trying not to laugh at my faux pas. Hey, I was flirting, I just wasn't very good at it.

"Let's try that again," he said after a moment. "Hi, Glory. I'm taking a break. Would you care to join me at The Lighthouse for a cup of coffee?"

"Sure."

I gave Bluebeard a stern warning before I locked the door and walked next door with Jake. I carried the store phone with me, and I noticed Jake did the same.

He suggested I grab a table while he ordered coffee. He spent a couple of minutes at the counter, conferring with Chloe before he joined me at a table by the front window. We could see the front doors of both shops from our vantage point—we might be on a break, but we were still both on duty.

When Chloe carried her tray to our table, the rich aroma of coffee and chocolate filled my nose, mingled with the delicate tang of lemon muffins. She had obviously advised Jake on my weaknesses. At least in regard to pastries. Well, I could skip lunch; glancing at my watch, I was shocked to find I had *already* skipped lunch. The car trouble had taken a bigger chunk out of my morning than I thought.

"So," Jake said once we were settled, "why a parrot?"

"I inherited him from my uncle Louis."

He quirked an eyebrow in question, and motioned for me

to continue. "You told me that much. What else? From the way you talk, your uncle must have been quite a guy," Jake said, crumpling his muffin paper into a little ball.

"To tell the truth, I don't know that much about him." It felt funny saying that aloud to someone other than Linda or Karen. "I wish I knew more, but I was just a kid when he died."

"But there are family stories, aren't there? Someone like that, there are always stories."

I didn't answer right away, and Jake instantly caught the hesitation.

"I said something wrong, didn't I?" He looked down at the table, crushing the muffin wrapper even smaller. "Sorry." His voice was soft and apologetic.

I reached across the table and laid my hand over his. At the touch, he looked up at me. I pulled my hand back, my fingertips tingling from the brief contact.

"There was no way you could know," I said. "My parents were killed in a hit-and-run accident when I was seventeen. All the family stories I thought I'd hear when I was older never got told."

I took a sip of the cooling mocha, letting the sweet liquid slide down my tightening throat. I knew it was Kevin's death combined with realizing Uncle Louis's ghost was still with me that had my emotions so exposed lately. But I couldn't tell Jake that.

"Oh, man." Jake shook his head. "Let me introduce myself. I'm Donnie Downer, the guy with his foot in his mouth."

That made me smile. "You didn't know," I repeated. "It was a completely innocent remark."

"Right. Great way to make a first impression."

Jake had already made a good first impression, and his reaction just reinforced it. Not that I was going to actually tell him so. At least not yet.

"You must have been reading my mind, though. Lately I've been trying to find out more about Uncle Louis." I didn't mention why.

"Any success?"

I told him about the newspaper articles I'd found, and he suggested doing an online search. "There should be some archives for the *News and Times*," he said. "And if you have enough information you might be able to find his service records, too."

"But I don't have any information. That's the problem."

"I bet you could find what you need. Was it a local lawyer who drew up the will? Those guys never throw anything away."

I got the distinct impression that was the voice of experience speaking, but he didn't give me a chance to ask.

"If not his lawyer, then maybe yours. Or the probate records when you inherited the store. You said you were just a kid. Ten, right?"

I nodded.

"So there's probably still people around that knew him. After all, that's only, what, twelve, fifteen years ago?" His eyes twinkled, telling me he was deliberately guessing way low.

"More like twenty-five," I answered.

"Not quite," a voice said from behind me.

I turned to see Karen standing just inside the door, grinning like a crazy woman. "You're not that old yet, Martine."

"Close enough," I argued as she pulled a chair over and sat down at the table with us. "Not staying," she added hastily. "Just saw you sitting here and wanted to know if I should pick you up for dinner." She shot Jake an appraising glance, and stuck out her hand. "Karen Freed, WBBY. I think we've met, but it's been a while."

Jake took her hand and shook it briefly. "Yes, we have. A Chamber of Commerce dinner or some such, as I recall. I'm a fan of your work, by the way."

"Thanks!" She looked back at me. "So. Dinner. You want a ride?"

"Actually, yeah. My car's been acting up, so I'd just as soon not have to drive."

"Great!" She stood up again and scooted the borrowed chair back to the adjoining table. "See you about six thirty."

At the door she turned back. "By the way, I talked to Boomer. I'll fill you in at dinner."

The thought didn't fill me with anticipation as much as dread.

"I gather you're friends," Jake said, looking a little dazed. I understood the reaction; Karen at full throttle could be overwhelming.

"We've been best friends since first grade." It seemed like an inadequate answer after Karen's whirlwind visit, and I began telling Jake about our weekly dinners. "You know Ernie Jourdain and Felipe Vargas? They own Carousel Antiques. We trade off cooking dinner for each other every week."

I explained about our current emphasis on traditional Southern cooking, and my recent experiment with creamed corn and hush puppies, relieved he hadn't asked why Karen was talking to the chief of police and telling me about it.

I stopped, feeling as though I'd been babbling. Jake was way too easy to talk to, and I was running on. "You really didn't want to know all that."

"Actually, it's great," he said. "I know a few people, but mostly I'm the new guy in town, like I said yesterday. It takes a while to make friends, especially in a small town."

"You just have to stick around. A lot of people last one season; then, when we hit the slow time, they bail. Or they can't take the long hours during the busy season. I guess it's not very friendly, but why spend time getting to know someone who's going to leave again in a few months?" I shrugged and drained my coffee. "But you haven't run away, so you'll be fine."

Reluctantly, I glanced at my watch. "I am going to have to get back to the store," I said. "I have been putting off working on my website for weeks, and I really need to do something with it." I sighed at the prospect. "Not that I know very much about setting up a website . . ."

Jake picked up the empty coffee cups and wadded paper napkins and tossed them in the trash. "I don't know a lot," he said, holding the door for me, "but I'm happy to share what I do know. And I have a couple books in the store that might be useful. Stop over when you have a minute and see if one of them might help."

He paused on the sidewalk. "Thanks for joining me. I enjoyed it. Let's do it again soon."

He started across the street, his long strides carrying him to the far curb in seconds. He stopped in front of Beach Books and waved back at me with a smile.

Yes, definitely soon.

Chapter 24

I WAS CLOSE TO A MELTDOWN BY CLOSING TIME. I'D battled the computer all afternoon, first trying to find information about Uncle Louis, without much success. While I searched, Bluebeard kept hopping back and forth between the counter and his perch, stopping to stare angrily at the display of memorial T-shirts.

His agitation showed in every movement, and each time he crossed the shop, I had to warn him about damaging the shirts. After every outburst, it took several minutes of soothing and petting to settle him down before I could go back to my research.

Frustrated, I'd finally abandoned the search and pulled up the website, determined to make some progress with the design project.

Why I thought I could do anything, though, I don't know.

I wasn't any kind of computer whiz; just the opposite, in fact. I blamed my problems on my teacher—and I was self-taught.

I was ready to throw something when Shiloh Weaver came through the front door.

"You okay?" she asked from the doorway, as though she wasn't sure she should come any farther into the room.

"Some days I purely hate computers," I said. I closed my files and shut down the system. "What can I do for you?"

She walked over and leaned against the counter. "Just doing some running around for Mr. Fowler. Bank, office supply, the usual. I was driving past and figured I'd stop and check how the shirts were doing."

"Moved maybe a dozen today," I answered. I remembered my conversation with Danny Bradley in the gym the night before. "There is one question you can probably answer for me, though, since you're here."

"Happy to, if I know the answer."

"It's about shirts for the team." The computer blinked off, and I walked around to the front of the counter. "I ran into Danny Bradley at the gym last night, and he said something about setting shirts aside for the team. Said Fowler usually did that for him, but he'd have to check since I was distributing them this time. This is awkward, but I kind of got the impression that I was expected to not charge them. How do I account for that?"

Shiloh put her hand over her mouth, a stricken look in her eyes. "I can't believe I forgot to tell you about that," she said. "I am so sorry! Team shirts are at cost. Six bucks each. The guys will probably come in together, so just keep track of how many you sell at that price. You get the same handling fee, of course," she added. "Used to be most of them had cash. Now it's mostly debit cards, except for a few," she rolled her eyes, "whose parents think they can trust them with a credit card."

"A high school kid?" I was incredulous. "With a credit card?"

"I know!" She was closer to being a teenager than I was, but we were both doing the geezer can-you-believe-these-kids routine. It made me laugh.

"Lordy! We sound like we're ancient!"

Shiloh laughed with me. "I know. Makes me feel like an old granny sometimes." She sobered and continued. "Anyway, you aren't expected to give the shirts away. Just let the boys have them at cost. They'll probably want to get them for their girlfriends, too. And Mr. Fowler usually gives them the nod on that one."

"Got it. Team shirts at cost. By the way," I switched the subject, "I wanted to thank you for getting Jimmy out here so quickly. It turned out to be a simple fix, but I was feeling a little panicky at not having a running vehicle."

While we talked, I fed Bluebeard and draped the old blanket over his cage. He wasn't ready to go to sleep for the night, but I wanted him to have a dark place to retreat to when he was ready.

"You're welcome, but it wasn't a big deal. The truck was available, and Jimmy came in just a few minutes after you called. Just glad we were able to help."

"Bad man!" Bluebeard screeched. "Bad man!"

I reached out and laid my hand on his head. "It's okay," I said softly. "I know about the bad man. But he isn't here. We're all safe here."

He calmed slightly, but his agitation was evident in the way he continued to fidget on his perch and to ruffle his feathers. Even a shredded-wheat biscuit wasn't enough to make him happy.

"I don't know who the 'bad man' is." I lied to Shiloh. I was certain the bad man was her boss, but I wasn't going to tell her that. "But whoever it is, he's really upset about it."

"Strange, isn't it, how animals react? My cat absolutely hated my last boyfriend. *Hated* him. Barf-in-his-shoes hated him. Turns out the scumbag was cheating on me." She shook her head. "So, whoever this 'bad man' is, you might want to listen to the parrot."

"You could be right." I switched the subject back to Jimmy and the tow truck. "Just wanted you to know I was grateful to Jimmy," I said. "He didn't charge me for the service, said it was an easy fix and he'd waive the fee if I promised I'd bring the car in soon."

Shiloh laughed. "I won't tell Mr. Fowler he did that. He only promoted the kid to the truck a week ago. In fact, his first tow was Kevin's car, after the accident."

"So the car was towed to Fowler's?" I asked, surprised. I had assumed it would go to some police lot somewhere for inspection.

"We have a fenced lot in the back," Shiloh explained. "The cops use it as an impound when they need to secure a vehicle. It doesn't happen that often in Keyhole Bay, as you can imagine, so it doesn't make sense for them to maintain a lot of their own."

I filed that piece of information for later. If the car was at Fowler's, someone there might know more about how the accident happened.

Or they might not. But according to Bluebeard, somebody in this town had to know what really happened to Kevin, and I was determined to find out who.

Shiloh was still standing at the counter when Karen pulled up in her SUV at the curb outside my door.

I checked the vintage kitchen clock next to the quilt display. She was a half-hour early.

Shiloh stayed long enough to say hello to Karen, but then she excused herself, saying she had to get back to her office.

The minute the door closed behind her, Karen pounced. "Making nice with Fowler's Girl Friday?"

"She brought more T-shirts over yesterday, and we got to talking. Truth is, I think she doesn't like Fowler much, but she talks a loyal game. Did you know," I continued, "that Fowler is talking about running for the School Board?"

"She told you that?"

I nodded. Karen tagged along as I got ready for dinner, picking up the folder of newspaper copies off my desk, grabbing a sweater from upstairs, and checking on Bluebeard.

He had quieted down after Shiloh left, but when I approached, he started muttering again about the "bad man."

"What's his issue?" Karen asked. "Somebody steal his crackers?"

"I don't know. He just gets upset every time there's a mention of the accident," Bluebeard ruffled his feathers at the word, reinforcing what I'd said, "and he keeps talking about a 'bad man' that I think means someone who hurt Kevin."

"You sure he didn't mean Shiloh? He's a parrot after all, might not be too accurate on gender."

She'd meant it as a joke, but I thought about the idea. Was Shiloh Weaver loyal enough to Matt Fowler to cause Kevin's accident? Or could she have some other motive?

It didn't seem likely—Bluebeard was adamant that it was a bad *man*—but at this point I was willing to consider any possibility.

"Which reminds me," I said. "Shiloh was just telling me the car is at Fowler's. There isn't an actual police impound yard in Keyhole Bay—did you know that?—and they towed the car to Fowler's secure lot."

Before Karen could reply, Bluebeard ruffled his feathers again and squawked loudly before he spoke another clear sentence.

"Go look."

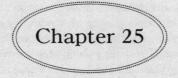

Chapter 25

KAREN AND I LOOKED AT EACH OTHER. I KNEW MY expression was as stunned as hers. "You aren't thinking . . ." She left the thought unfinished, as though that could stop the idea we both had.

"You heard him. We need to get a look at that car. There's a clue there, and we need to know what it is."

"Glory, I talked to Boomer today about the accident. I didn't tell him about Bluebeard or your uncle Louis because I knew you really didn't want me to. But I did ask him if he was sure it was an accident."

"And did he tell you not to worry your purty lil' head?" I knew I sounded whiny, but I didn't care. I had accepted that Uncle Louis was talking to me and that Kevin's death wasn't an accident. I didn't need some good old boy telling me I was meddling.

"Boomer's not like that, Glory, and you know it."

Defensive as I was, I knew she was right. I just didn't have to like it.

"Anyway," she went on, "he said there was no question Kevin was out at Thompson's Corner, and there was no question he'd been drinking. A bunch of the kids that he talked to said they saw Kevin with a beer in his hand."

"A beer? As in one? For a guy his size, that doesn't exactly make him a drunk driver."

She shook her head, pulling me toward the door. "No one is quite sure how many he had. Could have been one; could have been several. Boomer wouldn't tell me what his blood-alcohol reading was—claimed he didn't have accurate results yet—but that there was evidence in the car that Kevin was drinking. Besides, how much does it really take to affect a kid's driving? Especially when he's got a car with that much horsepower. Listen, I do think there's more to it, but we have to look at this from all angles."

I looked back to see if Bluebeard was okay before we left. He had retreated into his cage and settled down for a nap.

"I still need to go look," I said as I climbed into her SUV. "There must be something in the car that will help us figure out what happened."

We were still arguing over whether we should go try to see Kevin's car when we pulled into Ernie and Felipe's driveway. We carried the discussion inside, and soon the four of us were trying to figure out how to get a look in the secure lot at Fowler's.

"I'm telling you," Felipe said as he stirred the gravy on the stove. "It's Fowler. He did it, and now he's got the car in his lot. Nobody is ever going to know what he did if we don't do something about it."

I took a chilled oyster from the bed of rock salt on the appetizer plate, inhaling the tang of the salty liquor before letting the soft morsel slide down my throat, followed by a sip of Chablis.

Ernie put down his wine glass. "And just what do you think we should do, cher? March up to Matthew Fowler and ask him why he killed the quarterback?" He shook his head. "No, this is not our fight. In fact, I am not sure there is a fight."

He gave me a long look, his eyes dark. "Your haint says the boy's death wasn't an accident, and it tells you to go look at *something*. But how do you know what?" He shrugged, an elegant gesture. Ernie didn't know how to do anything that wasn't elegant. It was one of his most maddening qualities.

"I understand how you feel, Ernie. Really, I do." I held his gaze. "I thought the same thing myself until a few days ago. But too much has happened lately," I thought of the out-of-place quilt, "for me to dismiss it."

Karen came to my defense. "I was there, Ernie. I heard him. I don't really remember Glory's uncle, but I believe he's in that shop."

"Are you all forgetting that just three days ago, you," he pointed to Karen, "thought it was Coach Bradley; and you," he waved long fingers in my direction, "said it was Travis Chambers?"

"I didn't say it was Travis," I protested. "I just said he was out there at the kegger."

"And I didn't think it was Bradley," Karen said. "I just pointed out that he had as much motive as Fowler."

"And I," Ernie countered, "said it might not have anything at all to do with football, although the three of you were convinced it did."

We went around and around for a few minutes, debating the possibility that Kevin's death wasn't related to the football team and the current season. To no one's surprise, we didn't reach any agreement before Felipe brought the food to the table.

Steam rose from the vegetable bowls, one with greens

cooked with bacon and a touch of red-pepper flakes and one of sautéed yellow squash. A platter piled with golden pan-fried chicken took the place of honor in the middle of the table, flanked by fried grits and a bowl of the rich gravy Felipe had been stirring when we came in.

"I know," Felipe said, pouring sweet tea to accompany the hearty meal, "it's a festival of frying—the chicken, the grits, the squash. But it's *traditional*." He arched an eyebrow at Karen, who seemed to be the arbiter of what was or wasn't traditional Southern food.

Karen nodded, already helping herself to a piece of the chicken, still faintly sizzling from the heat of frying. "It looks good," she said. "Let's see how it tastes."

Kevin Stanley, Matt Fowler, Coach Bradley, and all the rest were left behind as we dug into the meal Felipe had prepared.

The chicken, seasoned simply with salt and pepper, coated with flour, and fried in a cast-iron skillet, was almost too hot to eat—and too good to wait for it to cool. The aroma made my mouth water, and I took a thigh and a drumstick, vowing to visit the gym again in the morning to work it off.

Karen spooned thick cream gravy, rich with browned bits from the bottom of the frying pan, over the slices of fried grits. Our plates looked amazing: dark greens, yellow squash, pale-gold fried grits, and dark, golden fried chicken. Felipe had outdone himself.

"How long did you simmer the greens?" Karen asked after her first bite. "They're incredible."

Felipe shrugged in an offhand manner, as though he hadn't worked all day on the meal. "A few hours," he said casually. "I think I started them right after lunch. You know how collards are; they need a long simmer."

I nodded in agreement, my mouth too full of searing-hot

chicken for me to speak. I took a quick sip of tea to quench a bit of the fire. When my mouth had recovered, I tasted the greens. The bite of raw collard greens had been mellowed by the long, slow simmer, and the salty bacon had added to the rich flavor.

Karen was right. They were incredible.

"The grits were leftovers from breakfast," Felipe explained as he put another slice on his plate and ladled gravy over it. "Ernie made a double batch this morning so I would have plenty to fry for dinner." He glanced at his partner sitting on his left. "Thanks, darlin'."

"Of course, cher." Ernie's smile showed his perfect white teeth against his dark skin. Felipe often said he fell in love with that smile first.

Felipe gave us more details about his cooking as we ate. He promised us he'd made copies of all the recipes he'd used, just as we had all done over the last few weeks. Another month or two and we would each have accumulated an impressive collection of new dishes.

We took a break after dinner, too full to have dessert right away. Felipe had scored some late-summer peaches and turned out a cobbler that filled the small house with a sweet, cinnamony scent, and we wanted to savor the last fresh peaches of the year. It deserved our full gastronomical attention.

Felipe cleared the table with efficiency born of long practice, stowing the dirty plates and silverware in the dishwasher.

As he refilled the tea pitcher, I got the ice bucket and refreshed the ice in our glasses. Ernie crushed fresh mint leaves into the pitcher and topped off all our glasses.

The conversation quickly returned to my shop, and my ghost. "Did you bring the newspaper copies?" Karen asked.

In answer, I hopped up from my place at the table and dragged the file folder out of my shoulder bag.

"This is all I've found so far," I said as I handed copies of the faded newsprint to all three of my friends. "It's darn little to show for sixty-seven years."

"He died *young*," Ernie said.

The comment caught me off guard, and I shot him a quizzical look before I remembered that Ernie was several years older than the rest of us. For him, sixty-seven was closer than it was for Karen, Felipe, and me.

"I think he had a hard life," I said. "I don't know exactly why I think that, but I have some vague recollection of my parents talking about Uncle Louis when I was little. I think he was still alive at the time, but they would always stop talking when I came in the room, like there was something I wasn't supposed to know."

"Maybe what happened to Kevin will give us a clue to what happened to your uncle," Felipe suggested. "We still need to figure out how to get a look at that car."

Ernie's face soured when Felipe went back to his earlier argument. His reluctance was clear. "Is there any way to do this without actually having to see the car?" he asked. "Perhaps there is someone who could tell us about the car without any of us actually having to get into the secure lot?"

"How about Glory's new pal, Shiloh?" Karen suggested.

"I don't think she'd tell us anything," I said, remembering my earlier suspicions. "She's very loyal to Fowler. Or at least she won't say anything against him. She works extra hours and does a lot that Fowler should do for himself," I went on, "but she says that frees him up to do the *important*," I made finger quotes around the word, "things."

"Really?" Felipe's voice dripped sarcasm. "And what are the important things Mr. Matthew Fowler is doing?"

"All his civic activities, from what Shiloh says," I answered. "The Booster Club, the Merchants' Association, that sort of thing. Oh," I suddenly remembered the other thing Shiloh had said the day before, "and she says he may be considering a run for School Board in the next election."

Ernie groaned—he even groaned elegantly—at the thought. "Fowler on the School Board? He must have really expected great things from the team this year."

"How do you mean?" I asked.

"Simple," Ernie explained patiently. "Fowler needs a lot more support than he currently has if he expects to jump into a political race; he'd need financing and endorsements."

"Which means he had a lot more at stake," Felipe said, his voice rising with excitement. "I told you it was him."

Ernie shook his head. "It also means that he had a lot more reason to keep his reputation clean. Causing that accident would have been a stupid move, and Matt Fowler isn't a stupid man."

"Define *stupid*." Karen jumped back into the discussion. "He has taken some huge risks over the years—most of them personal, not business."

We all turned and looked at her expectantly.

"There have been stories," she said softly. "Remember a couple years ago? Fred and Molly Curtis moved up to Arkansas because Fred supposedly got a transfer?"

We all nodded. Molly had been the office manager at Fowler's, Shiloh's boss and Matt's "right-hand girl." Yes, Fowler actually called his female employees girls.

"Fred didn't have a job, per se," Karen continued. "The story got spiked, but I talked to him before they left. He was opening a small car lot outside Little Rock. He wouldn't actually say so, but he hinted that he had financial backing from someone here in town."

"You mean—?" I stopped. This was confirmation of all the rumors I'd heard for years.

"Yep." Karen shook her head. "Absolutely. It was clear Fowler was paying them off for something. And right after they left, Kerrie Fowler got a new Cadillac. You know how that works. Every time Matt does something, Kerrie gets expensive jewelry or a fancy vacation. Or a new car."

"So you think Fowler and Molly . . . ?" Felipe left the rest of the question hanging in the air.

"No, I really don't," Karen said. "The way this got covered up, I think it was something—or someone—else. Kerrie might have suspected, but when she got the Caddy she settled right down. I think Molly found out about some antic of Fowler's that he didn't want made public, and he paid to get them out of town where she couldn't slip up and cause trouble. I don't even think Fred and Molly instigated it. The way I heard it, Fowler approached them. He said he wanted to branch out, and Molly knew how to run a dealership, so he put them in charge of his operation in Arkansas and gave them a little piece of the pie."

"Good plan," Ernie said. His voice held a note of something close to admiration. "Very smooth. And he undoubtedly got the newspaper and your station," he nodded at Karen, "to spike it with the argument that he didn't want to disclose his business dealings."

Felipe bounced out of his chair and started a pot of coffee. I rose and lent a hand as he got dessert plates and forks out and carried them to the table.

"You have to give him credit," I said as I set the cobbler next to the carton of vanilla ice cream Felipe retrieved from the freezer. "He's good at this kind of stuff. He knows what other people want and how to get them to do what *he* wants. And he knows how to keep himself out of trouble."

"Which is one argument against him being our bad guy,"

Ernie pointed out. "But he does have a temper, and he doesn't always control it completely," he conceded.

"Which is why he's still at the top of my list." Felipe set a shallow bowl of cobbler and ice cream in front of his partner. "Besides, he might not do the dirty work himself, but he could have hired someone."

I couldn't help laughing at that idea. "Really, Felipe! I don't much like the guy, but I really don't think he has the connections to be hiring a hit man."

I spooned up a bite of the warm cobbler and soft ice cream. Cinnamon, sugar, vanilla, and peach combined in my mouth and sent my taste buds into overload.

"I didn't say he hired a hit man," Felipe protested. "I just think he could have had help, and he seems to think he can buy his way out of anything."

"He can." Karen's cynical reaction was exactly what I expected. Her job gave her a jaded view of our little town and its power structure.

"Not everything," I said. "I'm sure there are things he couldn't get away with."

"You're a dreamer, Martine," Karen muttered, turning her attention to her own dessert.

"Karen," Ernie tried to deflect the argument, "what did the police chief say when you talked to him?"

Karen shrugged, gesturing to her mouth, which was full of cobbler. "Not a lot," she said after she swallowed.

"That's really good," she added as an aside to Felipe. "Anyway, back to Boomer," she continued. She gave the two men the same information she had given me. No blood-alcohol results, but Kevin had been seen at Thompson's Corner with a beer. Nothing to rule out an accident.

"But nothing to say it *was* an accident, either," Felipe said darkly. "The man does not know what exactly happened, but he's just going to write it off as an accident?"

"A kid, a beer, and a hot car," Karen repeated her earlier argument. "Sounds like a recipe for disaster to me."

"Disaster," I said, "is not necessarily an accident."

"It also isn't necessarily murder," Ernie said.

In the end, we decided that someone had to go to Fowler's and try to find out about Kevin's car. Because I had promised to bring my car in for service, I was elected.

And because my friends thought I shouldn't go alone, Ernie volunteered to go with me, ostensibly to drive me home if I had to leave the car overnight.

It was just a question of when we would go.

With the weekend coming, neither Ernie nor I could get away unless we did it the next day. Ernie said he could be ready first thing in the morning.

I groaned. "I don't want to do anything first thing on a Friday morning," I protested. "You guys keep me out way too late on Thursday nights."

"If we don't go tomorrow," Ernie said, "we'll have to wait for Monday, or later in the week."

"Can we at least make it later in the day?" I asked.

"If you go after three, I can watch the shop for you for an hour or so," Karen volunteered.

"That might be better," I said. "Fowler's gone a lot in the afternoons, according to Shiloh. It would mean we might be able to look around a little more if he's not there."

"I'll meet you at Fowler's at 3:30 then." For Ernie, the matter was settled. Once he decided to do something, he was committed 100 percent.

Our sleuthing would start tomorrow afternoon.

Chapter 26

BEFORE I COULD DO ANY SLEUTHING, THOUGH, I STILL had the question of Uncle Louis. None of us had gleaned much of anything from the newspaper clippings, beyond the bare facts of a few dates and his military service.

Jake had suggested a couple avenues to explore, so I spent part of Friday morning following up on his ideas.

I started with our family attorney. Clifford Wilson had practiced law in Keyhole Bay since he graduated from law school, which I suspected was sometime around the middle of the last century. Mr. Wilson—I couldn't bring myself to even think of him by his first name, a concession to my proper Southern upbringing—had to be eighty if he were a day.

He'd been the Martine family attorney my entire life, and he had worked for my parents and their parents before that, though he must have been a young man back then. He had had an established practice when he drafted Uncle Louis's will thirty years ago.

I wondered how much Mr. Wilson knew about my great-uncle and how much he might be willing to share with me.

Having learned over the years how to corral my tendency to jump from one project to another, I started two lists. One for clues to Kevin's death, and one for clues to the mystery that was Uncle Louis. I suspected the two would overlap, but I needed some way to keep the jumble of information from overwhelming me.

On the first list I put the names of the people who might know something about Kevin's death. Matt Fowler and football coach Danny Bradley were at the top of the list, but there were others, like Travis Chambers, whose star had been mostly eclipsed by Kevin, and Julie Parmenter, the former cheerleader whose devastation over Kevin's death was so extreme.

Any one of them—all people who were connected to Kevin in some way—might know something that could help me figure out why the football star ended up in a crumpled car in a cornfield.

I tried to think of where I could look for clues, but the only place I had so far was Fowler's secure lot.

I put it at the top of the list.

As for Uncle Louis, the list was much shorter and much less personal. His contemporaries were all in their eighties, the ones who were still alive. And as Linda had reminded me, he was a solitary man who kept himself to himself. No one knew him very well. Newspapers, service records, old yearbooks—they all might yield a fact or two, but the only actual person on the list was Clifford Wilson, and I wasn't sure how much he would be willing to share with me. How long did client confidentiality extend after the death of the client? And were there things he could tell me but would choose not to?

I dialed Wilson's office and made an appointment for the following week. His office hours had grown shorter in recent years, down to three afternoons per week, and the earliest I could see him was Tuesday at two.

Frustrated at the delay, I went to the computer and started searching for information. I wasn't sure where to start, but the Veterans Affairs website seemed like a logical first step. I browsed through the various menus, not really knowing what I was looking for and not sure I would recognize it if I found it.

There was information on military funerals, and something triggered a memory from my childhood. A flag in a shadowbox, hanging on the wall of my parent's living room. Both my grandfathers had been too young to enlist when the war started; only Uncle Louis had served during wartime.

It had to be his burial flag.

But what had happened to the flag? I couldn't remember. So many things had been packed away by Linda and a group of ladies from her church. I never unpacked most of them, and there were boxes stacked in the attic, waiting for the time when I would face the task of sorting through the personal effects of my parents. The flag was probably in one of those boxes, but I didn't know which one, and I wasn't willing to dig through all of them looking for it.

Besides, how much would the decades-old shadowbox be able to tell me, really? Likely nothing more than dates I already knew. But it made me think about his funeral. I was only ten, and my parents had left me and my cousin Peter at home with Linda while the adults were gone.

Uncle Louis had been buried in a military cemetery rather than the family plot. I did a search on the VA page, and found the address for the cemetery in Pensacola.

How strange that I had never even visited his grave. My

parents had taken my grandmother a few times, but I had always been left at home, and they stopped going after Grandma Antoinette died.

I checked the gravesite locator and found Louis Marcel Georges. I promised myself I would go visit my uncle soon. He would like that.

It didn't get me any closer to his service records, however. Those would be somewhere else.

I found a military-records site, but I needed more information to even begin a search—information I would have to get from Mr. Wilson.

I continued that way for most of the morning, one dead end after another. The *News and Times* had an archive, but it required me to register and wait for a confirmation, which didn't come.

Bluebeard spent the morning muttering on his perch, occasionally stopping to stare at me and beg for coffee. Each time I turned him down, the muttering increased, and he would demand a biscuit.

A trickle of customers kept me distracted. One man spent half an hour examining every pocket watch in the case before dismissing them as "ordinary." I politely referred him to Carousel Antiques, pointing out that they carried the more unusual items, with price tags to match.

As soon as he left the shop, I called Ernie and told him about the guy. "He won't think it's worth anything if you don't make him pay three prices for it," I said.

Ernie chuckled. "I will see to it that he pays an adequate price for my time. And for yours."

I felt better after I hung up. Some people didn't feel like they got value for their money unless they spent a lot of it, and I suspected this guy was one of them. If I couldn't sell him something he'd value, maybe one of my friends could.

I kept checking the clock as the morning dragged into afternoon. I continued with the computer as traffic allowed, but I wasn't getting anywhere.

I thought about closing for a few minutes and going across the street to ask Jake for advice. Since this line of research was his idea, he ought to be able to point me in the right direction. But every time I gathered the courage to walk across and ask for help, another customer wandered in.

When Karen finally came in, at a quarter after three, I was a bundle of nerves tied up with tightly strung wire.

Not the best choice for a clandestine mission, but I'd promised to meet Ernie at the lot. I had to go through with it.

Crossing my fingers, I turned the key on my battered sedan. It coughed to life, sputtering in its usual manner, and we were on our way.

I deliberately hadn't called ahead, in case Fowler might hide or destroy the evidence we were looking for—whatever it was. By the time I pulled into Fowler's service entrance, I had convinced myself I was on a fool's errand and was nearly ready to give up before I started.

What did I really hope to accomplish with this silliness? To prove that Kevin Stanley's death wasn't an accident? Based on the word of a parrot? Or a ghost?

Was I out of my mind?

I was on the verge of driving through the lot and back onto the street when Ernie strolled up to my driver's-side window and leaned down to peer in at me.

"I was wondering where you were," he said when I rolled down the glass. "I thought perhaps you had changed your mind."

I couldn't admit to him how close he was to the truth.

"No," I lied. "I just had to wait for Karen to babysit the shop." I parked the car and climbed out.

"Did that guy come by Carousel?" I asked Ernie as we walked into the service department.

His laugh was answer enough. "I sold him a pocket watch, a fob, and a wristwatch," he answered. "And, yes, he was very happy to pay dearly for his purchases."

"Good."

I know it wasn't very charitable of me. But if Mr. Big Spender needed a high price to make him feel he'd bought something of value, why shouldn't we accommodate him?

At the service desk, a young man with "Joe" embroidered over his shirt pocket asked if he could help me. Over his shoulder, I saw Shiloh in a glass-walled office, and I waved to her when she looked up.

Shifting my attention back to Joe, I explained about the car-starting problem and Kevin's advice to bring it in for some TLC. "I don't know exactly what's wrong, but it does run a little rough. Kevin said the starting problem was just dirty battery terminals but that it needed service."

He scribbled notes on a work order in handwriting that must have been the despair of Miss Minton at Keyhole Bay Elementary. She had drilled us on handwriting every day, expecting us to develop the graceful penmanship necessary for proper handwritten invitations, letters, and thank-you cards.

I hadn't had much use for elegant handwriting once I was past the fifth grade, but it was nice to know I had the skills if I ever needed them.

As Joe continued his notes, Shiloh came out of her office and stopped at the counter. She offered to let us wait in the small employee lounge overlooking the service area while Joe got someone to pull the car into the service bay.

"Any idea how long this will take?" I asked. "Ernie came with me in case I need a ride home."

Joe glanced at the intricate chart on the wall. "If there's

no calls, we can get to this in about fifteen minutes. Don't know how long the mechanics will need, but they usually give you an idea after a quick look."

"Come on back and have a cup of bad coffee," Shiloh offered. "We'll get it all sorted out within the hour." She glanced up at Ernie. "Unless you're in a hurry?"

He gave her a smile. "No, my partner's taking care of the shop for the afternoon. I'm just here to help Glory out."

Something shifted in Shiloh's eyes as she recognized Ernie and caught his meaning. "You're one of the guys from Carousel, aren't you?" Her posture visibly relaxed.

"Ernie Jourdain. And you?"

"Shiloh Weaver. A new friend of Glory's." She laughed a little self-consciously. "We bonded over memorial T-shirts."

She turned to me. "Which reminds me, have the boys from the team been in to pick up their shirts yet?"

I shook my head. "Homecoming's only a week away, isn't it? Coach Bradley must have them practicing night and day, trying to get ready for the game. Especially without—" I stopped suddenly, as I caught sight of Fowler and Jimmy Parmenter behind her at the far end of the service bays. Whatever was going on, it wasn't a happy conversation.

Shiloh jumped into the sudden silence, trying to smooth over my apparent distress. "I know; it's so difficult right now. I feel so bad for those boys."

Ernie, however, had caught the reason for my hesitation. While he closely watched the drama unfolding behind Shiloh's back, I kept her distracted, making long-winded comments about how upset we all were and how devastated the team must be by the tragic accident that had thrown them into such turmoil.

That much was true. I had seen those boys at the memorial service. They all seemed overcome by grief. It was possible one of them also suffered with guilt. And I was the only one in town—along with the friends I'd recruited—who believed it.

Shiloh and I chatted for a couple minutes more; then she excused herself, saying she had to get back to work. I wondered how I had ever suspected her, even for a minute. She was too open and trusting to be on my suspect list.

As soon as she left the room, I turned to Ernie.

"What's going on?" I whispered. Even though we were alone, I didn't want anyone to overhear our conversation.

"I'm not sure." He spoke softly, his lips so close I could feel his breath on my face. "Looked like Mr. High-and-Mighty Fowler was issuing orders, and the 'roid ranger there didn't care for what he was saying."

"Road ranger?" I didn't quite see how that fit Jimmy.

"'*Roid* ranger," Ernie repeated. "If I've seen anyone who was on the needle, it's that guy. Maybe not right now, but he has been. See how his skin's messed up and his hair's thinning? He's too old for the one and not old enough for the other."

I glanced over my shoulder to where Jimmy was puttering around the tow truck in the far bay. It hadn't occurred to me, but I trusted Ernie's judgment. Still, there was that question about Jimmy's wife.

"Don't steroids make you, uh," I stammered for a moment, looking for the right word, "sterile?" It wasn't exactly what I meant, but it would have to do.

Ernie laughed softly. "Not usually. But that wasn't really what you meant, was it, girl?"

The blush that colored my cheeks was all the answer he needed.

"They can purely mess you up in that department," he continued. "But usually it's only temporary—unless you've been on 'em a lot longer than that young buck." He gave me a sharp look. "But what's that to you?"

The question took me by surprise. Certainly Jimmy's virility—or lack thereof—was none of my business. I was just being nosy, bless my heart.

"I saw his wife the other day," I explained, "and for some reason I wondered if she was pregnant. Which would be a real bad thing if he couldn't, uh, you know."

This time his laugh boomed through the tiny room. Heads turned from out in the service bays, and now I was the one muttering curses under my breath.

Ernie quelled his amusement at my discomfort and continued in a serious voice. "Now they think we're just having a grand time while we wait, and they aren't going to pay much attention to the strange woman and her gay best friend."

"Nice try," I said drily. "But I don't believe for a second that was the reason you laughed."

"I gotta admit," he said, "you surprised me with that one."

"It was a serious question," I shot back. I was a little put out by his laughing at me. I didn't know about this stuff, and I had to ask *somebody*.

"And I gave you a serious answer, darlin'," he drawled. His voice was like honey, warm and sweet when he wanted it to be, and he could get me over a little hissy fit any time.

Like now.

"So what you're saying is that if my guess is right, and his wife is pregnant, it isn't any big thing?"

"Not from the 'roids." He shrugged. "There could be other things going on—you never know what's in some people's heads—but no, the 'roids wouldn't have anything to do with it."

We fell silent for a few minutes, staring out at the activity in the service bays. The mechanics all wore a kind of dark-blue, heavy-duty jumpsuit, with loops and pockets for tools. From a distance, without being able to read the names over their pockets, it was impossible to tell one from the other.

Jimmy stood out, though. As the tow driver, he wore a short-sleeve sport shirt and pants, both the same dark blue as the mechanics wore. I suspected if I got close I could spot the small tags that gave the size and the name of the uniform company.

My car was in the next-to-last bay, right in front of the tow truck. A mechanic was just pulling his head out from under the hood and wiping his hands on a shop towel.

On impulse, I opened the door into the service area. The earthy smell of motor oil mixed with the tang of solvents assaulted my nose, and the noise level was far louder than I expected. The glass wall that separated the employee lounge from the service area must have been well insulated to keep that much noise out.

I made my way around rolling tool boxes the size of my dining room table and stepped carefully between snaking hoses that delivered compressed air to the tools the mechanics were using.

As I approached my car, the mechanic turned and caught sight of me.

"Hey, you're not supposed to be out here," he hollered. "You either," he added, looking over my shoulder to where Ernie followed behind me.

I batted my eyelashes in a vain attempt to play innocent Southern belle. "I didn't know that," I said, smiling like a fool. "I just came out to see what you found out about my car."

He wasn't buying it. "Joe will give you the report at the service desk. But you have to get out of here. There's too many ways you can hurt yourself."

"And you wouldn't want to get sued, right?" Ernie's cynical tone implied he believed a lawsuit was a much greater motivation than any concern for the welfare and safety of the customers.

"That's why the boss worries," the young man (his shirt said his name was "Chet") said. "Me, I just hate the sight of blood. Even when it isn't mine."

That brought a grin from Ernie, and he stuck his hand out to Chet. "Ernie Jourdain. Glad to meet you, Chet."

A confused look flashed across the man's face, and he glanced down at his chest, then shook his head. "Damned uniform service. Pardon my French, ma'am," he nodded to me. "Sent over the wrong batch of uniforms. But I wasn't going to work in my own clothes, so I guess I'm Chet today." He shook Ernie's hand. "Any other day the name's Roy."

"Miss Glory!" Jimmy Parmenter appeared around the front of the tow truck. "Glad to see you got the car in. Roy here's one of our best guys; he'll do right by you."

"Thanks, Jimmy," I said. I walked around the front of my car, stopping in the narrow space between it and the tow truck, which was backed into the bay.

Jimmy had been tweaking something on the back of the truck when we first walked over. He hopped back up on the flatbed and went back to whatever he was fiddling with, looking back down to catch my eye.

"I appreciate you bringing your car in," he said quietly, as though he didn't want anyone else to hear. I doubted it was possible in the din of air-powered tools whining and pounding and the clang of metal on metal, but he kept his voice low.

"You were right," I said. "It did need a good checkup."

"Well, thanks anyway."

I wanted to ask if he got in trouble for not charging me, but I never got the chance. From behind me I heard a disturbance and turned to see what the problem was.

Matthew Fowler stood close to Ernie, his head bent back so he could look him in the eye, and he was telling him quite forcefully that he needed to get out of the shop.

Behind me, Jimmy cleared his throat noisily. When I turned around he caught my eye and gestured at me to squat down so I wouldn't get kicked out, too. Or maybe he was just protecting himself for not throwing me out on his own.

Not wanting to get in Fowler's line of fire, or make trouble for Jimmy, I took the suggestion and crouched down near the cab of the tow truck, straining to hear what was going on.

Looking under my car, I saw Ernie's immaculate white sneakers pivot smoothly and head out the open bay doors. Fowler's expensive loafers remained where they were for a minute, and I could picture him with his fists on his hips and a grim smile of triumph on his face.

I stayed in my hiding place until I saw Fowler's tasseled loafers turn and head back toward the office area. Once they were out of sight, I steadied myself against the running board of the tow truck to stand up.

That's when I saw it. A faint blemish on the shiny black finish of the oversize truck that hit me like a hard right to the midsection.

A tiny streak of baby-blue paint.

Chapter 27

HEART POUNDING, I RETREATED TOWARD THE FRONT
end of the tow truck. Jimmy was still on the flatbed and
couldn't see me.

I crouched next to the front wheel, which towered over my
head, and peered carefully around the back of my car, toward
the rest of the service bays. No one appeared to be looking
in my direction.

I sprang to my feet and ran out of the service area into the
parking lot. My head swiveled frantically, looking for Ernie.

I had to tell someone what I'd seen, and right now Ernie
was the only person nearby that I could trust.

Trying to look every direction at once, I walked quickly
across the parking lot and around the corner of the building.

Still no Ernie.

I leaned against the wall for a moment, savoring the relative security of having something solid at my back.

"Are you all right?"

I jumped about a foot, and my heart hammered like it was going to burst right out of my chest.

"Easy," Ernie pulled me into a tight hug and stroked my head as though I were a small child.

I must have looked as panicked as I felt.

I stood, leaning against Ernie for a minute, while my galloping heart settled into something resembling a normal rhythm. I opened my mouth a couple times, but I couldn't force any sound through my trembling lips.

Finally I drew a deep, shuddering breath as the adrenaline rush subsided, leaving me weak-kneed and tired. I managed to squeak out an assurance to Ernie that I wasn't going to pass out, and he let me go.

"What happened, Glory? I purely thought some demon was chasing you the way you came barreling out of that shop."

"That's kind of how it felt," I replied. I braced one arm against the wall for support. My legs still didn't feel as though I could trust them to hold me up.

"I don't want to talk about it here," I went on. "Let's see if I can get my car out of here, and I'll explain once we're safely back home."

His brows drew together at my choice of words, and I tried to soften what I had said. "I saw something, that's all. And I don't want to talk here. Okay?"

"Why don't you just let me take you home right now, and you can call to check on the car later? I'll even volunteer to be your driver until the car is ready if that's what it takes to get you out of here."

The decision wasn't difficult. The car could wait until the next day. Or the next week. Just as long as I got far away from Fowler's and that damning scrape of blue paint.

"Let's go."

I followed Ernie to his vintage red Miata. The van was the

shop vehicle, and Felipe had a motor scooter for anywhere that was too far to walk. Ernie had his prized Miata, which he'd purchased new in 1991, and I always felt privileged to ride in it.

We pulled out of Fowler's and rode in silence to Southern Treasures. Ernie parked on the highway in front of the shop, preferring to keep the car where he could see it.

To his credit, he held his questions until we were through the door. Fortunately, Karen was alone in the store.

Unfortunately, Bluebeard was awake. The moment I came through the door, he unleashed a string of cursing and flapped his wings in agitation. "Bad man! Bad man!" he squawked, then added another string of curses.

"Language, Bluebeard!" My voice was back to normal.

He flapped his wings again, then settled down to his usual muttered invective. The words weren't distinct, but the meaning was clear.

He was upset.

Angry.

I had been around the Bad Man.

I spent several minutes with Bluebeard, talking to him, feeding him biscuits, and generally making sure he knew I was okay. It was weird to be fussed over so protectively by a bird, but then I didn't really think it was the bird doing the fussing. Uncle Louis was trying to watch over me and protect me from the Bad Man.

Once Bluebeard had settled down, he retreated to his cage, and I draped the blanket over it. It was becoming a pattern: he got upset, I reassured him, he calmed down, and then he needed to retreat and recuperate.

It was like having a very young child.

With Bluebeard settled into the cage, I was able to turn my attention back to Karen and Ernie, who had waited semi-patiently for me. I didn't realize how long I had spent with Bluebeard until Karen set a freshly brewed cup of chamomile tea on the counter.

"No coffee," she explained. "Ernie says you had some kind of freak-out and you need to relax. So I made you chamomile."

She pushed the cup toward me. "Now, tell us what happened."

Ernie had already given Karen the basics of our visit to the Fowler lot and why we had hurried back without getting the verdict on my bucket of bolts.

I bit my lip, not knowing exactly how to explain what I had seen. "I think," I said slowly, "I know how Kevin ended up in that field."

Karen's mouth dropped open.

"Was it something you saw in there?" Ernie demanded. "And you wanted to go back in? Are you crazy, girl?"

"How do you know what happened?" Karen always cut to the heart of every issue. "What did you see?"

"I was kind of hiding next to the tow truck when Fowler started talking to Ernie." I turned to Ernie. "What was that all about? It looked like you guys were arguing."

"He was just telling me to get out of the service area. Said no one was allowed back there but employees, for liability reasons. That part makes sense," he conceded. "If anybody got hurt back there—and there are a million ways that could happen—his insurance carrier would have a hissy fit. But that's beside the point. Go on with your story."

"Okay. So, I'm crouched down behind my car, next to the tow truck. I could see you and Fowler from the knees down. After you walked away, I waited for Fowler to leave. I didn't want him to find me in there, too."

They both nodded at my sound reasoning.

"But then I was going to get up and walk out. I reached out to steady myself on the truck, and that's when I saw it. A streak of baby-blue paint just on the underside of the running board of the tow truck."

"Is that all?" Ernie said, shaking his head. "Didn't they use that wrecker to get the car out of the field? It could have gotten a little paint on it while they were getting it towed out or when they took it off at the lot."

"No." I was as sure of this as I was of my own name. "That paint didn't get there because the car was towed. There's no way the car was even *near* that part of the truck."

"How do you know that?" Karen asked. "Besides, the truck wasn't there until after the accident. We passed it on the road. And *we* don't know what happened after it arrived."

I crossed my arms over my chest. I was being defensive, but I was convinced the paint didn't get on the truck when it was towing Kevin's car.

I couldn't convince Karen and Ernie, however. Nor could either Karen or I remember who had been driving the truck the day of the accident. We'd passed it on the road, sure, but neither one of us was paying much attention to the tow truck. We had both been focused on the accident and the kegger at Thompson's Corner.

I finally had to admit Ernie had a point. The paint could have gotten there while they were working to get the car out of the field. I was busy jumping to conclusions, based on my own panicky response.

Trying to divert the conversation from my overreaction, I asked Karen, "Do you know who called in the accident?"

She shook her head. "There was a 911 call, but it was listed in the police report as an anonymous female caller. The dispatcher said she sounded young, but beyond that I wasn't able to get any information."

"So somebody saw the car in the field and called the police," Ernie said. "But there wasn't anyone else out there when you two arrived?"

I thought back, trying to pull the details of that day from my memory. "We heard the radio call," I began. "Karen practically did a bootlegger's turn to get off the freeway, and we headed out to where it happened."

"I just made a quick lane change," Karen said. "We drove out to County Road 198, and on the way there, the dispatcher nearly lost his mind."

Ernie frowned. "What?"

"We told you," I said. "Everyone on site went tunnel vision, and the dispatcher couldn't get anyone to respond."

Ernie nodded. "I remember that. Strange description, but it makes sense."

"It's what the emergency responders call it," Karen said. "Anyway, the place was swarming with official types by the time we got there, and they were keeping everyone back."

She looked at me as though I might remember something more, but I just shook my head. "I don't remember anything but official cars and trucks," I said. "In fact, I do remember thinking you were the first newsperson at the accident. So there must not have been any other civilian vehicles out there."

"Whoever called it in," Ernie said, his voice low, "saw the car in the field but didn't stay to help."

"Maybe she couldn't," Karen said.

"Or maybe," I added, "she didn't want the police to know she was there. Even if it was an accident, maybe she was responsible somehow, and she didn't want to be there when the cops arrived."

"But who is it?" Karen asked, cutting to the chase. "We don't know of any woman who had a reason to hurt Kevin."

"Actually," I said, "I might. Remember, I told you. Frank

Beauford's niece, Tricia. She broke up with Kevin because he was 'getting too wild,' according to Frank. And since he was cleaning up his act, she wanted to get back with him. We don't know how Kevin felt about it. What if he didn't want to get back together? What if he had a new girlfriend? That would be enough to make some girls really crazy."

"Not Tricia," Ernie said, firmly. "I know that girl, she lives down the street from us. She might be upset, but she wouldn't kill somebody over it."

"Maybe she didn't mean to kill him," I argued. "Maybe she just meant to hurt him. I don't want to think that anyone deliberately tried to kill Kevin, but if we accept what Bluebeard said, it wasn't an accident, either."

I took a swallow of tea. It was cold, the bitterness of the chamomile reinforced by the chill. I made a face and set it back on the counter.

In the momentary silence, the ringing of my cell phone made us all jump.

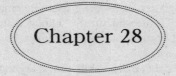

Chapter 28

MY HANDS TREMBLED AS I PULLED THE PHONE OUT
of my pocket and answered.

"Hello?"

"Glory? This is Shiloh."

Shiloh? Had she found out I'd been in the service bays?
Did she know I'd seen the paint smear on the tow truck?

My heart pounded, and my palms got sweaty. I nearly
dropped the phone.

"Shiloh." My voice squeaked, and I swallowed and tried
again. "Shiloh, hi! What can I do for you?"

"I thought you were going to wait to see about your car,"
she said. "But when I went back into the break room to look
for you, you weren't there. Mr. Fowler said something about
your friend being out in the shop and then leaving. I was
just closing up for the night, and I found the work order without any notes saying you got a copy. I wondered if you want
me to drop it by on my way home?"

"I, uh, I'm just getting ready to go out," I lied.

"Without your car?"

"I have some friends here, and we were just on our way out the door. Tell you what, you can e-mail it, or I'll switch the store phone over and you can fax it to me. Okay?"

"Well, if you're sure." She sounded tentative, but she agreed to fax the work order.

"I'll need a signature before we can order parts and start the work," she said before hanging up.

"What was that about?" Karen asked. "And where are we going?"

A shaky laugh escaped my lips. "Shiloh was worried because I didn't get the estimate for the work on the car," I explained as I switched the phone line to the fax machine. "I didn't want her to come by here, so I told her I was just on my way out."

Ernie laughed. "You feeling a little better now?"

He had me. Shiloh's call was completely innocent, and maybe I'd been freaking out over nothing. And we still hadn't found out anything more about Kevin's car, so the entire trip was wasted.

The fax machine whirred, and I walked back into the cubbyhole that I grandly called an office to retrieve the estimate.

I tried not to choke when I read the total at the bottom of the page. I could just about buy another car for the cost of the repairs if I did everything they recommended.

Shaking my head, I handed the estimate to Ernie. "So, just how rich do they think I am?"

His eyes widened at the total. "I don't think you'll be doing all this, girl. But they're gonna charge you for the diagnostics if you don't do *something*."

With Ernie and Karen's help, I winnowed the list down to a couple essential repairs that were within my budget. I would drop by the service department in the morning—with Karen this time—and authorize the abbreviated list. And I planned to try to find out more about Kevin's car.

I just needed to know which of the employees was the biggest gossip.

"That'll be easy," Karen said with a smug smile. "I just tell them I need to talk to someone 'off the record' for a follow-up on the radio. The biggest gossip is the person who is willing to talk to me as long as I don't divulge my source."

"Speaking of gossip—did you ever hear anything about Jimmy Parmenter and steroids? Ernie here seems to think Jimmy's been using."

"Not that I remember," Karen said. "But I don't always hear everything, despite what you two think."

Ernie glanced up at my clock. He dug his keys out of his pocket and bounced them on his palm. "I have to get going," he said. "Unless you two want to go grab a beer. I can call Felipe."

But when he got Felipe on the phone, there was some kind of customer emergency at the shop, and we scrapped the idea. Ernie trotted out the door with a wave after extracting a promise that we would give him a full report from our trip to Fowler's the next day.

I called my part-time clerk, Melissa, and she was free for Saturday morning, so I had time to deal with the car repairs. Which was a great plan, right up to the moment on Saturday morning that Karen's cell phone rang.

We were standing at the service counter, and I was discussing the repair options with Joe. He kept urging me to do "just a little more," and I kept juggling numbers in my head and saying no.

"I'll have to do this in stages as I can afford it," I said for the third or fourth time. "And that will depend on business at the shop."

Karen stepped away from the counter—and my Abbott-and-Costello routine with Joe—to answer her phone. I heard a sudden note of concern in her voice, and she returned a minute later, worry putting fine lines at the corners of her eyes.

"I need to go. There was a fight over at the Surf and Sand," she named a low-rent motel just outside of town, "and the station manager wants me to go interview the witnesses."

"Go ahead," I told her. "If I can't get my car out of here this morning, I can always call Ernie and get a ride home. Or I can walk—it's not that far."

Which might have been a bit of an overstatement. Fowler's was probably three miles from Southern Treasures. But I intended to ransom my car and bring it back for the actual repairs later.

Or not. Given the size of the estimate, I just might have to think about replacing it.

Karen hesitated, as though she didn't want to strand me. I turned my back to the counter and whispered, "Besides, Fowler isn't even here."

"Are you sure?" she said. "You could ride out there with me and we could come back here after, or I could make a quick detour to drop you at Southern Treasures."

"I'm sure. I want to try and get the car out of here today, and they close in about an hour, so I better stay. I'm already hating that I have to depend on other people to get around. You go on. I'll be fine."

Her phone rang again, and she glanced at the display. "The station manager. Again." She gave me one last questioning look, and when I shooed her toward the door, she went, putting the phone to her ear and snapping "What now?" as she headed out of the building.

I turned back to Joe, wondering what it would take to convince him I wasn't going to agree to any more work right now.

It wasn't Joe I saw at the counter, though. It was Roy, the mechanic who had been checking out my car the night before.

"You're the lady with the Civic, right?"

I nodded. "And you're Roy, not Chet."

He laughed. "Yeah. They got us the right uniforms today." He pointed to the name "Roy" embroidered on his coveralls.

Roy glanced around the reception area. "Is someone helping you?" he asked.

"Depends on how you define 'help,'" I replied with a little laugh. "I need to ransom the car, but this Joe guy that works here keeps trying to talk me into having more work."

"It does need attention," Roy said. "But," he glanced around again, "my personal opinion is that you'd be throwing good money after bad."

The sinking feeling in the pit of my stomach told me he had just confirmed my worst fears.

"That bad, huh?"

"Oh, it'll get you by for a little longer, but I wouldn't take it out of town." Since Keyhole Bay didn't stretch more than five miles in any direction, that was a pretty limited driving area.

"You mean I shouldn't drive it up to Montgomery?" Not that I had any intention of visiting Peter, or his parents, any time soon.

"I'd say not," he answered with a shrug. "But that's just my opinion."

"And you're the guy who's been under the hood," I said. "If I want to trust anyone's opinion, it's the guy who's actually inspected the car." I saw an opening and took it. "I mean, I wouldn't want to end up like the Stanley boy." I shivered delicately, betting that Roy would want to reassure a delicate lady like myself. If he only knew!

"Oh no!" His alarm was genuine. "Nothing like that. You

might end up stranded, or you might even run off the road, but," he smiled to take the sting out of his next words, "that Civic probably couldn't get going fast enough to do that kind of damage. It might slide into the ditch, but that's about it."

"So he was going pretty fast?"

"I'm no accident investigator or anything," he said, relishing the opportunity to show off his knowledge, "but it sure looks like he was traveling at a pretty good clip."

"But how did he end up all the way out in the field?" I dropped my voice to a conspiratorial whisper. "I was out there right after it happened, even before the ambulance. The car was way off the road."

"Like I said, I think he was going too fast. There was nothing wrong with that car. In fact, he'd just had it in here a couple days before, and we'd checked it out."

"That's right," I said, as if I had just remembered. "He was the new lot boy, wasn't he? You guys take good care of them, don't you?"

"Same as any other employee," he said.

"So it wasn't anything wrong with the car?"

"Nah, just too much car for a young kid."

"A young kid with too much beer in him."

We both turned to look in the direction of the voice. It was Jimmy Parmenter, and the scowl on his face didn't hide what he thought of Kevin.

Jimmy quickly arranged his features into a mournful expression, but I had seen the anger and resentment behind his sorrowful mask. "It was sad, sure. Nobody wants to wish that on a young kid. But everybody's acting like it's a big surprise that he had an accident. There was nothing wrong with that car; it was running like a top. It was just too much car for him, like Roy said, especially when he'd been out bangin' the brewskis." He paused, lowering his voice. "Hell, all the guys were out there. But Kevin was the only one with a car like that."

Jimmy shook himself, throwing off the moment of melancholy. He dropped a pile of paperwork in the wire basket below the schedule board. "I'm outta here," he said to Roy. "I'll have the cell with me if there's a call."

Jimmy turned to me. "Sorry for what I said, Miss Glory. I didn't mean to upset you none, and I know I shouldn't speak ill of the dead. But he got himself in trouble, and now nobody wants to admit it was his own fault."

He turned and stomped out. In a few seconds I saw him hop up into the cab of his overgrown pickup and roar out of the lot onto the highway.

Roy and I exchanged a glance, and Roy chuckled. "That boy does seem to know about driving a vehicle with too much power, doesn't he?"

Joe finally returned from wherever he'd been and reclaimed his place at the counter. He gave Roy a sharp look. "Aren't you supposed to be in the shop?"

Roy tossed my key ring on the counter. "Just bringing back Miss Glory's keys. I got the plugs done and the new battery terminals on. It should get her by for a little longer, but she'll need more work pretty quick-like." He turned so Joe couldn't see him and gave me a wink, reminding me that he'd told me something different.

With great reluctance, Joe accepted my check for the minimal service and gave me a receipt. I was beginning to think I was going to have to arm wrestle him for the keys when he looked at his watch—a too-big piece of shiny gold strapped to his bony wrist.

At least I understood why he was so determined to get me to agree to more repairs. He probably worked on commission, and he needed to support that watch.

"Closing time already?" he asked in mock surprise. "I had no idea it was getting so late!"

He put the keys on the counter, but he didn't turn loose of them. "You have to promise me you'll get that car back here soon," he said, his voice full of fake sincerity. "It needs some work before it's really safe to drive."

I managed not to roll my eyes. "I will bring it back just as soon as I can afford to." It was as much as he was going to get.

My impatience must have shown on my face. Joe took my hand, turned it over, and deposited the keys in my open palm. "I just don't want to see you get hurt, driving a vehicle that isn't 100 percent safe."

I tried to believe him.

I walked out of the building into the parking lot. My car was waiting at the far end of the lot—as far away as possible from the shiny models Fowler was trying to peddle.

Beyond my car I caught sight of a tall chain-link fence, with two rows of barbed wire running along the top. It had to be the secure lot—the place where Kevin Stanley's baby-blue Charger had been towed and was now waiting for the police and Kevin's family to determine its fate.

I *really* wanted to see that car.

Chapter 29

I STUFFED MY CAR KEYS INTO THE POCKET OF MY jeans and sauntered as casually as I could across the lot outside the service area. My heart raced, and I had to force myself not to run. But the service bays behind the big roll-up doors were deserted; everyone had bailed out as soon as the clock reached noon. This might be my only chance to look at the secure lot.

I followed a wide arc, avoiding going near my car, and craned my neck as though looking for something.

As I neared the gate to the secure lot, I spotted a chain and padlock holding the gate closed. The padlock was open, with the hasp holding two links of the chain.

Ernie had asked me if I was crazy, and I guess I had his answer. In spite of every nerve in my body screaming at me to run away, I reached for the chain.

I slipped the lock from the chain, watching to see if I attracted any attention. No one on the sales lot was concerned with the closed service area.

I pulled the gate open just wide enough to pass through and slid into the enclosure.

It shouldn't have been that easy, but no one seemed to care. So much for the superspecial secure lot.

I looked around, wondering where the Charger was. The secure lot was like a mash-up of a wrecking yard and an impound lot like you see on TV cop shows.

Near the fence, where they were visible, sat two rows of passenger cars and small trucks, maybe twenty in all. They appeared to be reasonably intact, with grease-pencil markings of dates and times on the windows. Behind the cars, a row of a half dozen large trucks created a barrier that shielded the rest of the lot from public view.

Behind the wall of pickups, steel racks held a massive collection of car parts. To my inexperienced eye, it looked like an engine supermarket: blocks of iron with mysterious metal appendages filled three levels of shelves, reaching higher than my head, and a small forklift stood ready to retrieve the chosen piece from the rack.

I continued exploring, gingerly making my way around the racks to see what was hidden from view.

That's where I found Kevin's Charger—and about a million other cars. Well, that might be an exaggeration, but there were a lot of cars, and a lot of them were wrecked.

The thought crossed my mind that Fowler must pay some hefty "fees" to maintain what amounted to a wrecking yard in the middle of Keyhole Bay. It looked like the kind of place you'd find out in the piney woods, far from any kind of city.

But here it was, in the middle of town.

A small cinder-block building sat in a patch of hard-packed

dirt in the middle of the lot. On the bare earth next to the flat-roofed structure were the remains of the once-pristine Charger. A couple forlorn loops of bright-yellow "Crime Scene" tape flapped from the mangled door handles.

I approached the Charger, feeling the hair on the back of my neck stand on end. As I got closer, an air of menace seemed to surround the car, and a deep foreboding settled over me.

I didn't want to get any closer.

But I had to. If there were any clues here, anything that would help me—help us—figure out what really happened to Kevin, I had to find them. I couldn't let this opportunity slip through my fingers just because it gave me the heebie-jeebies.

When I reached the car, I realized the utter futility of my plan. The car had been pummeled by the repeated rolling, and there wasn't a single place on the entire body that hadn't been bent or dented or scraped.

"Hey!"

The shout startled me. I spun around to face a wizened old man with skin the color of walnut shells and dark eyes, clouded with suspicion. He glared at me for several long seconds before he spoke. When he opened his mouth, I saw several gaps where missing teeth left bare gums exposed.

Beside him an immense black dog stood at alert, held in check on a heavy chain. His head looked as big as a basketball, if basketballs had mouths full of sharp teeth—which were currently on display. For good measure, he gave me a low growl, as though daring me to move. I had never heard a basketball growl.

"You ain't supposed to be in here." He gestured to the dog. "Bobo come and got me." Bobo looked up at the sound of his name, then focused his attention back on me before I could move. "He said there was somebody sneakin' around the yard, and I better come quick."

The dog had told him all that? For a moment I considered the insane notion that the dog could talk, just like Bluebeard, and had ratted me out to the old guy.

Which was ridiculous. The dog had found the old man and dragged him out into the lot. That was all.

"I'm sorry," I said, smiling innocently. "They gave me back my keys inside and told me the car was out in the lot. But I didn't see it, and the fence was unlocked, so I thought maybe it was in here."

I resisted the impulse to bat my eyelashes, or pour on the sugar any more than I already had. I could Southern belle with the best of them, but it usually worked best when applied with restraint.

"Don't have no repaired cars back here." He looked around like he was checking the lot. "Just impounds and parts." He turned his attention back to me. "What kinda car you got?"

"An old Honda Civic," I answered. "It's old enough that somebody might think it was a parts car, but it's really what I drive every day."

I laughed nervously and tried another faint smile.

It seemed to be working. He pulled on the dog's chain, and the pooch immediately dropped his haunches to the dirt, though he didn't relax. It was clear that as far as Bobo was concerned, the jury was still out on me.

"Is that . . . ?" I let the question hang in the air and nodded toward the wreckage of the Charger.

"Yep. That's the car that damned-fool kid got hisself killed in." He spat in the dirt. "Nobody's supposed to be around it on account of the po-lice ain't released it yet. But it just been sitting there for a week gone, and they haven't paid a lick of attention to it."

Of course they hadn't. Like the rest of the town, Boomer had decided Kevin's death was a tragic accident. Nobody had any reason to look at the car.

Nobody but me.

"I really am sorry to be somewhere I don't belong," I repeated. "I didn't mean to cause trouble."

I turned back to look at the car and a knot formed in the middle of my stomach. I had to find a way for him to let me take a closer look. I didn't want to miss something important.

"It's just, I got back in here, and I saw that car. I had to come and look."

I turned back to the man and dog. "My parents were killed in an accident a few years back, and I never looked at their car. Never tried, never wanted to."

To my horror, very real tears burned my eyes and threatened to roll down my face. I blinked rapidly. I'd been taught that crying in public was unseemly, that a true lady controlled her emotions in front of others. And here I was blinking back tears in front of a complete stranger.

I shook my head, glancing back over my shoulder at the wrecked Charger. "It's just such a shame."

"I guess just lookin' won't do no harm," he said. "But me and Bobo will have to stay with you. I can't let nobody touch this until the po-lice say so. That okay with you?"

I nodded.

"Name's Sylvester," he said, tugging gently on the dog's chain and urging him toward the Charger. "Most folks call me Sly, like that actor feller."

"Gloryanna," I answered. "Call me Glory."

"Well, Miss Glory, let's get a look so you can feel better about things, and then I can get back to my movie."

With my escort close behind, I walked over to the Charger. Up close, the damage was even more pronounced. Every window was broken out—whether from the crash or from the rescue efforts I didn't know—and the doors hung open. Dirt and mud had caked on the wheels and covered the headlights.

Sly, now that we were on a first-name basis, was happy to give me a running commentary on the indignities that had been visited on the vehicle. The tires were flattened, the trunk was sprung, and the famous baby-blue paint job had deep pits from the rocks in the ditch.

We walked around the car, Bobo occasionally sniffing at my shoes and pant legs.

The sun had reached the early afternoon peak, and the heat baked the yard, releasing the smell of old motor oil that had soaked into the dirt over the years.

I made a slow circuit, not knowing what I was looking for, but hoping I would see something. All I could see was crumpled metal layered with dirt.

Then, as I slowly scanned the driver's side, I spotted an odd dent. Unlike the others, which appeared to be direct impacts, this one was a long crease along the side of the car, just above the door sill.

It looked like something had been dragged along the side of the car, digging a furrow into the sheet metal of the door.

Like maybe the side of another car. Or the running board of a truck.

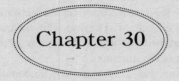

Chapter 30

I LEANED IN CLOSER, EXAMINING THE CREASE. IT WAS low, maybe too low for the running board of the huge tow truck.

Several inches above it, closer to the door handle, was another long scratch, this one with a flake or two of black paint.

Sly moved closer, pulling Bobo with him. "Ain't that just stupid? That idiot Jimmy—the pretty boy driving the tow truck?—managed to put another damn dent in this when we was taking it off the truck. Said he pulled in too close after they winched her off and scraped the side. The po-lice chief was none too happy 'bout that. He raised three kinds of hell—'scuse my language—with the kid and with Fowler. Told them they wouldn't be doing any more city tows if they couldn't keep from making things worse."

So Ernie was right. The paint on the truck had come from a mistake when they took the car off the flatbed.

There went my first real clue. Unless Jimmy had lied about how the dent got there.

I stood for a minute staring at the car, as though it would give me the answers I wanted. "So the police aren't through with it yet?" I asked.

"They say they aren't. But they haven't been out here since that first day, have they boy?" He leaned over and scratched Bobo's ears, earning the doggy equivalent of a smile. "Bo keeps an eye on the place for me, since I don't get around as good as I used to. Ain't been nobody back here since then, except you."

"Fowler doesn't check on his place?" I had him pegged as someone who kept his fingers in everything that went on, despite Shiloh's assertion that she took care of the dealership's day-to-day operations.

"Ain't his place," Sly answered. "It's mine. Been mine ever since my daddy passed, back in sixty-six. He ran this place for twenty years or more, and I'd just come back from the army. Took over when he passed, and I been here ever since. Now I lease part of the lot to Fowler, but I still live here—me and Bo—and I run the place."

He cast a glance toward the repair shop in the distance and spat again in the dirt. "Don't work for Mr. High-and-Mighty Matt Fowler. Never did, never will. Be my own man till the Good Lord calls me home to be with my mama and daddy."

I smiled at Sly and glanced down at Bobo, who waited patiently at his master's side. They were quite a pair.

"May I?" I reached a hand toward Bo, stopping to let him sniff my fingers and decide if I could be trusted.

"Sure thing." Sly laughed. "He looks ferocious, being black as night and all, but he's really the sweetest thing. Don't think he'd hurt a soul, lessen they tried to mess with me."

I waited for Bo to register his approval by nudging my hand with his snout, then stroked his broad back. "Nice Bo," I crooned. "Good puppy."

Bo rubbed his head against my leg, his bulk nearly sending me tumbling. I took a step to the side and regained my balance.

"Sometimes he don't realize how big he is," Sly said by way of apology. "He forgets himself is all."

"Oh, he's a sweet boy, yes he is," I said to Bo, scratching behind his ears as I had seen Sly do. "Aren't you a good boy?"

I hadn't learned anything useful in my excursion inside the secure lot in back of Fowler's, but I'd made a new friend. Two friends, if you counted Bo, and I certainly should.

I dragged my car keys out of my pocket and dangled them from my finger. "Thank you, Sly. I appreciate this more than you can imagine. But I better get back to the store; my clerk's supposed to get off in," I checked my watch, "fifteen minutes. Wow, I didn't realize it was getting that late."

"We'll walk you back to the gate so's you can find your car and lock up after you," Sly offered.

As we made our way back around the rack of engines and past the row of pickup trucks, Sly asked, "What store you work at?"

"I own Southern Treasures, the gift shop on Main, over by The Grog Shop."

"I know that place," Sly said. "Used to be owned by an old guy with a parrot?"

"I still have the parrot. My great-uncle Louis died when I was a little kid, and he left the place to me and my cousin."

Sly looked thoughtful. "I remember that guy, though I didn't know him very well. Kept to himself a lot." He glanced around the lot as we neared the gate. "Sorta like me."

I grinned at him as I stepped back through the gate. "Maybe I'll come back and visit you and Bo some time," I said. "I'd love to hear what you remember about Uncle Louis. I was just a little kid, so I don't know a lot about him."

"You're welcome back here any time, Miss Glory," he said. "Bo says you can come back whenever you want."

"Well, thank you," I answered. I leaned down and gave the big black dog a final pat. "And thank you, Bo."

I pointed across the lot, to where my beat-up Civic was parked. "There's my car. I'd swear it wasn't there before. I don't know how I missed seeing it the first time."

Sly pulled the chain through the gate and snapped the padlock closed. "Don't rightly know, Miss Glory," he said, but the bemused smile on his face told me he'd seen through me, and it was okay.

I waved good-bye and trotted across the lot. The car started a bit easier and didn't seem to miss as often as I pulled into traffic and headed home.

I'd just put a dent in my wallet trying to get information about Kevin's car, and I hadn't learned much of anything, except that Jimmy wasn't as good a tow driver as he thought he was.

At least my car was running a little better.

I parked behind the shop, glad to have my own car back. Most of Keyhole Bay was within walking distance, but I didn't much care for hauling grocery bags through town or carrying my dry cleaning down the sidewalk.

Melissa was at the counter with a customer when I walked in the back door. When the customer left, she turned to me. "I can stay a few minutes if you need me,"

I shook my head. "The car took longer than I expected, but I'm back, and it's your quitting time."

She sighed with relief. "I do have a date tonight, and I really need to get my nails done." She waved her manicured hand dramatically. The nails looked perfect to me.

"I'm wearing a blue shirt," she explained. "And this color totally does not go with my shirt."

Melissa, the daughter of my first boyfriend, Keith Everett, was a typical teenager, obsessed with clothes and boys and music.

But she also had a strong work ethic and a quick mind. She'd worked for me nearly a year and had displayed both on a regular basis. If I'd needed her to stay, she would have, no question.

Fortunately, I didn't, and a few minutes later, she trotted out the front door, cell phone against her ear as she arranged to meet a friend at the beauty shop to get her manicure re-done in an appropriate color.

It would be nice, I thought, to be able to go back and have that carefree life. To have parents to take care of the big stuff and let me obsess about boys and clothes. Then again, there was acne and curfews and exorbitant insurance rates if you wanted to drive a car.

Being a grown-up wasn't all that bad.

With the shop empty, I started straightening shelves and making notes of what needed to be restocked. Next week I would have to place an order with my supplier for more tourist trinkets, getting ready for the influx of snowbirds that came with the first bad storm up north.

Bluebeard was dozing on his perch, ignoring my puttering, when the front door opened and the entire football team spilled into the shop. The noise brought him instantly awake, and he squawked an expletive-filled greeting to the delight of the crowd of young men.

Bluebeard preened at their raucous laughter, and he bobbed

his head as though taking a bow. The boys responded by crowding around his perch and talking to him. His patience wore thin, however, with the continual singsong of "Polly want a cracker?"

"#$%#& Bluebeard!" he said, drawing more gales of laughter. "Give me a #^#^% biscuit!"

I made my way through the crowd of young men and looked up. "Language, Bluebeard!"

"Biscuit," he shot back.

"You gonna clean up your act?" I asked, keenly aware that we had an audience.

"Biscuit?" Bluebeard wheedled in a hurt voice.

"One biscuit," I answered. "But no more swearing."

He bobbed his head as though in agreement. "Biscuit!"

I reached in the tin under his perch and pulled out a single biscuit. He snatched it eagerly from my hand and chomped it in his powerful beak.

When it was gone, he looked at me. "Biscuit?"

"You had your biscuit," I told him. "No more right now."

He ruffled his feathers and settled back onto his perch, muttering.

With the show over, the boys milled around the memorial T-shirt display, looking over the selection. I made eye contact with one of them. "I have your shirts set aside over here," I said, motioning at the shelf behind the counter.

He nodded and went back to examining the shirts on the display. Well, Shiloh had said some of them would want to buy shirts for their girlfriends.

I pulled out my catalogs and started putting together the order for next week. As I worked, trying to be invisible to the boys milling around the display, I listened to their conversation.

From what I could observe, Travis Chambers took his new

role as team captain very seriously. He moved among the boys, talking with first one and then another for several minutes. Eventually, he stopped and called for their attention.

"So we're all agreed: we wear Kevin's shirts to the pep rally on Friday morning. Tricia says the cheerleaders will all wear theirs, too. If it's cold, we'll *only* wear letterman's jackets over them. And Friday night we'll tape the shirts to the front of our jerseys for the run into the stadium, since we can't get them over the pads and stuff."

Nods and murmurs of agreement went around the room. "What if we get in trouble for being out of uniform?" one of the boys muttered from the back of the group.

"I told you," Travis spoke sharply. "I already talked to Mr. Fowler. He said he'd get the Booster Club to back us up. Even Coach Bradley won't argue with the Booster Club."

I wondered why it was even an issue, unless the coach had a problem with having Kevin's face plastered across the chest of every player as they entered the field.

"Okay; if you say so," the protestor replied.

"I say so," Travis said. His voice carried a solid assurance and confidence in his authority.

He was showing his leadership chops, ambition clear in his every move. And he seemed to be good at taking command. But was it a command he would kill for?

I wasn't sure. There was attention and adulation, but those weren't reasons enough to take a classmate's life. There was also scholarship money, a lot of it.

Was that enough motive for murder?

A few feet from the counter, two boys talked in whispers.

"Did your folks ask you where we got the beer?"

"You kidding? It's been like the freakin' Inquisition or something ever since the party. They keep bugging me to tell them how we got the stuff, and I keep telling them I don't know."

"They don't believe we really don't know," the first boy agreed. "I gave Travis my ten bucks, and he said he was giving it to some other guy. But if I tell them about Travis, then they'll all gang up on him and try to make him tell."

"Yeah, and then we have to find someone else to buy the next time."

A third kid walked up and listened, then added, "Besides, if we tell anyone, the coach will go insane and start benching people, including Travis. Just what we need, to lose another captain three weeks into the new season."

The first boy nodded emphatically. "All because Kevin was a total lightweight, anyway."

"What do you mean?" asked Number Two.

"I mean," Number One lowered his voice, "I heard he didn't even drink a whole beer. He was mouthing off to one of the guys about how we were all going to get in trouble if we got caught, and the coach had told him he was going to bench anybody caught drinking."

"But I saw him with a beer," said Number Three.

"Right," One answered. "But he only had the one, and one of the cheerleaders said she saw him pour it out when he didn't think anyone was looking."

"But the police said—" Number Two stopped suddenly as Travis approached the conversation.

"You guys doing okay?" he asked.

All three nodded a little guiltily. "Just getting ready to get our shirts and get moving," Number One said. "Right?"

He glanced at his two companions, and they bobbed their heads in agreement.

Travis shrugged. "Okay. If nobody needs me, I'm gonna

shove off. It's getting late, and I got some stuff to do. I'll see you guys on Monday."

Travis left the small group and came to the counter to claim his shirt and pay for it. It was a signal to the rest of the team that it was time to go.

They drifted to the counter in twos and threes, most of them with a second, or even third, shirt. They paid for them, sometimes grumbling about not knowing the size for a girl-friend, or a parent, but anxious to get the discount for their friends and families.

By the time the last boy sauntered out the door, with a parting glance at a dozing Bluebeard, it was closing time. Or close enough, anyway.

I looked across the street to Beach Books. I had an evening free; maybe I should take Jake up on his offer of a good book on web design. Not that the prospect had me jumping for joy. On the other hand, there was Jake, so that was a plus.

What was I waiting for?

Chapter 31

I CLOSED THE SHOP AND CROSSED THE STREET, DE-
termined to get to work on the website.

My resolve weakened the minute I stepped into Beach
Books. Stories called to me from every shelf. Romance, mystery, and political thrillers. Fantasy and science fiction. Biog-
raphy and history and travel guides. Stories of places I might
never see but that I wanted to read about.

Jake appeared from behind a row of shelves, drawn by the
sound of the bell over the door. "Hi, neighbor. What can I do
for you?"

I did my best to gather up my resolve. "I came to ask for
your help. You said you had some stuff on web design, and I
really, really need to do something about my site."

"Sure thing." He came around the shelf and pointed toward the back of the store. "The technology books are back
there. Just let me put this away," he tossed the clipboard he

was carrying down next to the cash register, "and let's see what we can find for you."

But after several minutes, it was clear that my skills were below even the minimum requirements. "Don't you have one of those books for complete beginners? Something that starts with 'What is a website?' and builds from there?"

Jake laughed. He had a good laugh, which only encouraged my tendency to act the clown, if only to hear that laugh.

"You aren't that bad, Glory. I'd just bet you know a lot more than you give yourself credit for."

"Maybe." I sighed. "But every time I look at one of these books, I feel overwhelmed. There's so much to learn! I need to get the site working, and I sit down and try to figure out where to start and pretty soon I'm running for the chocolate. Or the tequila. I think I'm hopeless."

"If you promise to share that tequila," Jake replied, "I'd be glad to offer some private lessons."

"I'll even throw in dinner," I said.

Jake glanced at his wrist. "I close in an hour," he replied. "Can you wait that long?"

In the back of my brain a voice was shrieking "What have you done?!?" But it was too late to back out. "I have to run to the grocery store; the cupboards are a little bare. Anything I should avoid?"

"You don't have to cook for me," he protested. "I'm good with takeout."

I considered the idea but discarded it. "It's Saturday night. Everywhere will be jammed, and I won't be able to pick your brain." I mentally ran through my choices for quick and easy cooking. "You like pizza?"

"Doesn't everyone?"

I laughed. "True. What do you like?"

"Anything, as long as it isn't fish or fruit. Actually, I guess that isn't technically true. Tomatoes are a fruit, aren't they?"

"I will take that to mean tomatoes are acceptable." I headed for the door. "See you in an hour."

I crossed back to Southern Treasures, wondering what had come over me. I hardly knew this man, yet I'd invited him into my home and offered to cook him dinner.

Well, I'd offered to bake a pizza, but it was still technically cooking.

I grabbed my keys and wallet. I was nearly out the back door when I realized I could kill two birds with one stone, providing Julie was working tonight.

I stuck a bag with her T-shirts in the car. If she was there, I'd give her the shirts.

Cars filled the first few spaces near the door at Frank's, but the lot was mostly empty. Most of the locals chose to do their shopping in the middle of the week, so as to avoid the crowds of tourists who, unfamiliar with the store, wandered the aisles looking for some elusive snack or treat. Often they didn't even know what they were looking for; they just knew they wanted "something."

I made a beeline for the ready-made pizza crust and grabbed a couple of cans of tomato paste and a bag of shredded cheese. At the other end of the deli case, I found a package of salami and one of pepperoni. Now all I needed was vegetables.

As I headed for the produce section, I remembered the T-shirts, still on the seat of the car. I looked around, but I didn't see Julie. Maybe she wasn't working tonight.

I picked out a green pepper, an onion, mushrooms, and a couple of plum tomatoes. I even tossed in a few sprigs of fresh basil. This was a "healthy" pizza.

At the last minute, I threw in a carton of spumoni ice cream to go with the chocolate that I knew was in my freezer.

Julie waved at me from the customer-service desk when I got to the front of the store. "Frank's out back," she said. "Bring your stuff on over here, and I'll take care of you."

I moved from the checkout lane to the service counter.

"He's sneakin' a smoke," Julie said as I unloaded my basket. "He doesn't think we know, but we do. He swears to Cheryl that he's quitting, and he does quit. At least a dozen times a day."

She rang up my groceries, and I swiped my debit card. As she finished packing them into my shopping bags, Frank came to the front, just as two more customers wheeled full carts up to the checkout.

"I almost forgot," I said to Julie. "I have your T-shirts in the car if you want to take them."

She looked puzzled; then I could see the connections being made. "For Kevin," she said.

"Yeah. One for you and one for Jimmy, right?"

She nodded. "I told Jimmy I was getting him one, even though he probably won't wear it. But we need to support the team. They're going to have a rough season."

Frank was bagging the groceries of the first customer, and the second had already unloaded his cart onto the belt. I looked back at Julie. "Can you walk out to the car with me and get them? Or do you want me to bring them in? I mean, you can wait and pick them up, but I figured I had to come over here tonight anyway." I picked up my grocery bags and waited for her answer.

"Hey, Frank," she called. "Okay if I walk out with Miss Glory here for a minute?"

Without looking away from his customer, Frank nodded. "Go on; I got this."

Julie insisted on taking one of the bags from me, as though that justified her leaving the store. She followed me to the car, and I opened the hatchback, stowing the two small bags for the trip home.

I retrieved the T-shirt bag from the front seat, and Julie dug in the pocket of her jeans for a pair of crumpled twenties.

"It's so sad," I said, taking advantage of the opportunity to talk to Julie alone.

"Kevin was a good kid," she said. "A really nice boy." She choked up, and couldn't talk.

"That's what everyone says," I filled the awkward silence. "I didn't know him, just knew some of his family, but he seemed like he was going places."

"He was," Julie choked out. "I mean, he had his rough spots; don't get me wrong. I know Tricia dumped him." She looked up at the front of the store as if she expected Frank's niece to magically appear. "She was right to do it, too," she said, her voice growing stronger. "A girl shouldn't let a guy get away with being a jerk—or worse—just because he's a football hero. That's just wrong."

I had a feeling Julie wasn't talking about Kevin and Tricia. I thought her comments came from something a little closer to home, that she saw some parallels between Kevin and Jimmy. I was dying to ask about it, but I didn't think Julie trusted anyone well enough to talk about her husband. Especially about his failures.

"I think Kevin was getting the message, though," she went on. "He stopped partying and screwing around like some of the guys. He even tried to break up the party out at Thompson's Corner." She bit her lip, like she'd said too much. "At least, that's what I heard."

"You're still tight with some of the cheerleaders, aren't you? You were the captain of the squad just a couple of years ago."

"Yeah. I guess." She shrugged. "I just heard some of them talking, saying Kevin was getting to be a little too straight-arrow. But I guess maybe that wasn't true, not if the police say he was drinking and driving."

That was news to me. As far as I knew, the police hadn't released any information about Kevin's blood-alcohol test or the results of their investigation.

"Where did you hear that?" I asked. "About the police."

She screwed up her face, a study in concentration. "I truly do not remember," she said. "Maybe Jimmy told me. I just know somebody told me they were calling it an accident, but they knew he'd been drinking and they weren't saying anything so's not to make it any worse for his family."

"Did you know Kevin very well?" I pressed my luck, hoping to learn more.

"Pretty well," she said. "I was head cheerleader the year he made varsity, so we were in the same crowd. But I graduated over a year ago, so I wasn't around the team as much."

She looked back at the store. "I need to get back to work, Miss Glory. Thanks for bringing the shirts over."

"Glad to help," I said, climbing into the car.

I was out of the parking lot and heading home before the significance of her last sentence struck me. She said she wasn't around "the team" as much after graduation.

She hadn't said anything about Kevin.

Chapter 32

BACK HOME, WITH THE OVEN HEATING AND A PIZZA stone on the rack, I went to work on dinner. There was usually a pitcher of sweet tea in the refrigerator, but it was running low, so I started a pot of water boiling.

I grabbed a chopstick and knotted my hair up, out of the way, while I prepared dinner.

I dumped the tomato paste into a bowl and added spices: rosemary, thyme, oregano, garlic, and onion powder, with a dash of salt and pepper. I usually spiced my sauce heavily, but I tried to restrain my usual generosity, not knowing what my guest would prefer.

I chopped the pepper and onion, sliced the tomatoes and mushrooms, washed the basil leaves, and opened the bag of cheese, putting each in a small bowl, ready for the assembly process.

The tea water boiled, and I stirred in sugar and dumped in a handful of tea bags, leaving it to steep while I chopped romaine lettuce for a simple Caesar salad. With dressing from a jar, croutons from a bag, and a sprinkle of grated parmesan, it would dress up the table and offer some color and texture contrast with the pizza.

I opened the package of pizza crusts. There were two of them, and I decided to go ahead and make both. I could vary the toppings between the two and have leftovers for several days.

I may not have spent much time in college, unless you count the night classes in business at the local community college, but I understood the value of cold pizza for breakfast.

Working quickly, I spread a thin layer of olive oil on the skins, followed by a layer of the spicy tomato paste and a light sprinkle of cheese. On top of that I arranged the sliced meats and chopped vegetables, added a few leaves of fresh basil, gave the whole thing a light dash of garlic salt, and finished with a couple of handfuls of the cheese.

Ten minutes in the oven, and dinner would be ready.

I shoved the bowls in the dishwasher, grateful to have somewhere to hide dirty dishes since my dining area was in the kitchen.

Oven heating. Check.

Pizza ready. Check.

Salad made. Check.

Dessert? Ice cream was in the freezer, so I was good.

I took a clean tea pitcher from the cupboard and filled it with ice, then poured the freshly brewed and sweetened tea over the ice and set it on the table with tall glasses. I'd ice the glasses at the last minute.

Which it nearly was. Thanks to my talk with Julie, I had about five minutes before Jake would be at my door.

Up to this point, I had been too busy to worry about myself or the apartment. Now I glanced around, surveying the room. It was mostly under control, though the floor could use a vacuum. If I didn't take the time to do it, Jake was going to see how I *really* lived.

So much for first impressions.

I took the five minutes to let my hair down and run a comb through it, pulling it back from my face with a simple headband. I was still in the jeans and T-shirt I'd worn to Fowler's that morning. I grabbed a clean pink polo out of the drawer and pulled it over my head, hoping I didn't make a mess of my hair.

I realized there was one way to know if I had time to vacuum. I checked out the front window overlooking the highway. The rolling cart of sale books was still in front of Jake's store, so I had at least a few minutes.

I pulled the vacuum cleaner from the closet in the bedroom and made a rapid circuit of the room that comprised most of my apartment. If it were a modern house, I guess it would have been called a "great room" and would have been a feature. Maybe I should start calling it that. It sounded better than "one-room apartment."

I checked out the window after I stowed the vacuum. The sale cart had disappeared, and the lights were out. Jake should be at the door any second now.

The oven beeped, indicating it had reached the preset temperature. I could start the pizza now, or give the stone a few more minutes to reach the ideal heat.

Downstairs, I checked on Bluebeard and freshened his water while I waited for Jake's knock. I kept glancing at the window, expecting to see him come striding across the street any minute, but he didn't.

I was beginning to wonder if there was a problem when he knocked on the front door. The bag in his arms explained why I hadn't seen him; it was from The Grog Shop.

When I opened the door, he gestured with the bag. "I asked the lady next door what wine you preferred with pizza," he said. "She said you were more a beer kind of person, so I got a six-pack of microbrew. That work for you?"

"Sure. I probably won't be as good a student, but I never say no to free beer. Well, maybe once in a while. But not after a day like today."

"That bad?" Jake asked, following me up the stairs.

"Just busy," I replied. I wasn't about to tell him I was snooping around Kevin's death, based on the word of a parrot. Or a ghost.

"Beer first?" I asked as we reached the top of the stairs. "I have sweet tea, too, if you want to wait."

"Beer," he said firmly. "I'm still learning to drink sweet tea. I like it," he added hastily, "I'm just not used to having the sugar already in it."

"Yankee."

"No," he said. "I'm from the West Coast. Grew up in Northern California. Oh, wait, that's *northern*, isn't it?" he joked.

I cocked my head to the side and considered the question. "It is north," I said. "But I think the jury is still out on the West Coast. It's only been a hundred and fifty years. We Southerners take the long view, you know."

While I was talking, Jake removed the caps from two bottles. I reached for the glasses on the table, but he waved me off. "I'm fine with the bottle. Why make more dirty dishes if you don't have to?"

He handed me a bottle, and I took a long sip, feeling the cold all the way down. Now that I thought about it, I hadn't eaten since my early morning bagel and coffee. I'd better slow down on the beer until I had some food.

I slid one of the pizzas into the oven and set the timer.

Jake eyed the second pie on the counter. "You expecting an army or something?"

"Nope. I just figure when I'm messing up the kitchen, I might as well make enough to last a couple of days. Besides, cold pizza makes an excellent breakfast."

"I'll drink to that," he said, tipping up his bottle. When he lowered the beer and looked around, he added, "Although it doesn't look like you messed up the kitchen much."

Which was true. I had managed to disguise most of it. The cutting board was washed and hung back on its hook over the sink, and my knives had been wiped down and returned to their places in the knife block.

"In a place this small, I have to clean as I go, or it gets out of hand real quick. Around here, chaos is more than a theory."

Jake laughed at my joke, reminding me I wanted to hear more of that laugh.

I gestured to the table, set with casual place mats and heavy earthenware plates. One advantage of running a store like mine—I was able to pick and choose from the things I bought. I had furnished my kitchen with the kind of vintage pottery I liked most.

Jake took the invitation and pulled out a chair. I brought the salad to the table and joined him.

"Northern California?" I asked, filling time while we waited for the pizza to bake. "Like San Francisco?"

His answering laugh wasn't nearly as pleasant as his earlier amusement. "Hardly. That was way out of our financial range. More like Sacramento, but farther north. Agricultural area, mostly."

I wanted to ask more questions, but the look on Jake's face quickly shut down the impulse. Whatever was in his past, he was clearly uncomfortable talking about it.

Maybe next time.

Next time? We hadn't even had dinner, and I was already thinking about the next time? Time to get back to safer territory.

"You said you knew some things about websites," I said.

Jake's wariness relaxed, and I congratulated myself on the decision to change the subject.

"I'm no expert," he warned me. "I've done my own, and I've helped a few friends in the past. But I have learned my way around some of the design tools, and I know how the various services operate."

I nodded. "And where do we start?"

Just then the oven buzzed.

"We start with pizza," Jake said.

I got up and swapped the pizzas in the oven, then returned to the table. "Let it cool a few minutes before we try to cut it," I said. "It works better that way."

Jake started talking me through what I'd already done to get my site running, which wasn't a lot. I'd registered an address—what he called a domain name—and set up e-mail for Southern Treasures separate from my personal e-mail, but that was about it.

The second pizza finished baking. I took it out, turned the oven off, and cut the first pizza to bring to the table. For the next few minutes, the conversation slowed as we ate pizza and salad and finished our beer.

I cut the second pizza, and offered a piece to Jake. "Slightly different combination," I said as I placed it on the table. "There's no fish or fruit on either one," I added with a little smile.

"That must be what makes it taste so good," Jake said, helping himself to another slice. "You'll have to give me your recipe."

"What recipe? I got ready-made crust, spiced up some tomato paste, and added the toppings. I'd hardly call that a recipe." I thought about the elaborate dinners Karen, Ernie, Felipe, and I had been cooking recently. "Banana pudding from scratch—now that's a recipe."

"Really? What's the difference? You just slice some bananas, throw them in a bowl with vanilla wafers and pudding, and plop some whipped topping on it."

I shook my head and launched into a description of my latest dessert accomplishment. "You can make the quick kind, and I still do. But it isn't the same thing as cooking up your own pudding and baking it with meringue on top. Not at all."

"Sounds good. I think I'd like to try it."

"Maybe next time."

Drat! Did I just say that out loud?

Chapter 33

BY THE TIME WE FINISHED DINNER, I HAD A PRETTY good idea of what needed to be done to get my website working. I had no idea yet of how to go about it, but Jake had helped me wade through the tons of suggestions that had overwhelmed me every time I thought about the site.

"You have no idea how much help this is," I said. "I really didn't even know where to start."

"You really did," he demurred. "I just helped you sort out all the things you already knew."

Jake was being too modest. His patient questioning and explanations had allowed me to see answers to questions I hadn't even realized I had.

"You're a good teacher."

An odd look flashed across his face and was gone before I could figure out exactly what it was. "Thanks."

"I'll probably have a million more questions, once I get

past this stuff." I gestured at the list of notes I'd started writing halfway through our discussion. "I mean, this will keep me busy for a while, but I know I'll get lost again."

He looked at his watch, and back at me. "I had no idea it was this late. I didn't mean to monopolize your entire evening."

"I should apologize to you for keeping you so long," I answered. "I got a lot of questions answered, and I'm not nearly as scared of making a website as I was. I owe you for this."

His eyes twinkled with a hint of mischief. "Banana pudding," he said. "You can pay me with banana pudding, and I'll throw in another lesson for free."

The mention of the pudding reminded me of the ice cream I'd stashed in the freezer. "Oh no! I had ice cream for dessert—spumoni and chocolate—and I got so wrapped up in the web stuff that I completely forgot!"

Jake patted his stomach. "I'm so full of pizza, I don't think I would know where to put it. But for the record, spumoni is about my favorite flavor."

I was secretly pleased with that bit of information. Spumoni was my second-favorite flavor, after chocolate. Good to know we were ice-cream compatible.

I walked back downstairs with Jake and said good night. I watched him cross the street under the glow of the street lights and wave from the far side before letting himself into Beach Books's front door.

Everyone had secrets, and Jake Robinson clearly had his. He had sidestepped my questions about his past, and left me wondering what his life was like before he moved to Keyhole Bay.

I made one last check on Bluebeard, sleeping in his blanket-covered cage, and went back upstairs. There wasn't much cleanup, as Jake had insisted on helping me clear the table and put away the leftover pizza.

I started the dishwasher and sat back down to look at the list of tasks I had made, but my mind kept wandering.

Jake wasn't the only person with secrets. There was something in the way Julie had talked about Kevin that made me curious, especially what she'd said about football heroes. She hadn't been talking about Kevin, I was sure.

So what had Jimmy done that made his wife feel that way? She hadn't said *boyfriends* or *husbands*; she'd said "football heroes," as though that were the important part.

This was going to take some investigating. And I knew just the person to ask for help.

Unfortunately, if I called Karen at this hour, I could guarantee some serious grumbling. I would have to wait until morning.

But Sunday mornings are never restful when you work in retail. A drizzle forced a steady stream of tourists through my door and kept me busy until late in the afternoon.

Eventually, though, the tourists wandered off to their cars and clogged the highway heading home, leaving Keyhole Bay feeling quiet and empty.

I tried Karen a couple of times, but the calls went to voice mail. I wondered if she'd let her battery run down or if there was some new crisis I hadn't heard about.

I switched on the radio as I started the laundry and put away the dishes from last night. Nothing important on the news read by the relief announcer.

I tried Karen again and talked to her voice mail. Again.

Twenty minutes later my phone rang. I saw Karen's number on the display, and considered letting it go to voice mail. It would serve her right.

"Where have you been?" I said when I picked up the call. "I was beginning to think you'd fallen off the edge of the earth."

"Darn near," she grumbled. "Turned out one of the guys

in the fight was one of Riley's deckhands. I got caught up in the drama and ended up spending most of the night sitting in the police station with Riley while he tried to get his guy bailed out."

"Sounds exciting," I said drily.

"Tell me about it. The police strongly suggested I should put my phone on silent while I was in the station. I was so tired when I left, I forgot to turn it back on."

Now *that* was tired. Karen never got more than a few feet from her cell phone, and if she didn't get a call at least once an hour, she checked to make sure it was working.

"I finally got to sleep about daylight," she continued. "Just woke up a little bit ago."

"You hungry?"

There was silence on the other end for long seconds, and I could almost see Karen cocking her head to one side, thinking. "You know, I think I am. Heaven knows, I should be. Haven't eaten since Riley brought me a burger last night. Why?"

"I've got leftover pizza. Homemade. And information. You interested?"

"Sure." Karen yawned so hard I think I heard her jaw crack over the phone. "Let me shower first, and I'll be over." She yawned again. "What kind of information?" Her voice was suddenly sharp, as though what I'd said had just registered in her sleep-addled brain.

"I've had a busy day or so," I answered. "See you in a few minutes."

I think Karen set a speed record getting from her house to mine. She was at my back door in fifteen minutes flat, her hair still damp from the shower and an air of impatience surrounding her.

"What did you find out?" she demanded when I opened the door.

"Hello to you, too," I said.

Karen charged up the stairs, and I followed along.

I'd switched on the oven to reheat the pizza. As long as I had a good stone and a little patience, it was way better than the microwave. Not that Karen cared.

She charged into the kitchen, poured herself a glass of sweet tea, and plopped down at the kitchen table. "Spill," she commanded.

"Where did we leave off?" I asked.

She sighed. "When I left to cover the brouhaha at the Surf and Sand. Which, by the way, wasn't worth the time it took to get over there. Especially since Riley roped me into helping him get his hand out of jail."

I slid leftovers into the oven on a sheet of parchment paper. I couldn't put them directly on the stone, because the melting cheese would run all over, so the parchment was as close as I could come.

"Let me see." I set the timer and joined her at the table. "After you left, I talked to Roy—the service guy I told you about—and then I practically had to arm wrestle Joe for my keys."

"I don't doubt it. Fowler must have him on commission, considering the hard sell you were getting."

"Oh, and Jimmy Parmenter came in just before I left. I don't think he had much use for Kevin Stanley. Made it really clear he thought the crash was Kevin's own fault."

"Drinking and driving? Yeah, that pretty much makes Kevin responsible."

"But that's the strange part." I told her about the visit from the football team, skipping over Bluebeard's floor show. "Those boys said Kevin didn't even drink that beer. And Julie said he was out there trying to break it up."

"Wait! What?" Karen looked confused. "I just woke up

and all, but that still didn't quite track. Where did Julie come from in this whole thing?"

"I talked to her when I was in Frank's," I explained. "I took her T-shirts over when I went to get stuff to make pizza."

Karen stared at me for long seconds, her brows drawn together in concentration. "Start over, Martine. Let's take this from the top, and this time no jumping around, because I need to know what happened."

It was a long story, especially since I had to keep backing up and filling in details as Karen questioned me. I told her about the conversation with Roy and the one with Jimmy. About sneaking into the secure lot—I had to stop her from yelling at me for that one—and meeting Sly.

"You mean Fowler doesn't even own that lot?" she asked.

"Nope. Sly must be nearly seventy—he said he was in the army in the 1960s—and he inherited the place from his dad. Said he remembered Uncle Louis, too."

"So you got out of there without getting attacked by the junkyard dog. Then what?"

We finished our pizza while I told her about the football team and my trip to the grocery store, glossing over the real reason for my shopping trip.

"Hold on." Karen didn't miss anything. It was part of what made her a good reporter, but it also made her a pain in the neck when I wanted to keep something to myself. "Why did you go all the way over to Frank's to deliver T-shirts in the middle of the night?"

"All the way over? Are you kidding me? It's all of about four blocks. And it was hardly the middle of the night; I'd just closed up the shop and I needed some stuff for dinner."

"You never go grocery shopping on the weekend," she said accusingly. "You would have found something here to eat." She jumped up from the table and flung open the refrigerator, surveying the contents. Sure enough, there were at least three different things I could have had for dinner.

"So?"

She had me. I confessed that I'd had company for dinner and, under pressure, that it had been my hunky, book-selling neighbor.

The same neighbor she'd seen me having coffee with just a few days earlier.

"Is there something I should know?"

I rolled my eyes. "No. And anyway, isn't a person entitled to a little privacy?"

She grinned. "Nope. Not in a small town, and not from your best friend. So tell me about Mr. Tall, Dark, and Yummy."

"For heaven's sake! He's a neighbor who's helping me work on a website for the store, and he's willing to be paid in home-cooked meals. That's all there is to it."

Karen's look said she didn't believe me, and I knew the subject wasn't closed.

Chapter 34

"THE BIG QUESTION I HAVE," I SAID WHEN I FINISHED recounting the events of the previous day, "is what's going on with Julie and Jimmy Parmenter? There's something there, and I have the feeling it has something to do with Kevin."

Karen looked unconvinced.

"What if Ernie's right, and it is Fowler?" I pressed on. "Jimmy works for him. They might be in this together."

"Big Shot Fowler and the washed-up football star that drives a tow truck? That seems like a pretty odd couple to me. Besides, what's in it for either one of them?"

I shrugged, picking up paper plates and tossing them in the trash, along with the parchment I'd used to heat the pizza. "Fowler gets his problem cleared up, and Jimmy gets a job."

Even to me, it sounded lame.

"And Fowler gives the loser something to hold over him? Not likely. Fowler's too smart for that. Besides, what kind of problem did Fowler really have with Kevin? Has anyone come up with an answer for that?"

"No." I had to admit all I had was conjecture. "But those boys—when the team was in here—said he was getting to be a real goody-goody. Which might mean he wasn't willing to go along with Fowler's schemes. That would threaten Fowler's plan to ride the kid's coattails."

Karen shook her head. "I don't know. What about the theory that it might be someone else on the team?"

"Well," I ticked people off on my fingers as I ran down the names we'd tossed out over the last couple weeks, "it could be Travis or Coach Bradley. Ernie and Felipe swear it couldn't have been Tricia but she's still a possibility. Or even Shiloh, though I doubt it. And, of course, there's Fowler. But we're pretty sure he wasn't out there in the woods himself, so that means he had an accomplice."

"What if . . ." Karen hesitated, biting her lip. "What if it really was an accident? What if Kevin just lost control of the car and went off the road, even if he wasn't drinking?"

"And Uncle Louis is lying?"

"Not necessarily." She raised her hands, palms out. "Hear me out. I am not saying it isn't Uncle Louis talking to you. I've heard him through Bluebeard, and I can't argue with you. It doesn't sound like a parrot repeating something he heard. It sounds like a person. But what if Uncle Louis misunderstood something, and he's getting you all riled up over something that didn't happen? Isn't that possible?"

I couldn't lie; the thought had occurred to me. But there were too many things that didn't add up for me.

I shook my head. "After everything I've heard," I said, "I really can't believe this was just an accident. You didn't see that car, Karen. That scratch along the side didn't come from a roll-over accident." In fact, I'd spent some time that afternoon looking at gruesome roll-over pictures on the Internet. Lots of damage, but I hadn't seen anything that looked like the crease in Kevin's door.

"And it wasn't already there. You know how Kevin kept that car. If there had been a scratch on it, he would have buffed it out and touched up the paint immediately. In fact, it was in the shop just a day or two before the accident, according to Roy. And I don't believe that Jimmy could have made such a huge mistake when he towed the car. I don't think Sly was lying, I just think he was repeating what he'd heard from someone."

Silent minutes dragged on. We were at an impasse, and I didn't have an answer. Neither did Karen.

Finally I had to give up. "I have no idea," I admitted. "Maybe it wasn't anyone we know. Maybe it was a way-lost tourist who sideswiped the kid and didn't stop." I shrugged. "That would explain the anonymous call, too."

That call bugged me. "Can't they trace the number it came from or something?" I asked. "Find out who made the call, and make them tell what happened?"

Karen rolled her eyes. "You have been watching too many cop shows, Glory. Half that stuff isn't even possible, and Keyhole Bay isn't New York City. Or Los Angeles. We barely have a police department!"

"So they can't find the caller?" I was disappointed. Apparently the magic computers that could tell you everything about a phone call were right up there with flying cars.

"From what I hear," Karen said, "and it's all strictly off the record, they tried. The call bounced off a tower on County Road 198, near the crash, and it was made with one of those prepaid phones like they sell everywhere in town."

"Not in Southern Treasures."

"Only because Peter hasn't figured out you should. You could get a shipment of them any day now."

I groaned at the idea. Peter could help me right into the poorhouse if I let him. "Okay. The phone call is a dead end. We eliminated everybody who might have a reason to hurt Kevin, and if I'm not careful, Peter will bankrupt me with his brainstorms. Is that about it?"

"Yep." Karen waved away my defense. "Maybe you should just stop obsessing about this, and let Boomer take care of it."

"And sweep it under the rug as a tragic accident."

"Again, whatever. We haven't found anything that says different." She shook her head. "I know. I know. Except for Bluebeard. Or Uncle Louis."

She leaned on the table and levered herself out of the chair. "Much as I love you, Martine, I have got to go home. I did nothing but sleep all day, and I need to at least get a load of laundry done so I have something to wear to work tomorrow."

After Karen left, I pulled out my website notes and my laptop and started poking into the corners of my undeveloped website, trying to figure out how to make Southern Treasures as alluring as possible.

It occurred to me that this was the kind of thing Peter should be doing. It would keep him out of my hair, let him feel like he was contributing, and get the job off my to-do list.

And there was no way in the world I would trust Peter to do the job. No matter how many engineering degrees he had.

Stubborn only took me so far, and eventually I found myself wandering around the Internet, watching silly pet videos and generally killing time.

Frustrated, I got up from the table. It was too late for the gym, but I could do something useful. I needed more newspapers for the racks downstairs, and I could sort out some of the bundles from my storage area.

The 1960s were always popular with the baby-boomers that seemed to make up a large proportion of my snowbird customers, and I found three bundles from throughout the decade.

I carried the bundles downstairs and set them on the counter, intending to put some of them on the display. But when I cut the first bundle open, Bluebeard came hopping across the store. He glared at the pictures on the front page of the top issue and ruffled his feathers.

After a moment, he grabbed the paper in his beak and dropped it to the floor.

"Liars!"

He ruffled his feathers and reached for the next issue. I quickly snatched it away and bundled the papers back up. Whatever was in the *News and Times*, I wasn't going to find it while Bluebeard was supervising.

I coaxed him onto my arm and took him back across the room to his cage, scratching his head and talking soothingly. I settled him back in the cage with a biscuit, closed the door, and went back to work. Lately he was too agitated to be left free to roam when I wasn't in the shop.

Hauling the bundles into the storage room, I cut the string on the rest of the stacks and started laying them out on the empty shelves in preparation for cataloging and packaging. Despite my resolve, I caught myself leafing through the issues, reading about people and events in Keyhole Bay before I was born.

Many of the names were familiar, parents or grandparents of kids I went to school with, or neighbors from when my parents were alive. There were ads for businesses that had closed, and birth announcements for people whose own children were now grown and starting their families. It all reminded me Keyhole Bay was a small community, and it was all about family.

Was that the answer? Did all this go back to the basics, back to family? Or was it really just a random reckless moment that cost an innocent young life?

And if it was, why did my own uncle insist it wasn't an accident?

Chapter 35

BY TUESDAY I HAD SOLD OUT OF ALL BUT A COUPLE OF T-shirts, and I was ready to have them out of the shop. I called Shiloh and told her I needed to turn in the proceeds and return the last couple of shirts.

"I can come and pick them up," she offered. "If that's okay with you?"

"Sure. Why wouldn't it be?"

"I don't know." Reluctance tinged her words, but she continued. "When I called the other night with your work order, I kind of got the idea you were upset with me."

I laughed, hoping it didn't sound as false to her as it did to me. "I'm so sorry; I was just in a hurry. I had people here waiting for me. Tell you what," I continued. "Come by when you can stay a few minutes, and I'll buy you a coffee if the shop is quiet."

"You don't need to do that," she said. "I'll buy and charge it back to the dealership. It's the least Mr. Fowler can do for you, considering how much you did for him on the whole shirt deal."

We agreed she would come by in an hour. I hung up feeling a little less guilty. Shiloh's loyalty to Fowler was showing some cracks, which was a good thing for her.

I had the accounts totaled and an envelope of cash and checks ready for Shiloh when she came into the store. We spent a few minutes going over the counts, checking that all the shirts were accounted for.

From his perch, Bluebeard watched as I counted out the money and Shiloh verified the total of the checks. "Looks like it's all in balance," she said. "Which I totally appreciate. Most of the time, if Mr. Fowler ropes somebody into helping with these things, they do half the job and expect me to clean it up."

"Good job!" Bluebeard yelled at us.

"Thank you, Bluebeard," Shiloh said, "for the compliment."

Bluebeard loosed a piercing wolf whistle. "Pretty girl!"

Shiloh blushed. She *was* a pretty girl but so tentative she faded into the background. She probably didn't get many compliments, and she didn't quite know how to handle them.

I locked up, and we went next door for a cup of coffee.

Chloe made three lattes and brought them to our table with the morning's fresh cranberry-orange scones. She pulled out a chair and joined us, as she had before.

I took a sip of the sweet coffee, nearly burning my tongue. "Extra hot today?"

Chloe nodded. "Like you always ask for."

"And you never do," I shot back.

She rolled her kohl-rimmed eyes and turned to Shiloh. "Some people are never satisfied."

I took a bite of scone, enjoying the crunch of the crisp

outer layer and the decorative sugar crystals, followed by the mellow, buttery taste and the tang of cranberry.

"Someday I am going to con this recipe out of Pansy," I said for about the millionth time. Pansy, the eighty-year-old owner of The Lighthouse, did all her own baking and guarded her secret recipes with the vigilance of the Secret Service.

"She'll never give it up," Chloe said. "I've come in at four to bake with her, and she won't even let me know how she does it. She keeps everything in her head and goes so fast that I know I miss stuff."

"Is she ever going to retire?"

Chloe shook her head, her mouth full of scone. She took her time, savoring the bite, before she answered. "She wouldn't know what to do with herself. She comes in here before dawn, and it's all any of us can do to get her out of here at noon. Her son's over in Fort Walton, and he calls every day at twelve thirty to make sure she's gone home. About half the time he has to tell her to go."

We chatted for several minutes about Chloe's classes at the community college. She was studying to be a paralegal, and I wondered how her tattoos and piercings would fit in a law office.

It reminded me I had an appointment with Mr. Wilson in the afternoon. I couldn't imagine Chloe in Clifford Wilson's office. Old Mr. Wilson would have a heart attack the first time she walked through the door.

The talk drifted to work. Shiloh asked about the estimate she'd faxed over. "I heard you brought the car in Saturday."

"Yes. Took about ten years off my life, I can tell you."

She winced. "Sorry for the sticker shock. Joe is, well, I guess you could say he's thorough."

Chloe snickered. "Is that a polite way of saying he was padding the bill?" she asked.

Shiloh put her hand over her mouth. "Did I say that?" she seemed genuinely shocked.

I patted her arm. "No, you didn't. Chloe just likes to be an instigator."

"I was just asking."

"Right." I turned my attention back to Shiloh. "But you could answer a question for me, if it's not confidential or something. Does Joe work on commission? Because he sure seems anxious to make a big sale."

"You don't know?" Shiloh asked, then she shook her head. "Of course you don't, or you wouldn't ask. Joe is Mr. Fowler's oldest son. He dropped out of college to work for his dad, and he's trying really hard to make his dad think it was the right idea."

When I thought about it, I could see some resemblance between the two men. Especially in the pushy-salesman department.

"Oh, boy! Here come the daddy issues," Chloe crowed. She'd taken a semester of psychology last term, and it continued to creep into her conversations.

Shiloh shook her head. "It's not like that, really. He's just trying to impress his dad, just like every other guy."

Judging by her quick defense of the younger Fowler, I would guess that Shiloh had a crush on the man. I couldn't see why, but she knew him better than I did. Maybe he was great when he wasn't in salesman mode.

"Speaking of impressing the boss," I said, "when I was there the other day, it looked like Jimmy wasn't doing a very good job of it."

"He's a showboat," Shiloh said. "Always thinks he can get away with cutting corners. But he's not the big football star any longer, and he can't get by on his looks and reputation."

"He told me Fowler promoted him just a couple weeks ago," I pointed out.

"Got him out of the shop is more like it, before one of the other guys decked him."

"If he's that bad," Chloe asked, "why even have him there?"

Shiloh shook her head and drained her cup. "I don't know. I think he gave Mr. Fowler some sob story about how he was going to get back on the team at the university, but I'm not supposed to know about that."

I filed that piece of information. Maybe Fowler had had a backup plan if Kevin didn't work out.

Shiloh slipped the receipt for the coffee and scones into her purse and got up. "I need to get back to the lot. Joe's covering the phones for me, but he has his own work to do."

"I better get back to the shop," I said to Chloe after Shiloh left. "But if you figure out how we can pry that recipe out of Pansy, let me know."

She snorted. "And pigs will fly."

Chapter 36

BACK IN THE STORE, I DISTRACTED MYSELF WITH newspapers. I worked my way through two bundles of mid-1960s papers, scanning the pages for connections to Uncle Louis, putting them in protective plastic sleeves, and then logging them into inventory.

I turned the picked-over rack of papers and magazines into an attractive display—without finding anything more about my uncle—before my appointment with Clifford Wilson.

I coaxed Bluebeard into his cage, locked up the shop, and decided to walk. The weather was mild, and I had promised myself I would get more exercise.

I don't know quite what I expected from Mr. Wilson. He offered me a copy of Uncle Louis's will and identification numbers that would allow me to search for his military records, but he wasn't sure exactly why I was there.

Clifford Wilson was still an imposing figure. With an up-right posture that belied his age, and a snow-white pompadour that matched his ice-cream suits, he looked like someone who should be called Colonel.

"What is it you're looking for, Miss Gloryanna?" he asked after several minutes of conversation. "You said you wanted to know about your great-uncle, but as his attorney, and yours, there isn't a whole lot I can offer."

"I'm not really sure myself," I said, shifting uncomfortably in the ancient office chair. Mr. Wilson had furnished his office when he started practicing, nearly sixty years ago, and I don't think he'd changed anything since then.

"I just wondered about Uncle Louis, I guess. Now that I'm running Southern Treasures myself, I'm curious about him. I was so young when he died, I hardly remember him. I guess maybe I feel like I owe it to him to remember who he was—to have a connection with him, even though he's gone."

Or, more to the point, even though he *isn't* gone, though I wasn't going to give Mr. Wilson that explanation. It might be worse than Shiloh's tattoos.

The old man leaned back in his chair, the worn leather creaking with his movement. "A lot of what I know I still consider confidential," he said. "A lawyer has a sacred trust to carry his client's business to the grave, and I will not violate that trust. But I can tell you this: Louis Marcel Georges was a good and honorable man. No matter what you might hear, no matter what tales people might carry, your uncle was a good man."

Okay. Not what I was expecting to hear.

"Will I hear bad things about him?"

"I don't know," Mr. Wilson replied. "You could. Arguments and feuds die hard down here, and people carry tales for generations, even if they don't remember how they all started." He chuckled. "Don't forget, the Hatfields and McCoys were Southerners."

He turned serious again, leaning forward over the dark wooden desk, his arthritic fingers curled atop the leather blotter. "Just don't believe everything you hear."

It wasn't much, but I had to settle for what I could get. I thanked him for his time and for the copies, and let myself out.

The receptionist gave me a receipt for the photocopying and waved away my credit card. "No charge for this visit," she said. "Mr. Wilson's orders."

I stammered my thanks. Wilson must be getting sentimental in his old age; he had a reputation for never leaving money on the table.

As I turned toward the exit, I saw Coach Bradley sitting in the waiting room.

It would be rude not to stop and chat.

We traded greetings, and I told him about the boys coming in to get their T-shirts. "I guess they're planning to wear them at the game Friday night."

He gave me a sly look. "Yeah, they think I don't know about it—that they're putting something over on me. I'm letting them think that. They need something to bond over, and the shirts are as good a thing as any. I'll act surprised when they run out on the field, maybe even give them a little lecture about being out of uniform. But it'll be good for team morale."

My admiration for Bradley rose several notches. His concern for the needs of his players, and for the team, was a sign of a good coach in my book.

"How are they doing?" I asked. "They seemed okay when they were in the store. Travis looked like he was stepping up, too."

"You never know with kids," Bradley said. "Look at Kevin. I thought he was getting himself into trouble, was afraid I might have to end up benching him. But from what I'm hearing, he tried to break up the kegger and left when he couldn't. Probably would have messed with his authority as captain." A shadow passed over his face. "But now we'll never know."

I slid into the chair beside him, putting me at eye level with the coach. "You really think the rest of the team would have had a problem with that?"

"Maybe. No. I'm not sure." He frowned. "I think some of them might have challenged him, and he would have had to stand up for himself. But I think he was strong enough to do that. Unlike some of the boys I've coached, I think Kevin was learning to be a real leader."

I wondered what boys he was referring to, but I never got the opportunity to ask, as the receptionist called to him, "Mr. Bradley, Mr. Wilson is ready for you."

We stood up, and I offered Bradley my hand. "Hang in there, Coach. I'll be in the stands Friday night, cheering for the team."

"Thanks," he said, his voice husky. "We appreciate all the support. It means a lot to the kids." He released my hand, and swallowed hard. "And to me."

On the walk home, I kept coming back to the question of the beer. If Kevin hadn't been drinking—as Julie and his teammates said—then where were the results of his blood-alcohol test, and why hadn't the police released a final determination on the accident?

I pulled my cell phone out of my purse and called Karen. I didn't have any reason to question the police about the test results, none that I wanted to share with Boomer, anyway. But Karen made a perfect cover for me—as a reporter, she had every reason to question everything that happened in Keyhole Bay.

She wasn't on-air, luckily, and quickly answered her phone.

"Karen, I know you think I'm beating a dead horse here, but have you heard anything about blood-alcohol tests for Kevin? I just ran into the coach, and he's heard the same thing I did. Kevin wasn't drinking; he was trying to break up the party. So where are the test results?"

"Nothing's been released," she said. "I've been in touch with Boomer so often that he's sick of hearing from me. Last time I talked to him, which was just this morning, he said something about the state lab being backed up."

"Isn't that a simple test? Couldn't they just do it here at the hospital?"

"They do with live victims, or suspects," she said. "But there's some local ordinance that they have to send the tests to the state lab when someone dies."

"What?" I stopped in the middle of the sidewalk. "Are you kidding me?"

"I think it's been on the books for about fifty years," she said. "There wasn't a hospital in Keyhole Bay, and any serious injuries were sent to Pensacola. I know it doesn't make sense, but once these things get passed into law, they stay there forever."

I sighed heavily. "Well, that's ridiculous."

"Boomer agrees, for what it's worth," she said. "I have a hunch this is going to come up at the next City Council meeting."

"It should." I started walking again.

"I'm due back on the air in five," Karen said. "Gotta go."

I said good-bye and slipped the phone back in my purse.

I was only a block from home, on the opposite side of the street. A few yards ahead I saw the sale book cart on the sidewalk in front of Beach Books. It gave me an idea.

I hadn't talked to Jake since our pizza night. He was

behind the counter when I walked in, ringing up a stack of romance novels for a woman in a straw hat only a tourist would wear. I waved as I went by, headed for the computer-book section in the back.

A few minutes later Jake joined me. "See anything that interests you?" he asked.

I did, but since it had nothing to do with the volumes on the shelf, I kept it to myself. "Just looking back through some of these, now that I have some idea what I should be doing."

He picked up a bright-yellow volume only slightly smaller than a telephone book. "This series is usually pretty good," he said. "Most people are able to follow the instructions without any problem."

"When it comes to computers," I said, "I'm not 'most people.' I'm way worse."

"We had this discussion the other night," he reminded me.

Like I didn't remember!

"You aren't nearly as bad as you think you are." He repeated his assessment from our lesson on Saturday. "You'll get this, once you start working on it."

"I actually have," I said. "I poked around a little with the various templates, but I haven't decided which would work best for my store. Do you have a site for Beach Books? Maybe your template would be a good place for me to start."

I was either flirting or begging, and I really wasn't sure which. I liked Jake and would be glad to spend some more time with him, but I was also desperate to get the website running. Maybe it was a little of both.

He slapped his forehead dramatically. "I don't know why I didn't think of that the other night," he said. "I'm an idiot!"

"I don't think so. If you are, then I am somewhere below plankton on the intellectual scale."

We continued bantering for another couple minutes, until a real customer came through the door. Jake excused himself and went to greet the new arrival.

He was back in a minute, though. "She wanted to look through the mysteries," he explained. "And she made it clear she didn't need any help."

I glanced up, finding the concave mirrors in the corners of the shop, just like in mine. Jake saw my look and chuckled softly. "Yep, you're a retailer."

I nodded. "You have to be careful."

"So," he tugged at his earlobe, a gesture I'd seen before, "are you ready to make that banana pudding you promised? I'd be glad to give you another computer lesson in exchange."

My social calendar was pretty pathetic. The only thing I had coming up was Thursday's dinner. "Tonight?" I suggested. "Or tomorrow?"

"Tonight works for me," he responded immediately. "But you have to let me bring dinner if you're making dessert."

We bargained back and forth for a couple minutes, Jake occasionally casting a look at the security mirrors, where his customer was gathering up a stack of paperbacks.

We agreed I would provide a salad and chips, and he would bring sandwiches from a local shop. It seemed like we were both using computer lessons and promised desserts as an excuse to spend the evening together.

Not that I objected.

But I didn't have bananas or half-and-half, so I would have to make another trip to Frank's. I mentally reviewed the contents of my refrigerator and pantry and decided that was all I would need.

I left Beach Books and turned away from Southern Treasures. A few minutes later I walked into Frank's Foods.

Julie was alone at the register when I checked out with just the small carton of half-and-half and a bunch of bananas.

"Pudding?" she guessed. I nodded.

"Maybe I should make some," she said as she rang up the purchase. "Jimmy might like that."

"Most guys do."

"Yeah," she said. "Unfortunately for us, they burn it all off. We just put it into storage." She patted her backside, which didn't look as though she was storing much excess.

"It isn't fair, is it?" she continued. "'Course if they're athletes, they *run* it all off."

She shook her head. "Kevin sure did. I mean, *Jimmy* did. *Does*." She looked like a deer caught in the headlights, clearly distressed at what she had revealed.

I looked around the store, then back at her. "You knew Kevin pretty well, didn't you?"

She made the same visual sweep of the store I had before she answered. "You won't tell anyone, will you? There wasn't anything going on; it was more like a big-sister kind of thing, I swear. I just wanted him to straighten himself out before it was too late."

"Like it was too late for Jimmy?" It was the question I'd been wanting to ask her for days. Something had gone badly wrong in her relationship—I'd put money on it—and I hoped she was ready to talk.

"I don't mean to be disloyal—the man's my husband," she said, one hand drifting down to rest across her stomach, confirming another of my suspicions. "But he made some mistakes, and he lost a lot because of it. I just figured if I could talk to Kevin, make him see how much he was putting at risk, maybe I could save him some grief. Him, and Tricia, too. She was still in love with him, you know."

"I thought she was, from the way Frank talked about it."
I looked at her hand, and she snatched it away, her face coloring. "Does Jimmy know?"

She nodded but didn't speak. Maybe her young husband wasn't so happy about becoming a young father. It wouldn't be the first time a young buck found himself with a family before he wanted one.

I sensed that Julie wasn't going to answer any more questions. If I pressed, I might threaten the tentative bond I was forming with the girl.

"It'll work out," I lied, in what I hoped was a convincing manner. Even if it didn't, she needed the reassurance right now.

Chapter 37

I HURRIED ALONG THE SIDEWALK, ANXIOUS TO GET home. I had promised to make pudding for Jake, I had work to do in the shop, and I wanted to go through the papers I'd received from Mr. Wilson.

Besides that, I'd left Bluebeard in his cage for far longer than I'd intended, and there was a very good chance he would be in a nasty mood as a result.

I unlocked the front door to chaos. Bluebeard squawked from his perch, a string of curses interspersed with a screech of "Bad man!"

The damned bird had done it again.

But how did he get out of the cage? I was sure I had left it latched. Hadn't I?

I set my grocery sack on the counter and approached Bluebeard. He didn't look injured, but his agitation was so great I worried he might be. Parrots, though they have strong beaks and sharp talons, are still fragile in many ways.

I managed to coax him onto my arm and examined him closely for signs he might be hurt, but I didn't find anything.

Trying to calm him, I stroked his head and carried him to the counter, where I'd left my bag. I took out a banana and peeled it, offering him small pieces, which he eagerly devoured.

After several minutes of attention, he nestled his head into my shoulder. He was ready for a nap.

I finished the banana as I surveyed the damage to the shop. The newspapers hadn't been disturbed this time, but the T-shirts were scattered, merchandise was pulled from shelves onto the floor, and as I rounded the end of the counter, I could see that every paper on and under it had been pulled out and tossed around.

Receipts, checkbooks, order forms, inventory sheets—all piled haphazardly where they had fallen. I picked up the pile and put it on the counter. I would have to sort and refile every scrap of paper.

In the stockroom, I found proof Bluebeard wasn't the culprit. I stood there with my hand over my mouth. The back door stood open, the lock broken and the doorjamb splintered.

This time I had to call Boomer.

I waited in the store for the police, sitting at the counter because I didn't trust my legs to hold me up.

I tried to make an inventory of missing items, but from where I sat, I couldn't find any. In the back, my so-called office was a shambles, papers thrown everywhere.

Behind the counter, the computer had been turned on, but the welcome screen blinked enigmatically, challenging someone to enter a correct password.

At least they hadn't been able to breach my system.

After a few minutes, the initial shock subsided, replaced with red-hot anger. Someone had destroyed my back door and invaded my store—my home. A chilling thought occurred to me. If someone broke into the shop, they might have gone upstairs. And I hadn't heard anyone leave.

The idea was enough to send me to the front of the store, with its large windows overlooking the sidewalk. I suddenly needed to be where I could be seen.

My hands shaking with the realization that I might not be alone, I pulled my cell phone out and dialed the number for The Grog Shop next door.

"Guy?" I said when he answered. "Guy, could one of you come over here? I think someone broke in, and I'm waiting for the police, but I just don't want to be alone, and I had to call someone because I don't know if whoever it was has left, and I can't go upstairs in case they are—"

The front door burst open while I was still babbling, and Guy, the phone still in his hand, wrapped me in his strong arms.

"It's okay, Glory," he said, smoothing my hair as he'd done so many times when I was a kid. "I'm right here, and Linda will be right behind me."

He stopped. "Especially since I just ran out the door without telling her where I was going."

As if to reinforce his words, Linda came through the door a few seconds later, concern evident in every move. "Guy Morton Miller," she hollered, "are you trying to give me a heart attack? You pick up the phone and go running off without so much as a by-your-leave—"

The scene in front of her finally registered, and she ran to us, joining the family hug. "Glory, what's wrong?"

"Look around, woman," Guy snapped. "What does it look like?"

"It looks like that fool parrot trashed the place. Again."

I shook my head, pushing Guy and Linda away to stand

on my own feet. "No. Anyway, Bluebeard didn't break in the back door."

Linda craned her neck, looking past me to the storage room and the back door beyond just as Boomer Hardy came through the front door.

"Miss Glory." He tipped his Smokey Bear hat to me and took a pad and pen from his shirt pocket. "Can you tell me what happened?"

"Where do I start?" I asked. "I just came home and found it like this."

"How long have you been here?" he asked.

"Just a few minutes," I said. "I found the mess, and Bluebeard was upset so I tried to calm him down. It was after that I found the back door broken in, and I called you."

"And is this the extent of the damage?"

"I, well, I haven't been upstairs yet, so—"

"Upstairs?" he interrupted sharply.

"Yes. My apartment is up there, over the store," I gestured to the staircase in the back.

Boomer turned to the pair of patrol officers coming through the front door. "There's an upstairs apartment. She hasn't been up there yet." He turned back to me. "Is there anyone else living here, anyone who might be up there?"

I shook my head.

"Pets?"

"Just Bluebeard, and he's down here in his cage."

As if on cue, Bluebeard stuck his head out of the cage and fixed the police chief with a beady glare. "Keep it down. Trying to #$&%$% sleep here," he squawked.

All three officers chuckled, the bird's curses breaking the tension that surrounded them.

"Okay." Boomer gestured to the officers. "Check it out. Carefully."

I watched, wide-eyed, as the two men drew their guns and started up the staircase, flattened against the walls on opposite sides of the narrow flight.

Boomer turned back and continued asking questions. "How long were you gone?"

"I went out right after lunch. I had an appointment with Clifford Wilson, and I stopped at the bookstore across the street on my way home. Then I decided to go over to Frank's and pick up a couple things, and it was still nice out so I decided to walk, and that took maybe twenty or thirty minutes before I got back here—"

Boomer held up a finger, interrupting the torrent of words. "So you were gone from about one until," he glanced at his watch, calculating, "three fifteen? Three thirty?"

I scratched my head, trying to concentrate. "Probably closer to three thirty."

"And you left the shop closed for that time?"

I nodded. "Usually I get somebody to take care of it while I'm gone, but it's been pretty quiet around here the last week or so. It seemed like a good idea at the time."

"It might have been," the chief replied. "Nobody was here to get hurt when the intruder came in."

The thought sent ice water through my veins.

One of the patrol officers sounded an all-clear from the top of the stairs. "Doesn't look like he even got up here," he called down.

"Did you hear anything when you came in?" Boomer asked. "Like anyone moving around, or things being moved, or a door closing?"

I drew in a sharp breath, and my knees threatened to give way. "Do you mean—like was someone in the shop when I came back?"

He nodded. "That's exactly what I mean."

Guy offered an arm to lean on, but I waved it away. The moment of weakness had passed. All my stubbornness came rushing back; I was determined to handle this myself.

"No." I surprised myself with the force of my answer. "Bluebeard squawked when I came in, swore a lot, and yelled about a bad man. But that was it. The guy was long gone."

"Well, he was gone," Boomer conceded. "How long would be anyone's guess. As awful as this might sound," he went on, "it's probably a very good thing you didn't come home sooner. You could have walked in on him, and that would have been a bad thing."

Chapter 38

I HAD TO CONVINCE GUY AND LINDA TO GO BACK TO their store in the middle of the investigation, since there was nothing they could do, and they shouldn't be closed during the after-work rush minute.

Keyhole Bay was much too small to have a rush hour.

I finally assured Boomer nothing was missing, but that only seemed to make him more concerned, rather than less.

"It was probably just someone looking for cash or stuff they could easily fence," I said, showing him the monster safe under the stairs. "They didn't know I kept all the cash locked up, and the stuff I carry isn't easy to resell."

He didn't look convinced. "Or he was looking for something and hadn't found it yet when you walked in. Maybe he was gone, but maybe he wasn't. That back door was wide open."

I tried to dismiss his concerns. If I took them seriously, I wouldn't be able to sleep tonight. Not that sleep was very likely, anyway.

We were still debating the possibilities when Karen bustled through the front door, her face clouded with worry.

"Not you, too!"

"Yes, me, too!" she shot back. "I came as soon as I could get away from the station." She put an arm around my shoulders, and looked hard into my eyes. "Are you okay?"

"I'm fine," I reassured her. "It was just a break-in while I was out, and they didn't take anything. I don't think they even knew about the safe."

Boomer wedged his way between us, challenging Karen for control of the conversation. "What can I do for you, Miss Freed?" he asked, his tone clearly making it an official question.

"Glory's my best friend, and I heard the call." She tightened her grip on me. "I just came to see if there was anything she needed. Especially after the last time."

Boomer swiveled his head toward me. "The last time?"

I glared at Karen. "It was nothing." I looked back at Boomer. "The night Kevin Stanley crashed his car," I couldn't bring myself to call it an accident, "we came back here, and the place was a mess. But it was just Bluebeard having a tantrum, I'm sure."

"Your friend here doesn't seem so sure."

"My friend is a professional muckraker who doesn't know when to keep her mouth shut."

Boomer looked from me to Karen and back again before shaking his head in surrender. "Okay, so there wasn't a 'last time' according to you. But that bird did not break in the back door *this* time."

He gestured to the door in question, where the two patrol officers were erecting a rough barrier of planks to keep it closed until I could get it repaired in the morning.

"My advice would be to stay somewhere else tonight, just in case the guy decides to come back."

"Is that really necessary?" I asked, at the same time Karen offered her place for the night.

"Yes," they said in unison. It was the first thing they had agreed on since Karen came through the door.

I gave in but not without a lot of pouting. I didn't want to leave the place empty overnight, but Karen and Boomer ganged up on me, and I trudged upstairs to pack the essentials into my gym bag.

I was on my way back down when I heard a familiar male voice at the bottom of the stairs.

Jake!

I had completely forgotten our lesson in the aftermath of the break-in. I hurried down the last few steps, rehearsing an abject apology. At the same time, I remembered the half-and-half and bananas, the bag abandoned on the counter when I came back from the store. I would have to throw away the cream.

I never got the chance to offer my apology. The minute I came into sight, Jake spoke up. "You go with Karen," he said.

Since when were they on a first-name basis?

"The police are about through here," he went on, before I could offer a protest. "I'll be right across the street, and I can keep an eye on the place tonight."

"You don't need to do that," I argued. "You're going to want to go home at some point."

He shook his head. "I have a cot in the back, and I have stocking to do tonight." A momentary grin dispelled the worry lines around his mouth, then disappeared. "I don't think you're much in the mood for a computer lesson tonight anyway."

I could see this was one argument I was not going to win. Everybody was lined up against me, and all I could do was tag along as Karen loaded my bag into her SUV.

Boomer and the officers left, promising to increase the overnight patrols for the next few nights and to keep an eye on the place while I was gone.

I vowed to myself it would only be for one night.

Jake walked with us to Karen's SUV after I settled Bluebeard in for the night. I hated to leave him alone, but he got upset every time I took him out of the shop. He was safest locked in his cage with the blanket draped over it. I hoped.

Bluebeard looked as if he wanted to say something, but he remained silent in front of the other two. I gave him an extra biscuit, checked his water one more time, and locked the door behind me, rattling the lock to be sure it was latched.

When I was settled at Karen's with a shower, a snuggly robe, and a tall glass of wine, she started in with her own version of the third degree. Mostly about Jake.

I was quick to distract her with the copy of Uncle Louis's will and the tale of my conversation with Julie.

"There is something really wrong with her marriage." I told her Julie had basically confirmed her pregnancy, and I was certain Jimmy wasn't happy about it. Solicitous maybe, but not particularly happy. And I had the definite impression she hadn't told anyone else.

"My guess?" Karen replied. "There's something off with Jimmy. The guy's an ego on two legs, used to getting by on looks and charm. That's not enough to make a marriage work and it's certainly not enough to be a good dad."

Her assessment reminded me of Shiloh's description of him as a showboat. Was that only this morning? It seemed like at least a week ago.

I told her what Shiloh said, and Karen nodded emphatically. "Exactly. He's used to being the big star and not having to actually, you know, *do* anything. Remember, he was a big star with the lot-boy job and no real responsibilities last time he worked for Fowler. He probably expects the same treatment this time, and I can't imagine Fowler letting him get away with it."

"Except . . ." I repeated the part about Jimmy getting back on the university team. "Although a wife and baby could definitely put a crimp in that plan. He sure wouldn't be able to play the big man on campus with a wife at home."

Karen shook her head. "No, he wouldn't. But he could be the feel-good comeback story of the year. And Fowler would know how to spin it."

"So why hasn't Jimmy gone back already? Why is he driving a tow truck for Fowler? He sure doesn't look like he's still disabled. Not the way he's hopping around that truck and flexing his muscles around the shop."

A slow smile spread across Karen's face. "I think I know how to find out," she said. "An old friend of mine is covering the college sports beat for one of the big papers."

I would just bet the friend was male. Karen had dated several of her colleagues after her divorce. But she hadn't been ready to settle down, and eventually, they all moved on. But, just like with Riley, she stayed friends with them all.

She picked up her cell phone, punched a speed-dial button, and within seconds she was laughing and reminiscing with someone whose deep, unmistakably male voice leaked from the phone in a pleasant rumble.

I leaned back, sipped my wine, and closed my eyes. It had been a very long day.

I must have dozed off, because the next thing I knew, Karen was grabbing my wine glass. "You cutting me off?" I said, trying to snatch the glass back.

"Just trying to keep you from pouring it all over yourself in your sleep."

"I wasn't asleep," I said, though I was pretty sure I was close.

"Would you like to just call it a day and head for bed?" she asked. "Or maybe you'd like to know what I found out."

Like I said, she had a talent for torment.

"Of course I want to know!" I sat up straight and looked at her expectantly. "What?"

Karen sat back down on the sofa, her canary-eating-cat grin firmly in place. "I found out why Jimmy Parmenter got bounced from the football team."

"Judging from your smug expression, I'm guessing it wasn't because of an injury."

"Actually, it was. Sort of. But it wasn't *his* injury. It was the broken rib of the guy he punched."

"A fight?" I felt like a deflated balloon. I had been all ready for some real gossip, and all she found out was that Jimmy got into a fight and got suspended.

"Oh, way more than a fight. It was a frat party, and he went out of his mind. Nobody knew exactly what set him off, but he tore up the place, busted a couple windows, and punched out the chapter president when he tried to calm him down."

"Yikes!"

"But that's not the worst part." Karen leaned forward. "When the campus police took him in, they ran a drug scan. It's standard practice. Keeps them on good terms with the city cops, in case they have to be called in. Jimmy had a couple beers in him, not enough to account for his behavior. But he tested positive for steroids. He was juicing, and the fight was pure 'roid rage."

She clasped her hands and shook her head. "Fowler didn't have a backup plan, even though he might not have known it. Jimmy's banned for life."

Chapter 39

IN THE MORNING, I WOKE UP TO FIND AN EMPTY house and a note from Karen. She had the early shift at the station, but she'd left coffee in the carafe and biscuits and honey on the table.

She'd also called Felipe and Ernie, and Ernie was waiting for my call to take me home.

Once I was showered, caffeinated, and in clean clothes, the world looked a lot friendlier than it had the night before. The sun was out, but the temperature was mild, and I wanted some time to think about what Karen had told me.

I locked Karen's door carefully, put the gym bag over my shoulder, and headed home.

It was about a mile and a half from Karen's place to mine, and a light sweat had broken across my brow in the last quarter-mile as the sun grew warmer.

I was unlocking the door when someone approached me from behind. Heart racing, I turned, holding the gym bag in front of me like a shield.

"Whoa," Jake said. "Just wanted to make sure you were okay. I thought you were going to call me to pick you up."

"Call you?"

"I gave your friend Karen my number," he said. "Told her I could come get you if she needed me to."

I thought back to the note on the table. It said, "You don't have to walk. Just call for your ride home," and gave a number. It didn't actually say it was Ernie; I just assumed.

I smiled weakly. "I just needed some alone time, to think. Walking seemed like a good idea."

There didn't seem to be anything else to say, so I thanked Jake for his help and let myself in the shop. It was still a mess from the night before, but there didn't seem to be any new disarray.

So far, so good.

But after a few minutes picking up, I realized I couldn't concentrate. I'd already called someone to repair the back door, but the workman wouldn't be able to get there until late in the afternoon.

I needed to get out, to do something.

And I knew where I wanted to go.

On the way, I stopped for doughnuts.

I pulled up next to the tall chain-link gate and shut off the engine. In the silence that followed, I could hear the hiss and clank of the service department across the lot.

Male voices called to one another, and engines started and stopped in the still, warm air of late summer in the Panhandle. From inside the gate, I heard a single sharp bark and the rattle of a chain.

Sly and Bobo appeared on the opposite side of the gate, Sly holding tight to Bobo's chain. I stepped out of the car, the doughnut box held in front of me.

"I brought some doggy treats, too. Just in case you won't let him have doughnuts."

Sly's dark face split with a grin, and he hobbled quickly to open the gate. As before, the chain was held by an open padlock, and he slipped the lock off to swing the gate open.

"What can I do you for, girl?"

I walked through the gate and offered him the box of doughnuts. "When I was here the last time, you told me you remembered my great-uncle. Maybe not well, but there aren't a lot of people around who did know him. I was hoping I could bribe you to spend a little time telling me what you recall."

"Well that's mighty nice of you. Mighty nice." He took the box but looked sheepish. "I don't remember all that much, like I told you. You might be wastin' doughnuts on the pipe dreams of an old fool."

We started walking back toward the building he called home, past the two rows of cars and the wall of pickups, and around the end of the racks of parts.

Once again I found myself staring at the wreck of Kevin Stanley's baby-blue Charger. The impact wasn't as great this time, but I was even more curious about the crumpled mass of steel and chrome. There had to be some clue, somewhere, to how the quarterback died.

Sly balanced the doughnut box on the rails of an empty slot on the rack of engine parts. "Let me fetch us some coffee," he said. "And I'll try to remember what I knew about your uncle."

He started for his little house, then turned back. "Lessen you'd rather come in and set. I shoulda thought to ask that first," he said. "My mama would tan my hide for fergettin' my manners like that."

I could only imagine what the inside of the building might

look like. I demurred as politely as I could. "We won't be having this beautiful sunshine much longer," I said. "I think I'd like to stay out here and enjoy it."

"Suit yourself." I thought I saw a flash of relief on his face before he turned back around. His mama probably would have tanned his hide about the state of his housekeeping, as well as his manners, from the looks of it.

He disappeared inside his house, Bobo at his side.

I moved closer to the Charger, my hands clasped behind my back. I didn't want to touch it so much as just take a closer look, now that I was certain the driver hadn't been intoxicated.

Sure, the lab results weren't back, but I didn't need them to know the truth of what I had heard over and over: Kevin Stanley had cleaned up his life.

He hadn't been drinking the afternoon the car rolled over.

He wasn't responsible for the crash.

Kevin Stanley had been killed.

As I walked around the car, I tried to imagine Kevin sitting in the driver's seat, his right hand on the steering wheel, left elbow propped on the sill of the open window.

It was an image I'd seen frequently in the year since Kevin got his license. It was the way I would always picture him.

I bent forward until my nose was nearly touching the side of the car, close up on the deep scratch in the driver's door. It was shallow at the back end behind the wide door, with gaps in a couple places as though whatever made the scratch hadn't maintained contact.

But toward the front, in the middle of the door itself, the gouge ran deep, ending in a nasty depression.

I could picture it. A vehicle pulled alongside, barely grazing the side of the car as it started to pass. Kevin pulled away, trying to protect his prized Charger from further damage.

The second vehicle lost contact, touched again, and pulled in closer. The crease deepened.

Kevin pulled away, and the other vehicle edged closer, its speed nearly matching the souped-up muscle car's.

Kevin couldn't move any more without ending up in the ditch. He tried to hold the car steady as the other driver pressed his advantage.

Two vehicles flying down the country road side by side.

Until the driver of the second vehicle cut his wheels hard to the right, punching a deep hole in Kevin's door.

Forcing him off the road.

Into the ditch.

Into the field beyond.

I stepped back, shaken. Where had those images come from? I hadn't been there, didn't know how the accident had happened. I was making things up out of whole cloth.

But the certainty I was right wouldn't leave me, and I shuddered with the terror the young quarterback felt, knowing he couldn't stop what was about to happen.

"Served him right."

The voice was familiar, but it wasn't Sly's.

I whirled around and found myself facing a broad expanse of football-star muscle, stuffing a doughnut into his mouth.

Jimmy Parmenter.

"Shouldn't have been drinking and driving. And you shouldn't be here, Miss Glory. Nobody's supposed to be in here, except the old dude who runs the place and the tow driver." He swaggered closer. "And that's me. So when I saw a car parked at the gate, I figured I better come check it out."

Another step closer. "What are you doing here, Miss Glory?"

This time the title wasn't a sign of respect, making me feel old.

It was a challenge, full of menace, sending a chill of fear up my spine.

Up close for the first time, I saw some of the things Ernie had told me about. Jimmy's hair was oily and thinning, and I could see where he had covered acne eruptions with medication.

Muscles bulged in his arms and shoulders as he helped himself to another doughnut from the box.

"Brought these for the old geezer?" he asked around a mouthful of glazed cruller. "I'm sure he won't mind sharing. Especially with Fowler's football star."

"You're not a star anymore."

Julie emerged from behind the rack of engine parts. "You used to be a star, but you aren't anymore. And you're never going to be again."

She trembled with fear as she approached the hulking parody of the boy she'd fallen in love with. "You're just a tow truck driver whose wife brought him his lunch."

They stood in the sunlight, neither one moving, a tableau of anger and suspicion, desperation and courage. I couldn't move, still reeling from the images of Kevin's wreck, as another tragedy threatened to play out in front of me.

Jimmy ignored the brown paper bag Julie held out to him. "I am a star," he insisted. "And you'd know that if you weren't so busy playing up to that boy."

Julie shook her head, denying Jimmy's accusations. Pride stiffened her posture, and she held her ground as Jimmy stared hard at her.

Something shifted behind Jimmy's eyes. He thought he was being clever as he turned and advanced toward her.

A tremor passed through her body, but she refused to back away. Her back straight, she held her head high as he moved toward her.

"It wasn't just playing though, was it, Jules? Maybe you thought you'd dump ol' Jimmy and give the young stud a try?"

He lashed out, faster than I thought possible, and caught her across the face with the flat of his hand. Crimson fingers appeared on her fair skin as she fell into the dirt. The lunch bag landed a few feet from her, thrown aside by the force of the blow.

"Thought you could cheat on good ol' Jimmy and get away with it?" He reached down and pulled her to her feet again, holding her tight against him, in an insane parody of a passionate embrace.

I slid around the Charger, trying to get to Julie as she hunched over, using her arms to protect her midsection.

To protect the child she carried.

Jimmy turned his attention back to me. "Told you it served him right. Shouldn't go messing with a man's woman. No matter who you think you are."

He spat on the ground, and a trickle of blood ran down from his nose. He swiped his wrist across his face, surprise registering at the sight of his own blood.

"Damn," he muttered, wiping at his nose with the tail of his uniform shirt. "Damn."

Julie dropped out of his encircling arm while he was distracted and backed away, poised to turn and run.

Jimmy advanced on her, his hands curling into fists the size of Virginia hams. I could imagine one of those huge masses of bone, tendon, and muscle landing on Julie's tiny body.

"Leave her be," I shouted. I don't know what I hoped to accomplish, but I knew I had to try.

"It's none of your affair," he said, continuing to advance toward his terrified wife. "You wasn't the one she was running around on."

He whipped around long enough to glare at me, a look that froze me in place. "You just pay us no never-mind, y'hear? Me and my wife, we're gonna have a little talk about respecting your vows, and then I'm taking her home."

That one look told me Jimmy had gone over the edge. He wasn't thinking clearly; he wasn't thinking at all. And I knew that what had happened at the frat party was about to repeat itself, right here and now.

And I was the only one who could stop him.

"What did you do, Jimmy? Did you use the tow truck to run him off the road? Did you drive that big old truck up next to him and shove him in the ditch?"

Jimmy spun around and took a step toward me. Behind him I saw Julie slip behind the rack of engine parts.

At least she was out of harm's way. Her and the baby.

Now all I had to do was get away from this madman.

Easier said than done.

I stepped to the side, keeping the bulk of the Charger between me and Jimmy.

"Is that what you did, Jimmy? Was that why Fowler was chewing you out, he found out you used his tow truck?"

"I didn't use his truck," Jimmy growled. "I just borrowed one from one of my boys."

"Your boys?" I kept circling.

"The team," he said. "How stupid are you?"

"Borrowed? Someone let you take his truck?" I had to keep him talking.

A note of cunning crept into his voice. "I couldn't use the tow truck," he said, swiping a fist under his nose. His hand came away streaked with crimson.

"But you did, didn't you, Jimmy? We're talking about you using the tow truck and running Kevin Stanley into the ditch."

He lunged, grazing my side with his fist as I slid away.

I saw stars. I couldn't keep this up much longer, but I wanted to know, really know, if what I had seen was real.

"That isn't your team," I taunted, pain stabbing my side with every breath. "Your team graduated years ago."

"They're still my team. We party together, hang out. Kevin thought they were his guys, but they were mine."

He lunged again and I managed to sidestep, but I was tiring and I slipped, nearly landing in the dirt.

"They were tired of Mr. Goody Two-Shoes," he continued. "I brought the fun."

"Meaning you brought the beer."

With that, everything clicked into place. Jimmy was out in the woods that day, supplying beer for the kegger.

Jimmy, who was jealous of Kevin's position as captain.

Jimmy, who wanted to be back in the spotlight.

Jimmy, whose drug-addled brain had blown his wife's concern for a boy into a full-fledged affair.

Out in the woods with a high-powered tow truck and a hate-on for the quarterback.

It was a lethal combination.

I heard voices behind me, but I didn't dare turn to look. I didn't dare take my eyes off the raging pile of muscle in front of me.

"Did you mean to kill him, Jimmy?" I spoke softly, the taunting and baiting gone.

I was desperate to know, and I wasn't sure if I was asking for Kevin or for my parents. I wanted Jimmy to give me the answer I could never get from the driver who killed my mom and dad.

"Did you mean to?"

He never answered. Because at that instant Bobo launched himself from a spot a few feet behind me and sank his teeth into Jimmy's massive right arm, dragging Jimmy to the ground.

A high-pitched scream came from Jimmy as he batted futilely at the dog's head. Bobo wouldn't let go, no matter how many times Jimmy hit him.

I heard the unmistakable sound of a shell being racked into the chamber of a shotgun. "Bobo. Down."

The dog instantly turned loose of Jimmy and trotted back to sit at Sly's feet.

"You, boy!" Sly yelled at Jimmy. "You stay right there. Don't even twitch. I ain't fired this thing in twenty years, and I can't rightly swear I wouldn't hit parts you wouldn't care to lose, if you get my drift."

Jimmy muttered, but he took the warning and didn't move.

Julie had come back around the end of the engine racks when she heard Jimmy scream. "The police are on the way," she said. "I called them."

She looked down at the man on the ground. "I'm sorry, Jimmy. Sorry you couldn't believe me. Sorry that you did what you did. But mostly I'm sorry you'll never know your son."

"Ain't mine," he snarled.

"Yes, it is," she said calmly. "But you believe what you want to believe. You always have."

The wail of sirens drew closer, then cut off abruptly as tires squealed to a stop outside the fence.

"Back here," I yelled into the sudden silence. I looked over at Sly. "You might oughta put that shotgun down, though. Just so these boys don't get the wrong idea."

"Guard, Bobo," Sly commanded as he lowered the shotgun carefully to the ground.

Bobo trotted over to stand next to Jimmy, teeth bared in warning.

Jimmy didn't move.

Chapter 40

I SLID THE BANANA PUDDING OUT OF THE OVEN, golden-brown peaks of meringue covering rich pudding, bananas, and vanilla wafers.

A round of applause from the table greeted the dessert as I set it to cool.

"Fifteen minutes," I reminded the assembled group.

Ernie, ever the schedule master, checked his watch. "That should give us time for dessert and coffee," he tipped his head toward Felipe, "before we have to leave for the game."

He turned to our newest addition. "Jake, you're welcome to ride with us. We've got the van so there's plenty of room, and parking at the field is just impossible." He rolled his eyes to underscore just how difficult it was.

Jake took a sip from his glass of sweet tea. "I'd be glad for the ride," he said. "Thanks.

"And thanks to our hostess." He raised his glass to me,

and I felt a flush creep up my cheeks. Probably just the heat from the oven.

"I had a lot of help."

I did. We'd decided to go potluck before homecoming, and everyone had brought a dish. Karen fried up some chicken, Ernie made jambalaya that was so good I wanted to swim in it, Felipe brought a sweet corn salad, and I made dessert.

With the blessing of my friends, I had included Jake at the last minute, but I'd told him he didn't need to bring anything; he would be our guest.

Jake, however, was quickly learning Southern manners. He had shown up with a bubbling dish of potatoes au gratin and had everyone begging for his recipe.

With a showing like that, I suspected I might only be cooking every five weeks before long. But that was a discussion for another day.

For tonight, the agenda was good food, a football game, and an oversize helping of hope for the future.

I had shared my tale of the confrontation in the junkyard with them, answering questions and filling in blanks as I went along. Each time, I thought about the final question, the one I would never get answered.

The conversation flowed around me, Jake fitting into the group easily. I noticed, though, that he mostly listened, and asked questions about other people, volunteering little about himself and his background.

I added the hunky Jake Robinson to the list of mysteries I wanted to solve.

While my guests continued to visit, I excused myself and went downstairs to check on Bluebeard. I hadn't had much time to spend with him the last few days, and I was going out again tonight. I needed to give him a little of my time before I left.

"How you doing, big guy?" I asked as I slipped him scraps from our dinner. He gobbled down the sweet corn and the little bits of chicken I'd brought him.

"Bad man gone."

I gave him the half a banana I'd held back from the pudding. "Yes, Bluebeard, the bad man is gone."

The police had arrested Jimmy and immediately put him in a locked-down rehab unit to detox from the steroids. Karen told me they were afraid to put him in the general population until they had flushed the drugs out of his system. 'Roid rage in a jail was a recipe for disaster.

Bluebeard poked his bill into the bowl I'd brought, looking for more treats.

"That's all you're getting," I said. I filled his bowl with dry cereal and checked his water.

"Coffee?" he said plaintively.

"I wish I could, big guy. I really do, but it would just make you sick." I petted his head. "I can't give you coffee, Uncle Louis," I whispered.

"I know."

The voice, soft and strong, and unbelievably human. The voice that couldn't possibly belong to a parrot, and yet it came from the bird sitting on my arm.

Karen came into the shop, walking softly so as not to disturb us. "Dessert's ready," she said quietly. She chucked Bluebeard under the chin.

"Pretty girl," he said, and let out his best wolf whistle.

Karen laughed. "You're pretty special yourself." She stroked his head. "Can we steal your pal here?" she asked.

"Family."

Karen nodded. "Yeah, she's family."

Bluebeard bobbed his head. "Nighty-night," he said. He gave me a little head bump and hopped into his cage.

As I passed the counter, the phone rang. Without thinking, I reached for it, then stopped. It was after hours, and I didn't have to answer the phone. Besides, most of the people I would actually want to talk to were in my living room, waiting for me.

I glanced at the caller ID. The Montgomery number was way too familiar. Peter. No way he was intruding on my evening.

I looked back at Karen. "I'm ready for dessert," I said. Leading the way back up the stairs, I heard the click of the voice mail picking up. Whatever nonsense he was cooking up could wait for another day.

After dessert, we trooped back downstairs, heading for Felipe and Ernie's van. We were talking over each other, the way people do in a large, friendly group, as we headed out.

We were almost to the front door when a squawk drew our attention to the blanket-covered cage in the corner.

A brilliantly colored head poked out of the door, and beady eyes fixed us all with an angry-bird stare.

"Hey, trying to #^$&*& sleep here!"

Glory's Down-Home Dinner for Four (or More!)

BROILED GROUPER

1–1 ½ pounds grouper filet
½ cup each mayonnaise and mustard
1 teaspoon lemon juice
Salt and pepper to taste

Combine mayonnaise, mustard, lemon juice, salt, and pepper. Pat fish filets dry and coat with mayonnaise mixture. Broil 6 inches from heat for about 10 minutes, until coating is crusty. If the fish is not cooked through, finish in a 350 degree oven for 5 minutes, or until flaky.

FIELD PEAS WITH HAM HOCKS

The addition of okra will thicken your dish and give the pot likker (that wonderful broth that works so well for dipping cornbread) a heartier flavor and texture.

1 ham hock
4 cups fresh field peas, shelled
2 ½ cups water
4 fresh okra pods
Salt and pepper to taste

Wash and clean the peas, discarding any damaged peas. Brown the ham hock in a soup pot; then deglaze the pan with ¼ cup of the water to preserve all the pan juices. Add the rest of the water and the peas and bring to a boil. Skim any foam that develops and reduce heat to simmer for 15 minutes. Add the okra pods, cover, and simmer another 15 minutes, until the peas are tender. Season with salt and pepper to taste—the amount of salt will be determined by the saltiness of the ham hock.

CREAMED CORN

8 ears fresh corn
1 tablespoon flour
2 tablespoons sugar
Salt and pepper to taste
1 cup cream (36 percent milkfat or higher)

½ cup water
2 tablespoons bacon grease
1 tablespoon butter

Husk and rinse the corn. In a large bowl, cut kernels from the cob with a paring knife. Scrape the cob with the dull side of the blade, or with a table knife, to release the milky juices into the bowl. Stir together the flour, sugar, and salt and pepper to taste; then stir into the corn. Add the cream and water and stir until blended.

In a heavy skillet, liquefy the bacon grease over medium heat. When grease is hot, add the corn mixture, reduce heat, and simmer, stirring frequently, until corn is cooked and sauce is creamy—about 30 minutes.

Place corn in serving bowl, add butter, stir, and serve.

HUSH PUPPIES

Hush puppy recipes are as varied as Southern cooks. They can have herbs, green onions, chopped jalapeños, chopped tomatoes, or bacon bits added. Experiment with your favorite seasonings, and find the combination that works best for your friends and family. Here's a basic recipe to start with.

2 cups self-rising white cornmeal
½ cup self-rising flour
½ teaspoon garlic powder
1 tablespoon sugar
½ cup diced onion (optional)

1 large egg, lightly beaten
1 ½ cups buttermilk
Oil for frying

Note: If you can't find self-rising cornmeal, you can make your own. For each cup of cornmeal, substitute 1 ½ teaspoons baking powder and 1 teaspoon salt for 2 ½ teaspoons of regular cornmeal.

While you prepare the dough, heat the frying oil to 450 degrees. A deep fryer is recommended.

Mix together dry ingredients and diced onion. Add egg and half the buttermilk. Continue adding buttermilk until the mixture is a soft dough, but not runny. If the texture is too loose, add a little more cornmeal to achieve the proper consistency.

Drop the dough by tablespoons into the hot oil. Don't crowd the fryer (or pan); do just a few at a time. Cook until dark golden brown, turning once, about 2–3 minutes. Drain well on paper towels and serve.

BANANA PUDDING

Like hush puppies, there are as many recipes for banana pudding as there are Southern cooks. The recipes range from the elaborate, topped with meringue and baked (recipe follows), to the simple shortcut method that uses instant pudding and frozen whipped topping. They really are two completely different dishes. The basics, though, are always the same: sliced bananas, vanilla wafers, vanilla pudding, and a topping of whipped cream or meringue.

For everyday, use the shortcuts. It only takes a few minutes to slice bananas and whip up some instant pudding. Add a carton of whipped topping and you have a quick and easy treat. But for company, Glory is always going to make the "real thing," and made-from-scratch is wonderful!

> 4 ripe bananas, peeled and sliced
> ½ cup sugar
> ⅓ cup flour
> ¼ teaspoon salt
> 4 large eggs, separated
> 2 cups half-and-half
> ½ teaspoon vanilla extract
> 1 box vanilla wafers
> Pinch cream of tartar
> 2 tablespoons sugar

Preheat oven to 400 degrees.

Mix ½ cup sugar, flour, and salt in a saucepan. Lightly beat the egg yolks and add to the dry ingredients, whisking to combine. Add the half-and-half, and continue whisking until the mixture is smooth. Place the pan over low heat and stir constantly until the pudding reaches 172–180 degrees. This will require the use of a good cooking thermometer and *lots* of patience, but it will be worth it.

When the pudding reaches the correct temperature, remove from heat and stir in the vanilla extract.

In an ovenproof 1 ½ quart baking dish, pour a thin layer of pudding. Cover the pudding with a layer of vanilla wafers, then a layer of bananas, and finally about a third of the remaining pudding. Repeat the layers, ending with a pudding layer.

Set the pudding aside, and prepare the meringue topping.

In a mixer bowl, combine egg whites and cream of tartar. Beat at medium speed until soft peaks form. Continue beating as you gradually add the additional 2 tablespoons of sugar, and beat until the meringue forms stiff peaks. Spread the meringue on the pudding, making sure you seal the edges, and bake for 8–10 minutes, or until the meringue is evenly golden brown.

Cool 15 minutes before serving, and refrigerate leftovers (as if there will be any!).

SWEET TEA

Like the name says, this is tea that is served already sweetened. While Yankees up North and those in the West might find the concept surprising, it's the default drink in the South.

6 cups water
1 cup sugar
6 tea bags—traditionally, plain black tea

Bring the water to a boil, add the sugar, and stir to dissolve. Steep the tea bags in the sweetened water to the desired strength, and serve in tall glasses with ice. Garnish with mint sprigs or lemon slices, if desired.

Felipe's Festival of Frying

CHILLED OYSTERS ON THE HALF SHELL

These are really simple. Find the absolute best quality oysters you can, as fresh as possible. Wash them under cold water, pat dry, and shuck with an oyster knife, preserving as much of the oyster liquor as you can. Place the shells on a bed of rock salt or crushed ice, put one oyster in each shell with the reserved liquor, and serve plain, with hot sauce, lemon juice, or crackers on the side.

PAN-FRIED CHICKEN

Fried chicken is another simple recipe. Just be sure to control the temperature of your frying pan and oil, and you can't miss!

3–4 pound fryer, cut up
Salt and pepper

Self-rising flour
Oil for frying

Cut up your chicken, or ask the butcher at your market to
do it for you. Rinse and pat dry. Sprinkle with salt and pepper, and roll in flour.

Fry in a cast-iron skillet in a single layer, skin side down,
in hot oil (350 degrees) until the underside begins to brown,
about 10 minutes. (Don't mess with it while the first side is
frying. It should only need to be turned once.) Carefully turn
each piece and cook another 10 minutes. Serve hot!

FRIED GRITS

Fried grits take some advance preparation. Most traditional
Southern breakfasts include grits, and a Southern cook just
makes extra at breakfast to use later in the day. You can use
instant grits, but no good Southerner would admit to eating
them!

2 cups grits
9 cups water
2 ounces butter
2 teaspoons salt
Shortening for frying

Mix grits, water, butter, and salt in a large saucepan, and
bring to a boil over high heat. Reduce heat, cover, and simmer for 40–45 minutes, until all the water is absorbed and
the grits have a smooth, creamy texture. Cool the grits, pack

tightly in a 9 x 5 loaf pan, and refrigerate for several hours (ideally, overnight).

When you are ready to cook, release the chilled grit loaf from the pan, and slice ½ inch thick. In a skillet, heat the shortening to frying temperature (350 degrees), and fry the slices until golden brown, about 10 minutes per side.

Fried grits can be served with butter and honey, maple syrup, or pan gravy.

CHICKEN GRAVY

Made from the drippings in the chicken-frying pan, good gravy includes all the bits that fell off the meat while it was cooking. Rumor has it you can thicken gravy with cornstarch, but that may just be a Yankee plot.

Pan drippings
2–3 tablespoons flour
1 cup chicken stock or water
1 cup milk
Salt and pepper to taste

Deglaze the frying pan with 1–2 tablespoons of water to release all the juices and bits stuck to the pan. Remove from heat and stir in the flour; then return to heat and cook, stirring constantly, over medium heat until the roux mixture is smooth and the color of peanut butter. Add chicken stock and milk about a half cup at a time, stirring after each addition. Simmer to thicken—it just takes a few minutes—and season with salt and pepper to taste.

GREENS WITH BACON

1 quart water
1 pound slab bacon (or salt pork, if you prefer)
2–3 pounds collard greens
¼ teaspoon red-pepper flakes
1 ½ ounces vegetable oil
Salt and pepper to taste

Place water and the slab bacon (or salt pork) in a large pot with a tight-fitting lid. Bring to a boil, reduce heat to low, cover, and simmer for about 30 minutes. Add the greens and pepper flakes and continue simmering for an additional 2–3 hours, stirring occasionally. Add vegetable oil, simmer for another 30 minutes, season with salt and pepper to taste, and serve.

SAUTÉED YELLOW SQUASH

4 small yellow summer squashes, sliced
1 tablespoon butter or oil
¼ cup vegetable broth
½ teaspoon chopped garlic
2–3 thinly sliced green onions, optional
2 tablespoons fresh herbs—your choice of dill,
basil, marjoram, or chives
Salt and pepper to taste

In a large skillet, sauté the sliced squash in melted butter or oil over medium heat for 2–3 minutes, stirring constantly to prevent sticking. Add vegetable broth and simmer until squash is almost tender. Add garlic and green onions, if you are using them. When squash is tender but not completely soft, add your choice of herbs, season with salt and pepper to taste, and serve immediately.

PEACH COBBLER

Cobblers are counterintuitive. Although they come out with the crust on top, you actually put the batter in the pan first and then add the fruit on top. But don't worry; that fruit sinks to the bottom, leaving tasty trails of juice, sugar, and cinnamon to bake into the biscuit-like crust.

4 cups peeled, sliced peaches
1 cup sugar
½ cup water
1 stick (4 ounces) butter
1 ½ cups self-rising flour
1 cup sugar
1 ½ cups milk
1 teaspoon ground cinnamon, optional

Preheat oven to 375 degrees. Place the peaches in a saucepan with the first cup of sugar and the water. Mix well, bring to a boil, and simmer for 10 minutes. Remove from heat. (If you can't find fresh peaches, you can use canned, and substitute the juice for the 1 cup of sugar and water.)

In a 9 x 13 baking pan, melt the butter in the oven. While the butter is melting and the peaches are cooling, mix the flour with the second cup of sugar in a mixing bowl, and gradually stir in the milk. Continue stirring until the batter is smooth; then carefully pour it over the melted butter, but do not stir.

Spoon the cooked fruit and cooking syrup in an even layer over the batter. Again, don't stir. Sprinkle on the cinnamon, if you are using it.

Bake for 30–45 minutes. The crust will rise to the top and turn golden when it is done.

Serve warm or chilled, with a scoop of your favorite vanilla ice cream or a dollop of whipped cream.

Bonus!!—
Ernie's Easy Mock Jambalaya
for Four

The trick to a quick and easy version of this Southern Louisiana classic is flexibility. A traditional jambalaya contains chicken, shrimp, and spicy sausage, along with rice and vegetables. For Ernie's mock jambalaya, he simply used leftovers from the refrigerator.

1 to 1 ½ pounds leftover meat and/or shellfish
1 onion
2 stalks celery
1 small bell pepper (green, red, or yellow, or a combination)
2 tablespoons peanut or olive oil
½ cup broth (chicken or vegetable)
3 cups cooked white long-grain rice
1 14.5-ounce can chopped tomatoes with juice
2 bay leaves
Cajun seasoning to taste
Salt and pepper to taste

Chop the onion, celery, and pepper (the trinity of Cajun cooking). In a heavy skillet, heat the oil, and sauté the vegetables until the onions are translucent. Add the leftover meat (chicken, sausage, turkey), and cook over medium heat 3–4 minutes to heat. Add the broth, cooked rice, tomatoes with juice, and bay leaves. Add Cajun seasoning to taste (adjust the amount of spice to please the palates of your family and/or guests).

Simmer for 15 minutes, stirring occasionally. Although all the ingredients are already cooked, you want to heat the dish through and give the flavors a chance to mingle.

Just before serving, add any shellfish, and continue cooking over low heat only until the shellfish are hot—they will toughen quickly if overcooked.

Remove the bay leaves, season with salt and pepper to taste, and serve.